R.C.
BRIDGESTOCK
VENGEANCE

 CANELO

First published in the United Kingdom in 2022 by

Canelo
Unit 9, 5th Floor
Cargo Works, 1-2 Hatfields
London, SE1 9PG
United Kingdom

A CIP catalogue record for this book is available from the British Library.

Print ISBN 978 1 80436 056 9
Ebook ISBN 978 1 80436 055 2

This book is a work of fiction. Names, characters, businesses, organizations, places and events are either the product of the author's imagination or are used fictitiously. Any resemblance to actual persons, living or dead, events or locales is entirely coincidental.

Cover design by kid-ethic

Cover images © Arcangel, Alamy

Look for more great books at www.canelo.co

Printed and bound in Great Britain by Clays Ltd, Elcograf S.p.A.

1

As we emerge from the Covid pandemic and our lives return to the new normal, we think of those who lost their lives during that time, and especially those with life-threatening illnesses who lost precious time, in their final months, with their loved ones because of it.

We dedicate this book to two very special people.

Our dear friend, and 'Charity Angel', fundraiser Mandy Taylor, who had terminal cancer and died at the age of 53 in December 2021.

Mandy raised more than £2 million for good causes, and was recognised by Her Majesty and awarded an MBE in the 2022 New Year Honours. Before her passing in December 2021, she launched her #BeMoreMandy social media campaign and encouraged others to 'just do it'. Reach out to someone in need, help a charity, donate, pay it forward or just spread some joy. Together as a much bigger Team #BeMoreMandy we will ensure Mandy's legacy continues to blossom into something as beautiful as her. To find out more, visit bemoremandy.org

To inspirational teenager Abi, who with life-threatening conditions has chosen to spend her shorter life making and gifting bracelets, encouraging kindness and spreading joy. All she asks in return is a smiley picture, of you, wearing one of her bright and beautiful *Joy-lets* that are just as beautiful as Abi herself. Join in. Follow Abi on Twitter at @spreadjoywithabi, on Instagram at @spreadjoywithabi and on Facebook at Spread joy with Abi

Patrons:

ROKT Foundation – www.roktfoundation.co.uk

Encourages independence and builds self-confidence, providing adventurous activity in an urban environment, improving physical and mental wellbeing.

Isle of Wight Society for the Blind – www.iwsb.org.uk

Ambassadors:

Bethany's Smile – www.bethanyssmile.org

Helping to support children with life-limiting/life-threatening illnesses and their families since 2011.

Chapter One

Reverend Richard Radley threw the heavy studded doors of St Cuthbert's wide open to feel the warm rays of the sun on his face. In the distance, he heard the thumping of the baler – farmers were quite literally making hay while the sun shone.

The grass was dewy, but his favourite roses covered the latticework arch and were in full bloom. They were far too tempting to ignore and usually favoured by brides. He took care to avoid the thorny stems when reaching out to touch the glossy foliage. Tenderly, he cupped a glowing pink flower in his hand. He breathed in deeply, knowing that the Morning Jewel rose's sweet fresh scent was the best of all. Closing his eyes, he imagined he could already hear the clicking of the photographer's camera.

Today held great promise for the joyous festivities. The planning had already brought such happiness to two families who had patiently borne the disappointment of the cancellations caused by the pandemic.

He lifted his eyes and allowed himself a few minutes to look beyond the walled, well-manicured garden and take in the beauty of the Yorkshire countryside beyond. The ancient building stood on the east flank of the Pennine Hills overlooking the steep-sided Colne Valley. From here, he could clearly see the River Colne as it rose above the town of Marsden and flowed eastward towards

Huddersfield. Reverend Radley's heart was so full of gratitude that the sensation, it seemed to him, came directly from heaven.

It was in moments like these that he felt most peaceful and closest to God.

Then a movement at the foot of the hill below caught his eye. He watched as parishioner Bob Sullivan, already dressed in his finery, left his shop with a bundle of mail from behind his shop door. The reverend thought it an odd thing to do on his daughter's wedding day, but, knowing Bob's wife Josie, there would be a lot of fussing going on at home. Maybe he needed to get out from under her feet.

After the bride's father locked the door, he paused, and thanked God for helping him achieve this day. Despite many dark days and sleepless nights in the weeks leading up to the family business being forced to close, there had been the forthcoming nuptials on which the others could focus. For him, though, as the debts mounted while he tried desperately to save the business that had given three generations a luxurious lifestyle, there had been nothing else on his mind. With no income, and a wedding to pay for, the coffers were bare. Unbeknownst to his family, even the remortgaging of their home hadn't put the slightest dent in what he owed.

However, he was taking the blue sky and pleasant warm breeze as a sign that God was looking down on him favourably. If he could have offered his only child the perfect weather for her perfect wedding day, this would be it.

Back in the church, which was all ready for the wedding, the reverend sat for a moment. The heavy scent of lilies perfumed the building, and strangely, when he opened his Bible, he came across Luke 12:27–28. 'Consider the lilies…' He looked up with a smile and admired the floral decorations beside the lectern. He considered flowers bursting with symbolism, full of happiness at weddings, and solemn and serious for funerals. It seemed uncanny to him that the pew he had chosen was the one where he had first met Bob Sullivan, praying, in what appeared to be the end of challenging times for him. Crying, Sullivan had confessed to the clergyman that the Lord had touched him in his darkest hour. For what, Bob did not say, and the reverend hadn't asked, because the cleric was always glad to welcome another sheep into his flock.

—

After the service, the bridal party slowly made their way into the garden, throwing confetti and shouting their congratulations despite having just been asked by the Reverend Radley to wait until they had exited the grounds. To the side they had set up a traditional ice-cream tricycle with staff dressed in uniform. Waiters in tails offered pre-filled champagne glasses on silver trays to the guests as they passed. The louder the photographer shouted to organise the people into groups for photographs, the harder the ringers seemed to pull the ropes for the bells.

As the men in the bridal party lined up for the group photographs, with frightening suddenness, a man best described as a hermit appeared from behind a gravestone. In the moments that followed, everything seemed to happen in slow motion. Directly in front of his stunned audience, he calmly dropped to one knee, put an automatic handgun on his forearm, bared his teeth in a feral smile and opened fire. The shots were loud and frightening. Guests, screaming and shouting, rooted to the spot, were immobilised by fear as others dived to the floor and covered their heads, but most turned and fled into the sanctuary of the church. However, two brave souls sprinted towards the gunman, who by this time was on his feet and running away. Turning to look over his shoulder to see his assailants almost upon him, the gunman tripped, and a screech rent through the air when the men launched themselves at him. The gunman threw his hands forward, trying to save himself, sending the gun flying. Landing on the lawn with a thud, it skittered across the grass, coming to rest at the base of a lavender bush in the border.

Breathless and angry, the two men crouched over the hermit and pinned him to the ground. Panting they stared down at him.

For a second, the gunman, wide-eyed, stared back, then he began to laugh. It began as a snigger, and then crescendoed into wild uncontrollable, hysterical laughter.

The beating they gave him, no doubt fuelled by their surging adrenaline, was unforgiving.

Onlookers, were rendering first aid to the injured and comforting those who hadn't been able to flee. No one attempted to stop it.

Chelsea Clough, the photographer, stood with best man Jarvis Cooper and his girlfriend Ellie Yates under the shade of the gatehouse, waiting for the emergency services to arrive.

'Do you have any idea who the gunman is?' Chelsea asked.

Jarvis's face and clothes were splattered with blood. Shaking his head, he whispered, 'No.'

Ellie was sobbing uncontrollably. Jarvis took off his jacket, draped it around her shoulders, pulled her towards him and tucked her head under his chin, where it fit perfectly. He held her against his body tightly.

Chelsea continued. 'Why do you think that anyone do such a thing?'

Jarvis was comforting Ellie. 'I've no idea,' he replied, his voice sounding curt and irritated with the photographer.

Ellie turned her head, wiping her runny nose with a shredded tissue she had found up her sleeve. 'Perhaps he's a jealous rival?'

'Don't be bloody stupid. What do you know? You've only known them two minutes. Stacey and Mark have been going out together since we were at school.'

The sirens of the emergency services replaced the joyous sound of the church bells that had been ringing to announce the marriage of Stacey Sullivan to Mark James. It was now sending quite a different message down the valley. As the sirens grew louder, those in need were reassured.

'Hang in there!' went up a desperate cry from the woman tending to Bob Sullivan. 'Listen to me! Do you hear that? Help is on its way. You're doing really well. It's going to be okay.'

Despite her efforts to stem the blood bubbling up from multiple wounds to his head and chest, Trish, a district nurse, knew that her attempts to save him were unlikely to be successful.

Having been in front of the other men, and, following the photographer's request for him to be in the central position as father of the bride, Bob Sullivan, and those closest to him had been the ones directly in the gunman's firing line.

Now the bride's father and his nephew Ralph Bateman lay side by side upon the flagstones where they had fallen.

Blood gurgled in Bob's throat and oozed from his mouth; one more convulsion shot through his body, then death settled upon his face.

As Trish, uncurled herself from his body, her clothes, heavily soiled with blood, became more visible. Her tears flowed freely. She covered her face with her crimson-stained hands.

No matter how many years she had been a nurse, nothing could prepare her for losing someone she knew, in this way.

Two armed response vehicles were the first on the scene. Expertly screeching to a halt, they broadsided the vehicles at the gate, including the wedding car, a white Rolls Royce, thereby blocking the road and making certain that no vehicles could leave the scene.

The paramedic responders followed the police officers out of their vehicles, all adrenaline-fuelled, none of them certain what they would find.

Having ascertained what had taken place from those at the gate, the police took over the restraint of the bloodied, bruised gunman. Handcuffed, he was arrested on suspicion of murder.

Quickly, they established where the weapon lay when it showed itself to them, shimmering in the baking soil.

The officer retrieving the gun had a hostile, almost outraged expression on his face. 'Looks like a semi-automatic converted blank firing gun,' he said to his partner. He lifted his chin towards the wedding guests left standing. 'They've had a close call. There's ammunition in the clip. Fortunately, it looks like it jammed.'

Chapter Two

Refusing to stand on his own two feet, as if they had seized up, the gunman was half-carried, half-dragged to the roadway where a police transit van was waiting to escort him to the bridewell. It was hard not to notice the prisoner's deep-set eyes were dead and flat, glowering with an intense blackness. However, the officers were used to non-verbal intimidation and the neutral expression on a maimed face in situations like this. When the prisoner didn't react to their instructions, the arresting officer spoke more loudly, believing he might be hard of hearing, but this action only resulted in him flinching away as far as he could whilst still being hampered in shackles. Despite being outside, an acrid smell permeated the atmosphere around the gunman, and the senior uniformed officer present at the scene made a swift decision. They'd afforded him an opportunity to be compliant, and if that couldn't be achieved…

'Let's get on with it,' he said abruptly, walking away to put a call in to the control room to alert the duty SIO that they would be required at the scene.

Promptly and unceremoniously, the gunman was bundled into the rear of the vehicle, and this time there were no blue lights. No sirens. The cops had their prisoner, and he was going nowhere other than Peel Street Police Station.

The euphoria of the nuptials had lasted only twenty minutes before the treacherous man had put a stop to it. Distraught, the two families and their guests were at a loss as to why someone would target peaceful, law-abiding citizens in the sleepy village church. No one knew who the gunman was, or if they did know, they weren't saying.

DI Charley Mann grabbed her coat and bag and walked calmly but with a purpose into the main CID office. Three pairs of eyes looked up at her from their computers.

'Okay, look lively you lot, looks like we have a murder to deal with at St Cuthbert's. It's a shooting. The gunman has been detained and is currently on his way to the cells.'

Being a Saturday, there were only three detectives in the office, DS Mike Blake, DC Annie Glover, and DC Ricky-Lee.

'Annie, you're with me. Mike and Ricky-Lee, you follow us. I've asked the control room to divert Wilkie from whatever he's dealing with and asked him to rendez-vous with us at the church. We might have to call some of the late team in early, but I'll make that decision once we know more.'

'Strangest invite to a wedding I've ever had,' said Annie, pulling a parking ticket still in its yellow plastic cover out of her jacket pocket. She wrinkled her nose. 'Er… sorry, boss. I forgot…'

Charley shook her head and scowled. 'You do pick your moments, Annie. I'll deal with you later.'

As DI Charley Mann and Annie Glover travelled to the scene in her vehicle, the updates were coming in quickly from Inspector Ian Levitt back in the control room.

'The deceased is a sixty-six-year-old male, Robert – Bob – Sullivan, father of the bride. He has been pronounced dead at the scene by paramedics. Information suggests that he has been shot four times, once in the head, twice in the torso, and once in the leg. Also shot at this time in the thigh, was his nephew, Ralph Bateman, twenty-five years of age. He is believed to have arterial bleeding.'

'Is Mr Bateman still at the scene?' asked Charley, negotiating the narrow bridge that led into the village of Marsden.

'No, he's being blue-lighted to hospital.'

Charley grimaced as she asked. 'Likely to prove fatal?'

'I don't know.'

'Is the scene sealed?'

'I'm told so.'

'And the others?'

'Unbelievably, there is no report of any other injuries. However, I have been reliably informed by the firearms responders that not all the bullets in the automatic handgun were discharged. Which could explain why.'

Charley saw her brows had knitted together in puzzlement as she looked into the rear-view mirror to observe traffic piling up behind her as she waited at the traffic lights. 'Is there a reason for this, do we know?'

'They believe that the weapon jammed after six rounds.'

'Chuffin' hell they were lucky. Show me on the log as attending to take charge,' she told him.

At the scene, those who had been rendering first aid or restraining the gunman now joined those gathered inside St Cuthbert's Church. The guests' bloodstained clothes were a visual and immediate reminder of what had just taken place. Amidst the chaos and the panic, shouts of anger and agony ripped through the building, sending Stacey's heartbeat rocketing and leaving her shaking. Withdrawing into her husband's arms Mark led her away from the others. Sitting her down he comforted her. Stacey sobbed into his chest. All he knew was to hold her until she felt calmer as her father would have done. When finally she managed to get control of her emotions, she apologised, withdrew from his arms and tried to brush her tears off his shirt. He handed her his handkerchief to dry her eyes and her wedding make-up stained the pure white cotton. She spoke to him in a cracking voice. 'It's only a few minutes' drive from our house to the church, yet Dad had insisted I have the Rolls Royce I had always dreamed of to drive us here. This morning, he squeezed my hand tighter than he had ever done before. We shared a glass of champagne before we left the house, because I asked him to.' Stacey paused for a moment putting her trembling hand to her cheek. 'He kissed me and told me how proud he was. He even shed a tear. "Whatever happens in the future, you must never forget that I will always be with you," he said.' Pausing again her eyebrows furrowed. 'What a strange thing to say, don't you think?' she whispered.

'Do you think he had a premonition that he was going to die?'

'Or did he know that he was a target? *If so, for what?*'

Stacey's eyes were sore, she blinked and they burned. Looking down she saw her beautiful wedding dress. It was no longer white. It was torn, and smeared in dirt, grime, and blood from her father and her cousin whom she had been torn away from to let others render first aid. She swayed. 'Here Comes The Bride' whirled round and round in her head and the thought that she would never again be able to dance with her father was the last thing she remembered, before she fainted.

-

PC Tracy Petterson stood with a clipboard and pen at the police cordon. It was her job to record the name, time of arrival and departure of all who entered the scene. Having given their names to Tracy the detectives proceeded to get suited and booted in their protective gear.

'You're doing a grand job,' Charley said to her as she stood for a moment at the rendezvous point taking gloves from a paper-tissue-sized box, offered to her. 'Don't you be getting sunburnt now.'

Tracy smiled. 'No ma'am,' she replied. 'Don't you worry about me, I've got my sunblock on.'

Charley nodded her approval. 'Nobody gets past you without my say-so. Do you understand? Any problems, give me a shout.'

She nodded. 'I will, ma'am.'

Charley turned to Annie and Wilkie, then back to Mike. 'I'll keep Annie outside with me, along with Wilkie as exhibits officer, whilst we deal with the deceased and the scene.'

A police support unit van pulled up at the church gate. 'Things can now move forward at a pace beneficial for everyone,' she said, relieved to see that there were extra uniformed police officers arriving to help Mike and Ricky-Lee. 'If you two start the ball rolling with the uniform support team speaking to the wedding guests and the others, I'll join you when we have things dealt with out here.' She looked at her watch and frowned. 'CSI supervisor should be here anytime. I asked HQ to arrange for them to attend as a matter of urgency. We need the body screened from prying eyes, and quickly. No doubt the media will be on site before long.'

Charley's professional eye scanned back and forth. The scene was well-preserved and for that she was very grateful to the uniform staff, and made a mental note to send a memo to their supervisors for a job well done.

Detective Sergeant Mike Blake, her deputy on the enquiry was at her side. 'I want the officers speaking directly to those in attendance to obtain written statements where possible.' Turning to include DC Ricky-Lee she continued with her instructions. 'That includes the bride, groom and the deceased's wife,' Charley said, 'but, to start with, speak to the first-aiders and those who bravely detained the gunman. The sooner it's done, the better, and whilst they are assembled in one location and the incident is still fresh in their minds. I also want a comprehensive list of those in attendance, and their dates of birth, which might not seem of any relevance right now, but it's unknown at this early stage if we might need them at a later date. Intelligence gathered will be deciphered by the HOLMES database back in the incident room. If however they don't feel up to it, or it's not possible for any reason, have the officers make arrangements to do so at a later time, or date.'

Guests totalled forty in number. Then there were the others: the reverend, the verger, the bell ringers, the organist, the photographer, and those serving drinks and ice creams. Then of course there were the onlookers, those in the community just wanting a glimpse of the bride on a beautiful summer's day in the grounds of their picturesque church. The SIO wasn't naïve, though. Several 'call backs' would be required. Witnesses often remembered things a few days after the event or that they failed to mention when they were initially seen by the police. This was quite common, and the last thing that Charley wanted to do was miss any information that was available to her and the team, especially if it was ultimately of relevance to their investigation.

As Mike walked away, with Ricky-Lee, and towards the newly arrived support now out of the van, a thought came to her.

'Can you have the house-to-house questionnaire form modified, Mike? We need to make sure that we ask the right questions. Also, make sure we identify anyone who has taken any photographs here today, and make sure we seize any film footage. The last thing we need is any of this macabre incident being played out on social media.'

The DS nodded. 'It has been suggested that a video was being taken as well as the stills, according to one of the uniform lads I've just spoken to, but I'll check that out. If there was, we'll have that as well. Leave it with me.'

'Oh, and remind the team that, apart from zoom lens cameras, if there are any TV crews, they are also likely to have boom microphones so they could pick up any private conversations between ourselves. I don't want any of that to be the focus of attention on any newsreel.'

'Don't worry, I'll make sure everyone is aware,' replied Mike.

In the inner scene, Bob Sullivan's motionless body lay surrounded by confetti, saturated in blood. Isolated further by police tape, awaiting her arrival, there it would remain, sterile, until the removal of the body could be arranged. The sense of loss was palpable.

Annie looked from the body, to the officers beyond the cordon who were comforting the mourners outside the church. Her rational self began to fight with her deep-seated emotions, as they always did when she remembered her brother's suicide, the result of his abuse at the hands of the priests, at school. 'I often think of the police officer who helped me when Ashton died. Man's inhumanity to fellow man has different degrees of harm caused by the ripple effect doesn't it?' said Annie to Charley as they stood beside the body.

Charley eyeballed Annie. 'And, I've seen all manner of violent deaths but it's only been personal once before.'

'Your colleague in London that was a victim of Titus Deaver the cannibalistic killer?'

Charley sucked in her breath. The intensity of the feeling that washed over her shocked her. Quickly she changed the subject as her eyes once again found the face of Bob Sullivan. 'I've known him since I was knee high to a grasshopper. My gran wouldn't go anywhere else for her knick-knacks, except to Sullivan's Store. Mr Sullivan was a kind and patient man.' A wistful half-smile tugged at the corner of her lips. 'He had to be with my gran.' Charley went down on her haunches. Eyes scanning his body, she whispered to the bloodied corpse. 'What can you tell us my old friend?'

Chapter Three

DI Charley Mann and DC Annie Glover stared at the body in silence, alone with their thoughts for a moment or two. Whilst they waited for the CSI supervisor to attend, they each considered Bob Sullivan's injuries.

Annie adjusted the hood of her coveralls to get some air flowing across the top of her head. There was a ringing in her ears. 'Last thing you'd expect at a wedding.' There was a pause as she considered her work-related experiences at weddings. 'A few punch-ups afterwards, maybe, but not an assassination.'

Charley contemplated the bullet holes in the dead man's body. 'It seems highly probable that the father of the bride was the gunman's intended target.' She turned for a moment to look up at her colleague. 'One thing our man in the cells would have been sure of is where the father of the bride would be today.'

Annie felt confused. 'Why here though? Why today? Wouldn't it have been an easier task for someone who was after him, to find him in his shop?' The heat seared Annie's throat and lungs as it depleted the air, and she gasped sharply before she went on. '"If an injury has to be done to a man it should be so severe that his vengeance need not be feared." Niccolo Machiavelli.'

Charley's eyes dropped back to the corpse. 'Exactly! Okay, so what's the story here?'

'That's for us to discover,' replied Annie, stating the obvious. The younger detective squinted up at the sky, knowing that there was no shelter or shade from the sun directly above her. The shimmering lines of heat rising from the sweltering stone flags in the distance caused what could easily have been a mirage. Annie flapped her hand in front of her face. 'Phew! These suits don't half make you hot on a day like this, don't they? What I'd give for an ice lolly from that trike over there.'

Charley's mind was otherwise engaged looking at the bullet hole in Sullivan's right cheek. 'Clean point of entry,' she mused. The SIO's voice sounded distant. When Annie didn't reply, Charley turned to see her younger officer swaying towards her.

'Don't you dare faint on me, do you hear?' she hissed, pulling Annie to the ground next to her. 'The last thing I need is for you to fall on top of him!' Her wry comment was enough to stop Annie from fainting. She gave her a weak smile.

'As if. Any obvious clues?' she asked.

Charley shook her head. 'No, I think we'll leave that to the CSI. When supervisor Neal Rylatt arrives, we can move him. He's obviously been held up in traffic, but he should be with us soon.'

Charley's expression morphed into one of concern. 'You okay?'

Annie nodded. 'I'm okay. Do you think the gunman could be some sort of extremist or belong to a proscribed terrorist organisation? Firing an automatic weapon into a crowd is not what you could call normal behaviour, is it?'

Charley wiped the sweat that had accumulated on her brow with the back of her wrist. 'We can never assume anything, as you well know. However, no one has mentioned that they heard him speak, let alone shout anything indicating extremist support, so I'm not leaning towards that way of thinking at the moment, otherwise the anti-terrorism team would be all over it.' She looked towards the area where the shots were fired.

Annie followed her gaze. 'Wonder if the guests had hired their wedding suits? If so, the hire companies are not going to be best pleased, are they?'

'Honestly Annie, sometimes I wonder how your mind works,' Charley said with some bewilderment. 'I should think that will be the last thing on their minds right now, don't—'

Before Charley could finish her sentence, she could see the CSI van pulling up on the roadside and breathed a sigh of relief.

The body now screened from the public, CSI Neal Rylatt visually examined the scene around and in front of him. Almost immediately, he told Charley, 'There's no exit wound for the bullet wound to his head.'

Annie raised her eyebrows. 'The bullet's still inside…'

Neal nodded. 'That's right.' He continued to count four bullet wounds readily visible: one in his head, one just below Sullivan's right shoulder, one in the centre of his chest, and one in his right leg. 'It'll be interesting to see which actually killed him.' The CSI put his hands upon his hips and paused expectantly. 'Are we ready to turn him over then to see if there is anything else? We don't want any surprises at the mortuary now, do we?'

It was Charley's turn to nod her head.

Neal scanned the back of the dead man's body. 'As I expected, there are no exit wounds here either, which means that on this occasion, you will find the bullets have all remained within the victim's body, and will therefore be retrievable at his post-mortem.'

'That's a bonus,' said Annie, trying to sound positive.

Charley's mind, however, was focused on the precise opportunity that the gunman had chosen to shoot Bob Sullivan. 'I think we have established that for some unknown reason he chose this day. Is it that he wanted an audience too? If not then why didn't he just pull the trigger when Bob Sullivan first arrived at the church with his daughter? That way it would have been easier for him to escape unseen.'

Annie agreed. 'Of course, because most of the guests at this point would be inside the church waiting for the bride's arrival, wouldn't they? Even the ones that hung around outside the church to get a picture of the bride or who were sneaking a crafty fag.'

'Could it be he wanted witnesses?' Charley contemplated. She turned to face Neal. 'Onlookers tell us that they heard six shots fired. We know that one hit his nephew, so by my calculations we are still missing one.'

Now the immediate area outside the inner cordon was interesting to the CSI. Neal cast his eyes to the most obvious place the sixth bullet may have landed. He walked towards where the group of men had been standing for the photograph. To the rear was the rose arch. Sure enough, six feet from the ground, he found some damage to the climbing rose. Looking even more closely, he discovered a bullet lodged in a branch. After photographing it *in situ*, he proceeded to remove it carefully, cutting away part of the branch with it so as not to damage the exterior. Then he placed it in a transparent tamper-proof evidence pot. Returning to the others with a smile on his face, he held the sealed pot at shoulder height, not unlike a fisherman with a prize catch. 'Looks like a 9mm shell to me. Ballistics will confirm,' he said proudly.

Charley took the sealed container and studied the bullet through the clear plastic. 'I'd been considering calling Ballistics out, but now it seems to be a waste of time and money.'

Neal shrugged his shoulders. 'It's your decision, but I agree.' He counted on his fingers to make his point. 'Let's face it, they'll have the bullets, the gun and the pictures of his wounds, as well as video footage of the gunman firing. What more will they need?'

'When I was working in the Met, the National Crime Agency told us that ammunition was going for fifty pence a round, and you could pick up converted weapons imported from EU countries for as little as twelve hundred pounds apiece.'

'They're unrestricted and legal in those countries and it's not an offence, like it is here, to modify deactivated weapons, so they are then capable of being fired again,' said Neal.

'At least we don't have the number of gangs here that they do in the capital, thank God,' added Annie.

Charley pondered on the subject. 'Although, when I was at a cross-border management meeting to discuss current activity and best practice the other day, I discovered intelligence that there have been several new gangs identified in our county that were initially established in the cities, like Manchester, Birmingham, and Liverpool. Apparently, weapons are a status symbol, along with the designer clothes and bling jewellery that they swagger about in.'

Satisfied that all had been done that could be done in the inner scene, the SIO clapped her hands together and took a deep breath. 'Okay, let's get him moved to the mortuary, and we will head into church to speak to the family and friends,' she told Annie.

DI Charley Mann and DC Annie Glover removed their protective clothing at the rendezvous point and placed them in separate exhibit bags in case they were required for examination later. They left behind Neal Rylatt and his team to carry on gathering evidence, taking pictures, and searching for anything and everything that might be important to the enquiry.

The two detectives walked back to the building and in through the doors of St Cuthbert's Church when they were immediately hit by the sombre and solemn atmosphere.

DS Mike Blake and DC Ricky-Lee had liaised with Reverend Richard Radley, who had managed somehow to get the distraught wedding party calm, seated and drinking beverages. In the main the guests were praying with Radley. The others were being spoken to by detectives and the police support unit officers.

On seeing Charley and Annie enter the church, DS Mike Blake called for everyone's attention and introduced them.

Afterwards, Charley tugged at Mike Blake's sleeve to pull him to one side. 'Mike, have we seized the digital equipment from those who have taken pictures and video footage? My thoughts are that we could get these downloaded by the intelligence unit. I'm conscious of trying to give our team the opportunity to see what took place before, during and immediately after the event, as early as the briefing.'

'All taken care of, boss, and our modified question-naires are being completed by witnesses.'

'Did you come across any resistance?'

'No, not really. Some people frowned at handing over their mobiles, but they did because they wanted to help.'

'Have you spoken to the people who tackled the gunman and who rendered first aid to the victims yet? We need to get a feel for what they did at the scene.'

'It's done,' Mike assured her.

'Good.' Charley scanned the room. 'Where's the immediate family?'

Sitting down and speaking to Bob Sullivan's family to inform them that his body would shortly be taken to the hospital mortuary was not an easy task, but it was important.

'Can we see him?' asked his wife, Josie Sullivan.

'Arrangements will be made to do so as soon as it's possible and only if you're up to it, I promise. I know you will have a lot of questions and I'll try to answer them as soon as I can. First, we need to establish the facts and try to understand why someone would want to kill your husband and go to these extremes to do so today, because at this moment, it looks like he was the target.'

The following update that she received both alarmed her and made her furious at the same time. The arrested gunman had made a complaint to the custody sergeant of assault against the officers who had taken him into custody, and it was suspected that he had a broken nose and a fractured jaw. He was in the process of being trans-ported to A & E at the same hospital where Bob Sullivan's body was going, and where Ralph Bateman was under-going surgery.

He, however, was under close supervision and would remain handcuffed at all times. His allegation would need an independent internal enquiry, but importantly, this information told Charley that the shooter knew exactly where he was and what was happening. Even if he had taken drugs or any other substances that he might say clouded his judgement, they had not affected him so badly that he didn't know his own mind.

At the briefing two hours later back at the station, they repeated the facts with the team to purposefully reinforce what was required of them. The message by the SIO needed to be concise and clearly understood by everyone in these initial stages.

'According to the guests who spoke to the armed response officers, the gunman who we now know to be Benny Patterson came within a few yards of the male line-up before he opened fire. Intelligence sought on those attending the wedding, and the shooter, will hopefully throw up something that connects them. There's some suggestion that Patterson's automatic weapon jammed after six bullets were discharged. I don't need to tell you we could be dealing with far more casualties. I want to know if there is any previous history of use of firearms. In fact, I want to know everything about the obnoxious twat we're currently giving free board and lodgings to; and how come no one recognised the local idiot?'

At the end of the briefing Charley returned to her office to be informed that Ralph Bateman had died during the emergency surgery to save his life. She contemplated the grave news, and thought of his poor mother, not only had she lost her brother but she would also be burying her son.

Charley was now in charge of a double murder.

Chapter Four

Charley updated Divisional Commander Bobbie Stokes on the present situation in the enquiry, then the command team at HQ. The clock above her office door showed her it was two-thirty in the afternoon, and she had yet to eat that day.

As it was the weekend, Winnie the station cleaner, whose self-appointed job for the last forty-odd years had been to make tea and fetch sandwiches, was not working and since there was no canteen on site, Annie had offered to go to the supermarket for provisions.

'Breakfast, dinner and tea this,' said Wilkie Connor, stuffing a pork pie in his mouth and washing it down with a can of Diet Coke whilst unwrapping a sausage roll.

Annie was checking her list and distributing the food and beverage orders across the large incident room table to each detective who had asked for them. 'You mean breakfast, lunch and dinner.'

Mike flopped down in a chair next to Annie and opposite DC Ricky-Lee. He rolled his eyes. 'Can we not just enjoy our food for once without you two squabbling?'

The discussion between the team quickly turned to the enquiry regarding what had taken place that morning, where they were with the tasks and what was to still be done, when Charley took her seat.

'According to the initial statements given by family and friends of Bob Sullivan in the aftermath of the shooting, it is very obvious that he was a much-loved family man, a true gentleman, and a well-respected pillar of the community. Several people told me that they didn't know of anyone who had a bad word to say about him or Ralph Bateman,' said Mike.

'The news of Ralph Bateman's death means that the guests who knew him will perhaps have to be spoken to again,' added Charley as she took a bite of her baguette.

Mouth full, Mike nodded in agreement.

'Shocked mourners were leaving flowers and cards at the police cordon at the church gates when I left,' Ricky-Lee informed them.

Charley stated the obvious to the others as she sipped her mug of tea. 'We know who shot them both, but what we don't know is why, and the only person who may perhaps enlighten us as to the reason is Benny Patterson, who of course we haven't had the opportunity to interview yet due to the fact that he was taken to the hospital. We'll also have to wait until he's spoken with a solicitor before we can speak to him.'

'Maybe Bateman was also Benny Patterson's target?' said Mike.

Wilkie opened the office manager's biscuit tin and his eyes lit up. Annie shook her head. 'Tattie'll have your guts for garters if you dare eat those homemade cookies.'

The older detective shrugged his shoulders and dunked one after another in his coffee. 'Maybe Patterson was so drugged up that he didn't know who the hell he was firing at?'

Annie dipped her hand into her crisp packet. 'Yeah, I must admit I hadn't thought of that. Or maybe the bullets were meant for no one in particular just to ruin their day.'

'Don't be daft! He didn't have to kill anyone to do that, he could've stood up in church and shouted, "it should've been me!"'

Annie's lips were perfectly poised around the straw of her smoothie carton. She stopped drinking and glared at him.

Charley's mind was otherwise distracted, buzzing with questions that she had no immediate answers for, but that kept her from getting involved with the office banter.

Turning to Mike, she asked, 'Do we know if there's any CCTV around the church? If so, I want it seizing.'

Mike got out his notebook and his pen hovered over a new page. 'I think it's important we find out how Patterson arrived at the church, but more importantly, I want to know what's his connection with Bob Sullivan and his nephew, and where did he get that gun from?'

Annie finished her drink and tossed the carton in the bin. 'I arranged for Patterson's personal property to be seized as possible exhibits, and would you believe there was five hundred quid in new notes which was found in his pocket when he was detained.'

Charley shared her thoughts. 'It's a long shot, but can you locate the ATMs in the vicinity? ATMs have cameras which might be useful to us. I think the pictures are only stored for three months, though, so we must keep it in mind that we might need them.'

Ricky-Lee was listening in. 'To get that amount of money in one transaction, you'd need to go into a bank. Although, there is a way around it if you use two different cards. I know because I did much the same with credit cards when I was gambling,' he said.

Mike wound his pen through his fingers, typical of the detective sergeant when he was thinking. 'Perhaps it's also worth asking if it's possible to identify anyone requesting to withdraw five hundred pounds in one transaction at the local banks?'

'Most garages have CCTV. Which is the nearest to the church? If Patterson came by car, then maybe he called at the garage,' said Ricky-Lee.

Annie rolled up her litter and took a successful shot at the bin. 'He didn't have any bank cards on him. Five hundred smackers is a lot of money to a druggy, a nuisance, a beggar, and according to the intel we have on him, he isn't as prolific as he used to be,' she said.

Wilkie belched loudly. Annie pulled a face at him. Unperturbed, he carried on, 'Knowing Patterson, he'd sell his own mother for five hundred quid.'

Annie looked surprised. 'She's still around then?'

Wilkie frowned at her. 'How the hell do I know?'

Annie looked puzzled. 'But you said…'

'It's a saying. It means he has no sentiment or scruples and would do anything for money,' said Ricky-Lee.

'I've had a sheltered life,' she replied. 'I was taught by nuns.'

Charley nodded. 'The money's gone to be swabbed for drugs and prints. Let's see if that leads us anywhere. You and I know that folks have murdered for a hell of a lot less, and if he is a regular user then he will need money to feed his habit,' Charley paused. 'We also need to check all routes that lead to and from the church to see if we can find evidence of Patterson travelling to the church.

Someone must have seen him at some point this morning,' Charley told them.

Mike wrote the tasks to action with haste. 'I for one am interested to know who Benny Patterson's associates are of late.'

-

On hearing the door open, the SIO looked beyond the others and smiled warmly at young blonde Connie Seabourne standing in the doorway wearing a pretty summer dress. Charley stood to greet her and walked with her towards her office. 'I was just about to say to this lot that I would let you know the basics of what we are dealing with.'

Connie sat down at the other side of the desk from Charley. The SIO offered the press officer a sheet of paper. 'As usual, I've got a brief statement for you. However, we can't name anyone just yet.'

Connie sat quietly whilst she read.

> A murder enquiry is underway, led by DI Charley Mann, after a double shooting at a wedding that took place at St Cuthbert's Church, Slaithwaite earlier today. One man died at the scene after receiving fatal injuries, and a second man died in hospital during emergency surgery. A twenty-five-year-old local man was detained and arrested at the scene and a firearm recovered.
>
> Enquiries are continuing.
>
> Members of the public need not be unduly worried as this appears to be a targeted attack.

As usual, we would like to hear from
anyone who was in, or passing through, the
area of the church at the time.

Connie lifted her head and smiled. She stood.

'Thank you for that. I'll put it out on the news line. It
will keep the media wolves at bay for a while, or at least
until I get a further update from you.'

'You know that as soon as I can, I will. Just to note that
there will be no press conference or interviews because we
have a man in custody, and therefore we can't discuss the
details.'

Connie nodded her head. 'Understood.' Swiftly she
moved towards the doorway. 'I'll speak soon and thank
you.'

Charley was glad she was wearing a comfortable navy blue
cotton suit and white short-sleeved shirt, which was cool
and made her look fresh, despite the heat, when she stood
in front of the whole team in the incident room at five-
thirty for a full debrief.

'Some of you may have come across Benny Patterson,
who this morning was disarmed and arrested at the scene
of the shooting of Robert – Bob – Sullivan in the grounds
of St Cuthbert's Church, where he was attending his
daughter's wedding. Patterson is in police custody, and
I've been informed he has just returned to the cells from
the hospital, where he has been treated for a broken nose
and a hairline fracture of his jaw. He claims these were
sustained, along with other minor injuries, during his
detention at the church and transportation to the station.
For those of you who have been drafted in from other

Force areas, and haven't come across Patterson before, he is a known twenty-five-year-old local smackhead with previous convictions for grievous bodily harm, affray, robbery, burglary and weapons offences from these parts. However, there is nothing which suggests that he previously had access to firearms.

'At the time of his arrest, a search of his person resulted in the seizure of one wrap of cocaine and five hundred pounds in cash. The cocaine might explain his bizarre behaviour on his detention and arrest. As for the money, could this be blood money? Although Benny Patterson's appearance is one of a homeless person, according to the details he gave for his detention sheets, he does presently have a bedsit at the Oak Bank Bail Hostel, Gaol Lane. His room will be subjected to a search as a matter of urgency for potential intelligence and evidence.

'Presently, he is awaiting the arrival of his legal representative. Today I can tell you that the local on-call duty solicitor is Anne Jacobs. I am told Patterson is no stranger to Ms Jacobs as she previously represented him when he was a juvenile.'

DS Mike Blake updated the others. 'More than likely owing to the occasion, there was no resistance from people handing over their mobile phones or cameras to the police at the church. The stored data can be downloaded with the statements and transferred to the police HOLMES system, working twenty-four-seven in the incident room. This, as you are aware, is not always the case.'

'It's hard to comprehend why anyone would not offer evidence that would put a criminal before the courts isn't it? However, although they're in the minority, some as we know are reluctant to help us, even on a murder enquiry, for no other reason than they have a deep-seated hatred of authority.' Charley checked her notes. 'On that note, before anyone interviews Benny Patterson, I want them to view at least some of that footage to see for themselves what took place,' said Charley.

When the team dispersed, Charley headed to her office to speak to the coroner's officer by telephone.

'I'd like a suggested time-frame for the family to attend to view the deceased,' she said.

'I'm waiting to get an update as to the availability of the Home Office forensic pathologist.'

'I understand that, but it doesn't matter if it's before post-mortem. We need a formal identification.'

'Plus, the coroner will require a statement from the next of kin,' he replied.

'I'll await your call,' she said, and with that, Charley put down the phone.

In the cells, the custody time clock was ticking. It had started when Benny Patterson had arrived at the bridewell, and in these initial stages they had twenty-four hours in which to speak to the prisoner in accordance with the Police and Criminal Evidence Act, although it had been stopped for the duration of his hospital visit.

The photos of the wedding were available now to view as well as the video footage that had been downloaded to watch. Charley knew that, before long, they would need to interview Patterson and she looked forward to giving him the opportunity to explain his violent actions.

Charley's mobile rang. She answered, 'Detective Inspector Charley Mann.'

'Inspector Levitt, control room. An update for you in case you haven't been notified by the hospital. We've just been informed that Ralph Bateman died of heart failure, not the gunshot wound. Apparently, he had an unknown heart defect.'

When Charley put down the phone, she knew that at any future trial, Benny Patterson's defence team were likely to argue 'causation' in respect to Bateman's murder. However, that was for the future.

On hearing the news, though, Annie had no doubts. 'A jury will make the right decision when they've heard all the facts.'

'Ralph Bateman wouldn't have been facing emergency surgery if he hadn't been shot, and my argument would be that this heart defect could have been identified at any time, corrected, and potentially he could have gone on to live a long life if he hadn't been shot. It is no doubt murder. I hope that the Crown Prosecution Service and the jury will think likewise.'

'Yes, if he says that the shooting of Ralph Bateman was an accident, and he didn't cause his death, that might indeed confuse the jury.'

'Let's hope when we eventually get to that stage that the trial judge advises them on the law, and that common sense prevails.'

Chapter Five

The warmth of the incident room, coupled with the amount of heat created by the bodies within, produced a ruddiness on DI Charley Mann's cheeks. It was, however, unusually quiet as the investigative team on the case viewed footage of the shooting.

It was quite short, most of it being wedding guests in conversation and laughing until it was interrupted by the suddenness of the gunfire. This visual tool was of great evidential value, not only for the investigators, but also for any future trial. In fact, it was just as valuable as the senior investigator's personal policy log was to her. The SIO's policy log was often referred to as their bible, and Mike was showing Annie how to complete it.

Charley was sat within hearing distance and was duly impressed by both Mike's teaching skills and Annie's readiness to learn.

'All you have to remember is that it's a place to record the senior investigative officer's decision making on major incidents, which must also include decisions not to pursue a particular line of enquiry, and why. Each entry has to be timed, dated and signed in duplicate.' Mike slid the book across the table for Charley to sign. 'Each entry is then input onto the HOLMES computer database, as you are already aware, to give us clarity of direction and what is required,' said Mike.

Charley and Mike left the incident room together. As they walked to her office, Charley retrieved her mobile phone from her pocket. Mike opened the doors for her and she scrolled through her messages.

'No update on the time of the post-mortems yet?'

Charley shook her head, and cast him a glance. 'Thanks for updating the policy log, and for showing Annie despite how busy you are. I really appreciate it.'

Mike smiled. 'It's my pleasure. I don't know what uniform were thinking when she relocated from the south, and they seconded Annie straight into CID as soon as a vacancy arose.'

'Uniform's loss, and our gain,' Charley replied.

In her office, Charley sat behind her desk. She moved her overflowing inbox to the side to make room for the tray Annie brought in with her. The Tupperware box reeked of stale plastic and contained her pre-prepared meal from yesterday: peanut butter sandwiches with jam in two slices of brown bread, now curled up at the edges. The banana had turned an unattractive black and the slice of cake was stale.

Annie was apologetic as she sat. 'I made them for myself yesterday afternoon to eat on my late shift, but we were so busy that I didn't get a chance to have a meal break. They were still in the fridge, and I thought them better than nothing. Besides, I can't abide waste. Blame the nuns!' The young detective had cut the sandwiches into small triangles so they could share them. The three of them knew that there was no likelihood of any other sustenance because time was crucial. They were there to discuss the interview strategy for Benny Patterson.

Charley watched Mike and Annie going through their notes as the low sun shone gently onto Mike's face from Charley's window. Their disinterest in the food was clear, but they knew they needed to eat something. The bright light showed up the lines at the side of Mike's eyes and the corners of his mouth. It was then that she realised that he looked as tired as she felt. She appreciated the responsibility that rested heavily on the detective sergeant's shoulders, but the day was far from over. There were interviews to prepare and participate in for the two tier-five detectives, who were the experienced, specialist-trained officers who interviewed suspects for murder and major crime on a regular basis.

Charley's heart jumped at the noise from an incoming message. Two pairs of eyes looked at her questioningly. She read the message, which made her aware that there were two post-mortems for her to attend that night back-to-back.

'It's not going to be just a late night, it's going to be a long night,' she said. 'Let's crack on.'

The SIO was interested to hear first what her colleagues' thoughts were on the footage of the incident that they had just witnessed, which could affect the questions that they would put to Patterson in interview.

'It was obvious that the guests were totally oblivious to Benny Patterson's presence until he knelt down and started firing,' Mike said, flinching as hot liquid burnt his tongue.

'My God, those men were brave to step forward, overpower and disarm Patterson, weren't they?' said Annie.

'If his gun hadn't jammed...' Charley shuddered.

'They'd be dead.' It was Annie's turn to state the obvious.

'I know we are looking at the seized CCTV, but have either of you heard that we've got a confirmed sighting of Patterson earlier this morning, either on his way to the church or in the village?' asked Charley.

A collective shake of heads told her no.

Charley held their gaze. 'Strange that, don't you think?'

Annie's eyes glazed over. 'Hell yes, there were enough people to-ing and fro-ing at the church this morning.'

Charley lowered her eyes. 'Yet none of the witnesses to the crime mentioned in their statements that they saw him previously.'

Annie mused, 'So how'd he get there?'

'Can I suggest we ask the guests to check their dash-cam footage?'

'That's a good idea Mike!' Charley replied. 'We need to seize every opportunity to gather as much evidence as possible. Talking about evidence, please make sure we let Ballistics know that they will be getting the shells that will hopefully be recovered at the post-mortem examinations, as well as the gun used by Patterson, and a copy of the footage of the incident caught on camera. Also, remind them these exhibits need to be treated as a priority because we have the offender in custody.'

There was a knock at the door and a rather dishevelled-looking Wilkie popped his head in. 'Just a couple of things to report from the search of Patterson's shit-hole of a gaff, boss: a green Bosch drill box covered in gaffer tape and an empty brown envelope that had been torn open and discarded on the kitchen worktop.'

Charley looked puzzled. 'And the reason being?'

'The drill box was open in the middle of the room. Might be something, might be nothing, but a drill is not something that I'd have thought Patterson would possess.

Plus there was no drill inside, so what was the box used for? And the envelope was new, there was no writing on it, it had been torn open. My thought is we might get the sender's fingerprints from it.'

Charley half-smiled. 'Good thinking, Wilkie. That's great.'

–

Meanwhile, in his cell two floors below them, Benny Patterson was enjoying his rest period and eating a warm meal in line with his dietary requirements and religious beliefs, per the legally bound Police and Criminal Evidence Act of 1984, which states that the police must exercise a proper duty of care for people held in custody.

–

Charley continued to discuss the strategic approach to the upcoming interviews, and when the detectives left her office to prepare, she checked the link so she could watch those interviews from her office. This allowed her to multitask whilst she managed the rest of the investigation, making the best use of her time before she was required to attend the mortuary.

Charley made a mental note to make sure Ralph Bateman's family had been spoken to and to allocate a family liaison officer to assist them through the traumatic time. He, too, had been a victim of Patterson's.

After three interviews with Benny Patterson, Mike and Annie returned to Charley's office.

'Well, that didn't take long, did it? As you probably saw, he told us to fuck off,' said Mike, laughing.

Annie wiped a palm across her forehead and drank from the plastic cup that she'd filled up from the water dispenser in the main office. 'Yes, and fuck right off and fuck off you two,' she added, pulling a face and blowing her nose.

'Nice, what's the face for?'

Annie gulped her water. 'He stank of ammonia,' she gagged. 'I'm trying to rid my nostrils of the smell.'

Charley's face showed no emotion. 'On a positive note, and there's always a positive if you look hard enough,' she replied, 'just because he didn't answer your questions isn't going to stop us from asking them, giving him an opportunity to respond. Did he or his solicitor make any comment when you informed Patterson that he was also under arrest for the murder of Ralph Bateman?'

Mike shook his head. 'No.'

Annie turned to Mike. 'Didn't you see him smirk though? There was no sign of remorse. He thinks he's a gangster now.'

Stretching her aching back, Charley yawned. 'Well, he'll soon be remanded in prison, and with any luck he'll get a whole life tariff conviction. There's no rush on his custody clock. We'll wait for a bit to see if there is any further evidence to put to him. If not, then I'll run it past the Crown Prosecution Service, but as far as I can see, we have enough to charge him with the murder of Bob Sullivan and therefore we must do it.'

Annie mulled this over. 'Why not Ralph Bateman?'

'I want to wait and see what the post-mortem tells me because the suggestion from the medical staff is that he shouldn't have died from his injury, and we can get Patterson remanded back to the cells to facilitate any further interviews we might need.'

Mike was studious. 'We know Patterson is capable of the execution of an unarmed person in cold blood, but what we don't seem to have is any intelligence that shows him being firearms trained, or owning, using, or having contacts from which he could obtain a firearm, and yet he appeared to know exactly what he was doing.' The detective sergeant paused for a moment. 'And what confuses me is that he didn't try to conceal his identity. There's no question in my mind that the shooting was a deliberate act, in front of witnesses, which makes me puzzled as to why he is now not willing to answer our questions.'

Charley agreed. 'Good points, and let's not forget the gun jammed, and he was unable to, or didn't attempt to, fix it. Luckily it did curtail what could have been a massacre.' Charley paused for thought. 'You're right. He must have had some firearms training.'

'Maybe he learnt the basics on the internet?' suggested Annie.

Mike replied. 'He hardly seems the type of person to access the internet, let alone search and follow the instructions.'

'Does that suggest to you that he's not alone in this? It will be interesting to see if intelligence tells us that the weapon has been used in previous crimes.'

Charley's phone lit up. She looked up from reading the message. 'I've got to go to the mortuary, so we will catch up later. If there is anything you need, I have my mobile with me.'

The detectives stood, Charley grabbed her bag and as they headed towards the main office, a thought rushed into her mind. She turned to Mike. 'I've had a change of heart. Just charge Patterson and we'll go for the remand back to the cells as we discussed. We will know in the next few hours what exactly killed both men won't we, and he must have had help.'

'Time will tell. Let's face it, he got the gun off someone didn't he?' replied Mike.

Chapter Six

Charley slowly stepped over the threshold of the mortuary. With a heightened awareness of her surroundings, her eyes were instantly drawn to the large window which opened up to her the brightly lit room, where she saw the dissection table with the corpse of Bob Sullivan ready for examination.

Undertaking a post-mortem wasn't exactly the best way to spend a Saturday night, but in the SIO's eyes, it was a necessary one. Unless for some reason it wasn't logistically possible for her to attend, as the SIO of a murder enquiry, she would always choose to be at the procedure. Knowing how the victim had lived, as well as how and why they had died, was as important to her as the murder scene itself. However, not all SIOs agreed with her, and would sometimes dispute the need for her rank to attend the gruesome, disfiguring, and wholly destructive procedure. However, Charley argued that she needed firsthand knowledge of the facts to be able to lead from the front.

Charley and Ricky-Lee had this same debate on their way to the mortuary, where he would be presiding as exhibits officer. 'How can a designated person, who may not have actually been inside the murder scene, attending on my behalf, be able to ask questions that arise during the dissection of the body?' she asked.

Detective Constable Ricky-Lee was in total agreement. 'I don't think that it's humanly possible for someone to convey the sense and feeling of a post-mortem to another. The facts, yes, but in my mind that's not enough for such an important part of the investigation, and one for which the conclusion could potentially determine the final outcome of the case. Can you imagine how embarrassing it would be to be questioned by the pathologist about the scene if you hadn't been near the body, as the SIO or CIS would have?'

Hearing that Professor Emily Morton was in charge, Charley knew that they would have quick, sensitive and extremely thorough examinations. Charley settled in the viewing room, ready for the procedure to begin. She would be patient and await Emily's findings, aware that they could be at the mortuary for several hours. It wasn't just the body, but also them, who were in the pathologist's hands for however long this took.

The first examination to ascertain Bob Sullivan's cause of death showed that he had clearly died from a bullet to the head, although the other bullets from the automatic weapon would also have meant death was instantaneous. She looked up from the corpse and pointed her finger at the bullet's entry point in his face. 'The bullet that caused this wound came to rest in his skull and would have caused his death. That said, the shot to his chest caused the bullet to go through his ribcage and, as you can see, damaged his aorta before lodging in his spine, which would have also killed him, but I suggest not as quickly as the one to his head. The other two wounds were not immediately life-threatening, however they did cause him severe injuries which would have required surgery had they been the only ones.'

Bob Sullivan had bled internally, just as CSI supervisor Neal Rylatt had anticipated at the scene. His body cavity was flooded, and the pathologist's assistant required the use of a plastic jug to scoop out the blood before his internal organs could be removed, weighed, examined and photographed. Four shells were recovered where they had come to rest in his body, individually photographed *in situ* by Neal Rylatt before being removed and each placed in an evidence tube and labelled accordingly as to where in the body they had been discovered.

'All the signs indicate to me that Robert Sullivan was a healthy individual before he was shot,' said Emily as she outlined her findings. After the post-mortem was concluded, she looked up at Charley. 'Someone wanted to make sure he died, didn't they?' she said, blowing out a long breath.

The thirty-minute break between examinations allowed the detectives a drink, and gave the pathologist, her assistant, and Neal time to change their protective clothing before commencing the same procedure on the next victim, Ralph Bateman.

Charley took the opportunity to get some air from outside the confinement of the viewing room and found Ricky-Lee standing at the top of the steps of the fire escape, vaping. A few feet away from her, the white smoke billowing around him looked like it had come from the spout of a steam engine.

'Do you find that enjoyable?' she asked.

The detective screwed up his nose. 'Not really, but I've found that the Peppermint E liquid is a perfect palate cleanser and helps to take away the taste and odour of this place,' he replied. He offered her the electronic cigarette. 'Do you want to try it?'

Charley grimaced and shook her head. 'No thanks,' she said, wafting her hand in an attempt to bat away the smoke. 'Don't tell me that that's good for you?'

'Probably not,' he agreed. 'But what is these days? If we were to believe and adhere to everything that the media put out, then we'd just be eating lettuce leaves and they give me wind.'

Charley opened the door for them to walk back inside, a smile on her lips. 'Lettuce does not cause bloating, however, you've made your point. Come on back inside, they'll be waiting for us.'

The items taken from Bob Sullivan for the exhibits officer included his clothing, the body samples, and the recovered cartridge shells, which were passed through the hatch into the viewing room for the attention of DC Ricky-Lee.

He ensured they were sealed in tamper-proof containers to prevent any risk of contamination, and to make absolutely sure that there would be no mix-up, he took the precaution of taking the exhibits to the boot of his car before the second post-mortem began.

On his return, the post-mortem of Ralph Bateman began, and it wasn't long before Professor Emily Morton told the officers, 'The bullet that entered his thigh severed the main artery near his groin, which created uncontrollable bleeding.' For a moment, she stopped what she was doing, and referred to the medical notes that had been made at the time, which told her what procedures had been carried out in the attempt to save his life. Having opened the wound that the surgeons had repaired, the next step was for Emily to have it photographed.

The pathologist continued, and her next observations intrigued everyone. 'It is clear to me that this wound would have required immediate surgery, and the surgical team dealt with it and repaired the damage to the artery in his leg. This injury did not cause Mr Bateman's death.'

The revelation caused Charley to pause briefly. 'The heart defect?' she whispered, for she knew that Emily would continue with her examination until she found the exact cause.

Not hearing her, Emily opened up the torso and removed the internal organs for examination. Whilst the other organs were being photographed and weighed, she held his slightly enlarged, rounded heart in the air so that she could explain to Charley what she had found. 'When I dissect this heart, I expect to find evidence of a disease called dilated cardiomyopathy, which makes the muscle wall become stretched and thin.' Emily pointed to a tear in the heart wall. 'This I suggest could have been brought on by stress. Whether that was because of the operation or the shooting, we will never know; however, heart failure is the cause of Ralph Bateman's death, not the bullet in his leg.'

'What was his life expectancy prior to the shooting?' asked Charley.

'I can't tell you that. With an early diagnosis, this is not a death sentence. Although there is no pacemaker fitted to ensure that his heartbeat stayed regular. Undiagnosed, it could be a problem.'

In the following minutes, Bateman's heart was weighed and at each point during the dissection procedure, it was photographed.

'Apart from his heart condition, he was a healthy young man?' Charley asked.

'Absolutely.'

'For clarification, and this is really important, are you telling me that if Ralph Bateman hadn't been shot, which undeniably caused a huge blood loss, plus the trauma of the surgery on top of that, he could've been walking around for a while yet despite the heart disease?' queried Charley.

'There is no doubt that his heart would have been weaker, but by no means was he at death's door until he was subjected to the attack. In a case like this, like I said, a pacemaker may have helped,' replied Emily.

It was late evening when the two detectives set off to return to the incident room.

'Will CPS go for us charging Patterson with Bateman's death?' questioned Ricky-Lee.

'They'd better, otherwise they'll have an argument on their hands. I'm in no doubt that the defence will make a big play on it, hoping to confuse a jury, but if you've got a loaded weapon and fire it at someone at close range, not much more needs to be said, does it?'

'Not in my book, no. The intention to kill is there, we know what the result of firing the weapon was, and we also know that if Bateman hadn't been shot, he would still be alive today.'

Charley sighed deeply. 'It's too late for me to speak with the Crown Prosecution Service tonight, but I will do first thing in the morning. Let's face it. Patterson isn't going anywhere anytime soon, is he?'

Ricky-Lee was sitting in the passenger seat of her car. At the red traffic light in town, she glanced in his direction. He was shaking his head, looking out of his side window at the empty street, and seemed to be smiling in a disbelieving way.

'What?' asked Charley.

Ricky-Lee turned to face her. 'I was just thinking how unprofessional it would be seen to be if we interrupted Patterson's eight-hour sleep period to formally charge him with Bateman's murder when his custody clock allows us to do it tomorrow.'

Charley closed her tired eyes for a second and opened them to a green light. 'Exactly,' she said, taking a look in her mirror before she put her foot down to drive off. 'But we will sleep better in the knowledge that we understood how both men died and now have medical evidence to support the facts.'

The incident room was still a hive of activity, but the lighting was subdued and the feeling was one of fatigue. Charley was about to leave for home when Wilkie Connor, coat on, all ready to leave it with the night shift, caught her attention.

'Boss, just before you go, we've got a sighting of a black BMW saloon on CCTV dropping off someone who we believe to be Benny Patterson on Argyle Street two streets away from St Cuthbert's Church this morning. We can't make out the driver or a registration number, much as we've tried, but at least it's a start.'

'A time for the footage and another look at CCTV in the immediate area. Now we know there is a vehicle of interest.'

Heading for home, Charley felt in much need of her bed. Having set her alarm clock for six a.m., she laid in bed, staring at the timepiece, calculating how much sleep she would get if she fell asleep immediately. With a pen and paper at her side so she could record her thoughts if she woke up, she was sorely tempted to put a jug of milk on the doorstep – just as her grandfather and grandmother would have done as believers in the Yorkshire folklores, including the hobgoblin and its powers.

However, as soon as her head hit the pillow, she was out like a light.

Chapter Seven

At eight o'clock Sunday morning, the team were briefed on the outcome of the post-mortems. Now also arrested for the murder of Ralph Bateman as well as charged with the murder of Bob Sullivan, Benny Patterson would be interviewed again, this time regarding the younger man's death. The interview team had no more expectation than to be told to go away, but not so politely.

Given it was a Sunday, the next time available to the police to put Patterson before the court for a remand back to the cells was the following morning. After that, they could interview him further and his custody clock would be restarted, so they would have up to seventy-two hours to question him before charge. The charge would have to be agreed by the Crown Prosecution Service.

At the briefing, Charley observed the sea of tired faces, and she guessed that the few hours respite which the investigation had allowed hadn't offered any of them much breathing space, nor would they have much in the days to follow. The SIO's voice sounded brittle even to her.

'We are currently in pursuit of a black BMW that was captured on CCTV in the vicinity of the church yesterday morning, and which I believe could have brought Benny Patterson to the scene. Enhanced, I am hoping that this image will give us at the very least a partial number plate. If so, we'll run that through the ANPR. Potentially we could immediately have an owner and their address. I am also hopeful the picture might provide us with the driver's identity.'

There were a vast number of enquiries ongoing, but finding out what had taken place during and prior to the killing were top priorities. This information would provide details of any preparation needed to assist in proving the intent. Patterson had known where and when the wedding was to take place, so it seemed for some reason this was his chosen place to strike. He had acquired a gun, ammunition and now it appeared he'd even arranged a lift to the church.

Charley wouldn't leave any stone unturned. If there was something to be found, she was sure that her team would find it.

-

By the time she reached her office, Charley felt a headache looming. She had a lot of things on her mind and prepared to make use of her time wisely whilst waiting for updates. The bottle of painkillers in her desk drawer caught her eye. She reached for it, shook out a couple and swallowed them with a mouthful of cold tea.

Considering the pathologist's findings at the post-mortem of the younger victim, Charley was happy she'd gotten relief by the time she finally got through to the Crown Prosecution Service to discuss her thoughts on charging Patterson. It was important that Benny Patterson be charged with Bateman's murder; any less of a charge would not be acceptable. When she heard Caroline Maston's voice, full of authority, the SIO found herself feeling slightly anxious that she might have a fight on her hands, but this was not the time to feel down-hearted. This particular discussion couldn't be avoided or put off.

'You and I both know that the charge could be reduced at trial should the judge think it more appropriate. What we can't do is increase it. So, I'm standing firm on this one, Caz. I want him charged with Bateman's murder,' she said, well aware that Caroline's argument could be that Bateman had not died as a direct result of his injuries, and therefore she may want the charge to be reduced to manslaughter.

However, to her surprise, Caroline fully supported her, and readily agreed to the charge of murder. As Charley had been expecting a longer discussion, she replaced the handset and found that not only had her headache already subsided, but she had a spurt of energy that sent her out to check on the others.

Charley found every member of the team busy with their given task. The first group was researching the background of the two deceased victims and the wedding guests. The SIO felt the flutter of anticipation as she watched them busy at their work and a million questions popped into her head at once.

Had any of the information retrieved so far flagged up anybody of interest to the enquiry? What might the team tell her at the next briefing about Bob Sullivan, Ralph Bateman and their associates that she didn't already know? Was there any more intelligence to say that any of those already spoken to owned a black BMW? she wondered. Instead, she informed them, 'I want the background of all those in the photographer's line-up with Bob Sullivan put under the microscope. On the surface, it looks like our drug-crazed madman got his man, but we need to be absolutely sure that another person was not his intended target.'

The next group was scrolling through the seized CCTV footage. Charley willed them to find more evidence in relation to the black BMW. Clearer footage might give her the chance to consider using facial mapping to put Patterson there, along with the identification of his clothing, to show beyond doubt that the person alighting from that vehicle, at that precise time, was the man they had in custody. It might also help identify the driver of the car.

Charley found Ricky-Lee in the property store prioritising exhibits to send to Forensics, prepared in batches, in the hope that it would help curtail budget costs should Forensics get a damning result. The caged rooms holding the property in police possession were always locked and the doors in the underground garage where the property was stored kept closed.

'Starting with what we believe will yield the best evidence,' Charley told him, 'let's go through what we have.'

The impression she got as she spoke to the Home Office Large Major Enquiry System (HOLMES) team, who were constantly updating data submitted to the HOLMES system, was that the police file was slowly building, and its contents would ultimately ensure that the case against the offender was watertight and would help convict him.

They too were aware that Patterson's defence team would, in accordance with data protection, have access to anything that was retained and recorded by the police, unless there was an objection to an item that would lead to the identity of an undercover officer or a protected witness. However, she was assured that so far, there was nothing in this enquiry that raised such an issue.

Having been presented with Benny Patterson's background details, Charley settled down at her desk with a coffee and opened his file. It showed her that he was a loner and a bully, an aggressive individual, with references to police involvement going back to when he was a young boy. He was a person who should have been identified early in life as someone who clearly needed help. It wouldn't come as a shock to the locals that, yet again, he was going to prison – this time for the rest of his life. His previous convictions were well documented over several pages. He committed his crimes alone and had indicated to officers that he did so to ensure that he didn't have to share the proceeds of those crimes.

Charley reviewed her notes. There was a knock on the door and Annie walked in.

'Penny for them,' she said.

'MOPS, Annie, that's what I'm thinking. MOPS.'

Annie stopped in her tracks, startled, her face lighting up. 'Pardon?' she giggled.

Charley beckoned her over to sit opposite in her visitor's chair and continued to give her a knowing stare. 'Motive, opportunity, preparation and subsequent acts: basic elements of every crime. Tell me, did Patterson expect to get away from the scene? Because, if so, would the BMW still be cruising the area waiting for him? Or would you think it more likely to be parked nearby with the engine running for a quick getaway?'

Annie shrugged her shoulders. 'I've just come to tell you that Helen, our FLO, is calling into the incident room in about an hour to touch base with us. She says that both families are very nice and she hasn't detected any skeletons in their cupboards or a black sheep in the family yet. They're apparently still reeling from the shock and devastated, as you can imagine.'

Chapter Eight

When Charley walked into the Magistrates' Court the following morning, some words from Harper Lee's *To Kill a Mockingbird* sprang to mind, despite the heat of the day. 'The atmosphere in the courtroom was exactly the same as a cold February morning, when the mockingbirds were still, and the carpenters had stopped hammering.'

With the intelligence and evidence implicating Benny Patterson presented to the magistrates, his appearance before the court was short and swift. He spoke twice to confirm his name and address. It was nothing new for Patterson to be in the dock before the magistrates and it was nothing more than procedure.

The mood back at the station constituted a stark contrast to the atmosphere of the court.

With numerous lines of enquiry highlighted as essential, the paper being pumped out of the printer for the investigating officers was nonstop. Charley was pleased to see that the cogs were in motion and the incident room was buzzing with renewed energy. It was a new day and no one was more aware than her that there was a lot to achieve.

For Charley, leading an investigation sometimes felt like riding a horse; and for those who thought the horse did all the work they should think again! She loved the freedom that the title of SIO gave her, in choosing the route that the enquiry took. Sometimes, however, it felt like the enquiry was at a standstill, and at other times she had to pull back the team's reins to stop them galloping like the wind, in their desire to reach the goal too soon, and therefore make mistakes which could cause the case to fold. Her aim was to get as much evidence as possible before they charged Patterson with Ralph Bateman's murder and they had a maximum of seventy-two hours to do it.

Numerous arrests failed to convert to convictions through lack of evidence, absence of witnesses, or witnesses withdrawing statements, but Charley was certain this wouldn't be a problem in this case. It was rare to have witnesses to a murder and most of these witnesses were guests at the wedding as well as witnesses to the murder of Bob Sullivan.

As the SIO walked through the office to the morning management meeting, she was given updates from the team.

'A further two officers have been drafted in to assist with the viewing of the CCTV footage collated on the streets surrounding the church,' said Wilkie.

'ANPR is searching for BMWs,' reported Ricky-Lee.

Superintendent Bobbie Stokes congratulated Charley's team on their progress. 'Another murderer off the streets. The public will be pleased.'

'Yes, but we still have a lot to do. It's a misconception that once a person is arrested, the work is over.'

'What's the plan?'

'Now that he's remanded, we will continue with our interview strategy, but as you and I know, interviews these days are about giving the arrested person a chance to answer questions that we put to them, including the reason for committing the crime.'

'And is he talking?'

The fact that Charley's lip curled up at one corner told Stokes what he needed to know. 'No, but we are allowing him to assist us in proving or disproving his innocence.'

'Absolutely sir,' she said. 'May I be excused now from the morning management meeting as I have a lot to do.'

Charley hurried down the steps of the police station, not having had a chance to watch the interview. Mike and Annie caught up with her not long after she had returned to her office. She was working through the paperwork in her inbox, with an eye on her computer screen.

'Well?' Charley asked on seeing their emotionless faces at the office door. 'Come on in. I want to know what happened.'

Ever the gentleman, Mike gave Annie a little passing room to enter and followed her into the office, mimicking the prisoner's voice, as he did so. 'If he 'ad a bad heart, I did him a favour then. He'd have us believe he's got one!'

'Thereafter Patterson reverted back to his favourite two words: F off.' Annie cocked her head and stared at her with unblinking eyes. 'He thinks he's hard.'

'Sit down please,' Charley said as a throbbing pain began behind her eyes and spots appeared before them. *Please, God*, she prayed, *don't let this be the start of a migraine.* Charley reached in her drawer for two paracetamol and washed them down with the old coffee on her desk. The cold fluid made her flinch, and afterwards she gave the officers a forced smile. Taking a deep breath, she continued. 'Don't let that bother you. He's going to find out that there's always someone harder where he's going.'

Annie sat down slowly. 'What do you mean?'

Charley cast her eyes down to the file she had been reading and turned the pages over quickly until she found Patterson's sentencing history. She narrowed her eyes as she studied the piece of paper, pretending to concentrate and digest the content. When she looked up, she was glad the spots before her eyes had gone.

'Well, up to now, his prison history shows us that he's served time in juvenile detention, done a couple of stretches in Cat. D prisons for crimes he committed after coming of age, and then he did a stretch in a Cat. C prison, because by this time it was deemed that he couldn't be trusted in open conditions, but was considered to be unlikely to make a determined escape attempt. Also, because he had a previous sentence of twelve months for the escalation of severity of crime including violence, threat of violence, and the rest...' She sat back in her chair. 'However, a maximum-security prison? Well, now that's a different ball game, isn't it?'

Annie looked thoughtful. 'Maybe we're barking up the wrong tree here. Have you ever thought that going to prison could be a bigger deterrent before you go? The thought of going to prison is...' Annie shuddered. 'No, I can't even imagine. It's horrendous. But because he's pretty much institutionalised, it might actually be a relief for him.'

The younger detective observed the mischievous glint in the SIO's eyes 'You think he might go to Monster Mansion, don't you?' she said.

'Why not? HMP Wakefield is local to the court, and it's the largest high-security prison in the UK. It has about six hundred of Britain's most dangerous people serving life sentences. Pretty scary, eh? And he'll have heard the stories from the elders inside who speak about an "easy time", of "doing bird", but wait until he hits the wing. He won't know what hit him.'

Mike agreed. 'Absolutely, and mark my words, if he hasn't done so already, he'll start to think about the fact that he's facing a prolonged loss of his liberty, identity and dignity. There will be no lads he went to school with, lads from the corner, or lads he committed crimes with to take care of him, because he's always been a loner.'

An alert on Charley's computer told her that she had a message from Ballistics acknowledging the receipt of the weapon, the copy of the wedding footage, the recovered ammunition from the scene, and those from the victims' bodies. The tests were commencing.

Suddenly, with that information, the mood in the office changed. 'When we get more intel on the BMW, the driver, and results from Forensics, we'll have more questions to put to him. Until then, let him stew. We could never begin to imagine what's going on in his head. He's a murderer and we will put all the evidence we find on him before the court as soon as possible.'

Annie voiced her thoughts. 'I wonder what he will say when we ask him outright if he got paid to do the job.'

Charley shrugged her shoulders. 'We'll soon find out, won't we?'

Her telephone rang, and Charley managed to quash her surprise when she heard Maurice Gaunt the Ballistics expert on the other end until Mark had closed the door behind him.

Charley didn't speak to Maurice often, but when she did, the deep, dishy sound of his voice sent a ripple of awareness chasing down her spine. It was a pity his looks didn't quite match up to his voice.

'I don't know if you're aware, but the bullet retrieved from Mr Sullivan's head is a .22-calibre slug, which means it couldn't possibly have been fired from a handgun.'

Charley's pulse quickened. 'So there were two killers on site at the church wedding?'

Maurice said that the second shooter wouldn't have had to have been on the grounds. 'The .22 slug came from a rifle, so it's likely that they would have been positioned somewhere outside the church grounds but had a clear view of the target.'

When Charley put the phone down she sat for a moment digesting the news. 'Bloody hell,' Charley said, on the end of a long breath.

All of a sudden the evidence blew the investigation wide open.

Charley raced to the door. 'Mike, my office. Now!'

Chapter Nine

Charley was staring at the phone on her desk, her mind still racing, when Mike joined her. On seeing his concerned face as he stood stiffly in the doorway, military style with his hands behind his back, she shuffled in her chair and straightened her blouse.

'Come on in and close the door behind you,' she said.

Mike pulled a chair up to her desk, sat down sideways, and leaned in so close she could practically taste the subtle spice of his aftershave. 'What's up? You look as if you could do with a drink.'

Somehow, Maurice Gaunt's words had grown into a dark cloud that hovered over her. 'There was a second gunman at the scene. Whoever it was, they had a clear shot at Sullivan's head. The .22-calibre slug was fired from a rifle.'

Mike stared at Charley for a moment or two, processing the information. 'Where from? I take it he looked at the footage before he rang you?'

Charley nodded. 'He thinks the second shooter was positioned some way off, strategically placed at a high vantage point. Let's face it, if the shooter lived in the area or had done any research on it, they would know that the rose arch was favoured by brides and wedding photographers at St Cuthbert's Church. So it doesn't take a genius to presume that the target, being the father of the bride, would be standing there for pictures at some point.'

Mike shook his head. 'But we were only saying that Patterson's MO has always been to work alone, so what made him change his mind this time?'

Charley shrugged. 'Money, drugs. He had both on him when he was arrested.'

'Patterson was paid to be the fall guy?'

'Maybe. The only other explanation that I can think of is that whoever was the mastermind behind this, and we know it wasn't Patterson, was doubling his chance of success. What this confirms to me is that, if two shooters were involved in trying to take him out, Sullivan definitely was the intended target as we suspected all along.'

'What else do Ballistics say they can tell us?' asked Mike.

'Maurice is doing more tests. From the rifling on the bullets, he'll be able to find out from the computer system if the guns the bullets came from are linked to previous criminal activity.'

Mike frowned. 'If they aren't pool guns used by all and sundry, this might give us a link to the owner by way of the firearms licence.'

'In theory, yes, although it would be a miracle if the guns being used by criminals are not stolen or illegally owned. In which case, there will be no trail.'

Mike twisted his lips. 'Whoever supplied Patterson with the handgun would have known that this would be seized when Patterson was arrested, which was almost certain given the amount of people at the shooting. However, in the rifle's case, that may be different. Perhaps the shooter wouldn't think that the bullet shot from that weapon would give them away. Maybe that will be their downfall. What else did Maurice say?'

Charley sighed. 'Just that the shot wouldn't have been a difficult one, not for a trained shooter with a fitted telescopic sight and a silencer to suppress the noise.'

Mike's eyes lit up. 'Well, we now know that we are looking for a trained shooter. Another piece for the jigsaw.'

Charley looked through her office window into the incident room, where several of the team members were looking towards them from their desks, in anticipation, after the tone in which the boss had commanded her deputy's attendance in her office. 'Appears so. You don't just pick up a rifle and hit a target a few hundred metres away with that accuracy, do you? Maurice is coming out to do a recce to find out possible hiding places where the rifle could have been fired. We need to update the team.'

Mike brushed his hand over his short thick dark hair. 'This is the last thing I expected, and still we don't have a motive.'

Charley pressed her lips together. 'Not yet we don't, but it is early days. Could it be that Bob Sullivan's killer intended to cause his family as much distress as possible?'

'Who would benefit from Sullivan being dead?' asked Mike.

Charley pulled a face. 'That's a piece of the jigsaw that we're missing.'

–

The other officers were just as surprised and baffled, when Charley revealed the new information at the debrief, though everyone seemed to have an opinion.

'Do you think the perpetrators planned for this to happen at the previous cancelled wedding ceremonies?'

Charley shrugged her shoulders. 'Who knows, Annie, but I can't help thinking that in the two years running up to this event, and with two previous cancellations owing to the Covid epidemic, there would have been other opportunities with less witnesses for someone so determined to kill the man.'

'Maybe it's not something that has been festering for a while. Maybe the feud happened more recently, perhaps something to do with the closing of his business. Did he have debtors?'

Charley saw Wilkie chuckling and whispering behind his hand to Annie who was sitting next to him.

She abruptly walked in front of him. 'You find something funny, DC Connor? We could all do with a laugh. Please share.'

Wilkie Connor sat up from his slouching position and straightened his tie. 'I was just saying, boss, they weren't too bright, were they? Did they not think we'd check the recovered shells?'

Charley showed him her bottom lip. 'Perhaps they're not as clever as you, and they don't know what we can do. Maybe they expected the bullet to pass straight through Sullivan's body and be lost in the church grounds. Let's face it, if it hadn't lodged itself in his skull, it might never have been found, and they might have got away with murder.'

The SIO was keen to move on. 'I see that we have no trace on the BMW. In the coming days, we need to continue looking at vehicles that have been reported stolen and check on any burnt-out vehicles that are discovered.'

Ricky-Lee wasn't convinced that the owner of the vehicle would be so naïve as to draw attention to himself by burning the vehicle. 'It'd be far too risky. ANPR would pick up that it was a stolen car.'

'True, if it's been reported as stolen by the owner. Then again, the BMW could be on a cloned plate when we finally get the registration number. From what we already know, it strikes me that whoever planned this took their time and would have covered their tracks. They'd be aware of road cameras and CCTV. However, no one can plan for the unexpected, no matter how clever they think they are. They will have made a mistake. It's merely a matter of us finding it. Meanwhile, I want you to continue to dig up even the slightest bit of dirt on the wedding guests, especially the men who were in the line-up with our victims. These men have got to be our priority.'

Mike was unusually quiet but looked studious. 'It seems ever more obvious to me that Benny Patterson, a nobody, is a pawn in a much bigger game. In fact, I think it's probably doubtful that Patterson even knew there was a second gunman.'

Annie turned to face Mike. 'I think we've already established that he's not the brightest button in the box. I think he's done what he's been asked to do, and been paid to do it, like we've always said.'

Charley picked up the discussion. 'There were forty guests at the wedding, so, on the balance of probabilities, someone must have a skeleton in their cupboard or a dodgy link to someone on our system. This feels like it's some kind of a reprisal for something that's happened in the past. Something terrible.'

'Drugs involvement maybe? Patterson had drugs on him when he was arrested.'

'We must keep an open mind. I want to reinforce to you all that we are pursuing a cold-blooded killer, and if there is the slightest suggestion of anyone you are visiting possessing a firearm, then you must liaise with the Firearms team, and where necessary, request armed backup. I don't want any of you taking the slightest risk,' said Charley, winding up the briefing. 'Do you hear?'

Chapter Ten

Charley looked at the medication lined up on the small oak table next to Josie Sullivan's easy chair along with a stack of unopened mail. When DC Helen Weir introduced the SIO to Bob Sullivan's widow, she did nothing but stare into the empty air behind the police officers. Nevertheless, Charley crouched and laid her hand over the woman's, softly explaining that she was there to talk about her husband.

Charley offered Mrs Sullivan and her family her deepest sympathies. She recognised the ominous glazed look in her half-closed eyes, her grief nestled in a head separated from her body. Her chest rose and fell heavily with each mechanical breath.

The newlyweds sat on the sofa holding hands so tightly that Charley could see the whites of Stacey's knuckles.

'We don't have enough vases,' she said, by way of an explanation, when she saw Charley's eyes turn to the flowers and bouquets still in their wrappings on the floor.

A single tear rolled down Josie Sullivan's cheek unchecked. The SIO reached into her bag for a tissue and passed it across as the tears that flowed developed into soft sobs. Charley reached out, placed an arm around Josie's shoulder and pulled her close. It was an unconventional gesture, and one not adopted by her colleagues. But at the end of the day, Charley was not just a police officer, she was a human being who had also suffered personal loss. She touched her lips. Funerals were the only time she wore red lipstick, since her beloved grandpa had died when she was seventeen. She had kissed his head and left an imprint of her lipstick on his silver hair. Mother said she was brave. Truth was even then she was a realist.

When Josie's tears slowed and her breathing started to regain some normality, Charley left her side to sit down on an armchair. From there, she could see the wall and sideboard covered in an avalanche of sympathy cards that surrounded pictures of the family in happier times. When Mark went to make coffee, Helen opened her notebook, and Stacey started talking about those happier times. Josie seemed to come around a little, wiping her nose and periodically joining in the conversation.

For the next twenty minutes, the detectives sat and listened intently to them talking about Bob's life, their family and the business. It was the legacy he had been left and had hoped to leave his children, but it had to close due to the pandemic.

The detectives were told that Jerry Campbell, a friend of Stacey's, had been in Bob Sullivan's employment in recent years and was considered a valuable member of staff.

'Employing Jerry meant that Dad didn't have to be in the shop all the time,' said Stacey.

'It was typical of Bob. When he heard that Jerry had been made redundant, and that he was disabled and didn't have a single job offer. Something which he justified to Jerry by saying he wanted to spend more time with me.'

'Was Jerry at the wedding?' asked Charley.

Stacey shook her head and a smile formed on her lips. 'No, he was invited, but if you knew Jerry, you would know that weddings aren't his thing.'

With the question still on her lips, Charley glanced at Helen. 'He is down to be spoken to later today, ma'am,' she said.

To hear these good things about Bob Sullivan was no more than the detectives expected as no one else had said a bad word about Bob Sullivan at all.

Charley needed to keep the family talking to get as much information as possible at this meeting. She couldn't afford to let her emotions get in the way. When she felt that they were settled enough to bear her news, she told them about the results of Bob's post-mortem as well as the second gunman who had fired a rifle at Bob and killed him.

Mrs Sullivan bit her lip and chewed on it for a moment.

Charley reached over and took her hand.

Josie's eyes filled with tears, her voice barely audible. 'Have you arrested him yet?'

Charley shook her head. 'No, we don't know the identity of the person who fired the rifle, but I can assure you that my team and I are doing everything we can to trace him.'

Mrs Sullivan appeared to accept the news.

When they stood to leave, Charley glanced around the room and advised them not to listen to rumours and speculation. Briefly, she glanced at Helen. 'Helen will update you with any developments as and when they happen.'

–

A red Mercedes with a personalised plate was standing outside the front door on the freshly laid shale driveway of Ralph Bateman's parents' detached bungalow.

'How are you?' Charley asked Frank after he opened the door to her and Helen. The SIO flashed her identity card. 'Please accept my condolences.'

Frank stood squarely in the doorway, blocking the entrance and puffing out swirling clouds of cigarette smoke. 'As well as can be expected, thank you for asking,' he replied politely.

The door was splintered near the handle and there were pieces of wood on the step she was standing on.

'Have you had some trouble?' Charley asked, pointing to the damage. However, before he could answer, Charley heard a door open, and a shadow appeared directly behind him.

'Look, I understand the need to speak to me and my wife, but I'm certainly not ready yet and I don't think she is ready for more questioning about her son and brother. At least not right now.'

Charley pressed her lips together. 'I'm sorry, I can't even begin to imagine what you're going through, Mr Bateman. However, it would be extremely helpful if you could let us in to talk to you. We need to update you on the investigation, as Helen explained to your wife when she rang her to arrange for me to come along to introduce myself.'

Frank Bateman pff'd.

At that moment, Charley saw that Margaret Bateman looked confused, as if she had just woken up, her eyes puffy and red. It was obvious she had been crying hard and when Charley sat down next to her and touched her arm, it became clear that she had been waiting for someone to listen as she began pouring out her grief through uncontrollable sobs. The void that her son had left in her life was palpable.

'How could a family wedding result in such grief?' she sobbed. 'Why did I not know about his heart defect? What kind of a mother does that make me?'

Frank looked at his wife. 'Don't be bloody ridiculous, woman. There is nothing in the family to suggest such a thing!'

Much calmer when Frank went to answer the door, Margaret lowered her voice so Frank couldn't hear. 'I don't want you to think badly of him. He's finding it really difficult. He's never been one to talk, or show his feelings, and I'm just the opposite, as you can see. He's a good man with every good intention and he was a very good stepfather to my son. Ralph idolised Frank when he was little, but their relationship changed when he became a teenager. Sadly they had little in common, and Ralph rebelled against what he called an over-authoritarian, and rigid step-father.'

Charley nodded an understanding. 'It's good to talk.'

'And to cry,' said Helen.

When Frank returned and handed Margaret a handful of mail, she smiled briefly, opened a condolence card and showed it to the detectives. 'People are so kind to think of us,' she said.

After a moment, she put the card down on her chair arm and Charley pressed on. 'I know this won't bring you much comfort, but I want you to know that we believe that Ralph wasn't a target. In fact, our investigation is leading us to believe that your son was simply in the wrong place at the wrong time.'

Margaret looked taken aback. 'But my brother was targeted?'

'Yes.' Charley paused for a moment. 'We think he was, but we have no idea why.'

They had been two hours away from the incident room, but for the SIO it was time well spent. Both families had been given an opportunity to talk to Charley, the person in charge of the investigation, and she hoped that they had taken heart from her tenacity and determination to solve the crime.

Back at her desk, she reflected on how surviving family members coped with the death of a loved one in such circumstances, and how it was they who served the life sentence because, no matter what sentence was handed down to the killer, it was never enough.

Charley turned to the sign hanging on her wall and read out loud the quote which perfectly fitted the present investigation for her. '*Murder is like no other crime, and the ultimate test for the detective.*'

The noise of her computer starting up brought her focus back as she saw the mass of data that had been added to the database whilst she had been out.

Feeling invigorated, experienced and confident in her leadership ability, Charley forged ahead with her admin work, prioritising new lines of enquiry. She was pleased to see that this was done in detail when it came to Jerry Campbell, Bob Sullivan's employee. Campbell was thirty years old and physically disabled, having lost the lower part of his right arm in a childhood accident. Campbell told the officers who spoke to him that he could think of no one who would want to harm Mr Sullivan, nor of anyone with whom he'd had an altercation. The officers attending reported that he appeared genuine, but of a nervous disposition.

The time on Charley's computer read three o'clock when Mike Blake stuck his head around her door. 'Boss, we've got the BMW on CCTV at the bottom of St James' Road.'

'Benny Patterson lives down St James' Road.'

'He does, and this time we've got a registered number of the car.'

DC Annie Glover and DC Wilkie Connor drove past Daisy Alice Wainwright's shop first to see if it was open.

'There is nothing on the system to suggest that Mrs Wainwright has any previous convictions, but the car is linked to the flower shop,' said Wilkie.

'It's parked in the space at the side of the shop,' said Annie.

Although the car had played a part in giving Benny Patterson a lift to the church, it didn't necessarily mean that Daisy was the driver or that she knew what was about to take place. Evidence was crucial, but the revelation would be a positive boost for the enquiry.

'I know you probably want to buy me a bunch of flowers while we're here, but really you don't have to,' she teased Wilkie as they walked towards the door.

Wilkie guffawed. 'Waste of money, if you ask me,' he said bluntly.

Inside the shop was a middle-aged woman wearing a green tabard, preparing a bouquet of flowers and singing to the music on the radio. She was behind a glass screen.

'Be with you in just one second,' she said on hearing the bell on the door announce their arrival. Putting down the blooms, she turned her back and they heard running water. 'Two ticks, just need to wash...' she called, but before she finished the sentence she was standing before them, drying her hands on a threadbare hand towel, smiling widely. 'How can I help you?'

Daisy's smile soon turned to a frown when DC Wilkie Connor produced his warrant card and began to explain to her that he and DC Annie Glover were working on the double murder at the church.

'Your car was seen in the area on the morning of the murders and as a matter of routine, we are eliminating any vehicle in the vicinity at the time.'

'You think I can help?' she asked. 'Of course, I remember that day well for obvious reasons. I delivered flowers to Argyle Street. I heard the church bells ringing, but I wasn't the one asked to do the flowers for the wedding if that's what you want to know, and I've no idea who did, I'm sorry.'

'Did you see anyone acting strangely on your way to and from Argyle Street?' asked Wilkie.

Daisy shook her head. 'No, it was a quick drop-off. The recipient had paid by card over the telephone, so it was just a case of handing the flowers over.'

'You were on your own then?' Annie continued.

'I was when I dropped the flowers off, but I gave a lift to one of my regulars, Benny.'

DC Wilkie Connor and DC Annie Glover looked at each other.

'Would that be Benny Patterson?' asked Wilkie.

'Is that his name? Scruffy young local man, unshaven with a beard, but it's not my place to judge. His heart's in the right place, I always think. Well, it must be. I know he has his problems, and he hasn't got a lot, but he buys flowers from me to take to his mum's grave. I gave him

73

a lift to the church on my way. Why? Has something happened to him?'

'I think you'd better sit down,' said Annie.

Chapter Eleven

Daisy's eyes moved quickly from one detective to the other.

'Obviously, you were unaware that Benny Patterson was arrested at the church on Saturday for shooting two of the guests,' Annie said.

Putting her hand directly to her stomach, Daisy could only stare at the younger of the two police officers in horror. 'No, I didn't know. I heard that the gunman had been arrested, but he wasn't named. I never thought for a minute that it could have been him.'

Daisy caught Wilkie's eyes narrowing and felt the paralysis of fear take over. 'Oh my God, you think I might be his accomplice?' The florist faltered and her colour drained. 'My God, he had a gun. I could've been killed, couldn't I?'

Annie reached out and gently touched her arm. 'Daisy, can you remember if he was carrying anything?'

As the young detective hoped, the florist's focus came back to her. 'Only the flowers he bought, as far as I'm aware.'

Annie smiled encouragingly. 'Do you work here alone?'

Daisy flashed her eyes towards the entrance to the shop. 'Yes, I do. I can't afford to employ anyone, but maybe I should?'

Wilkie's voice broke in, interrupting her thoughts. 'Tell me, how many times has Benny Patterson been into the shop?'

Daisy paused briefly, frowning as she thought. 'I reckon about four, possibly five times since his mum died last year. I must admit though, I haven't seen him round the village for a while and I assumed he had been inside again. I didn't recognise him until he spoke. In fact I felt quite sorry for him. He had lost weight, and he looked even more like a vagrant than he did.'

'Have you given him a lift before?' asked Annie.

Daisy shook her head. 'No, no... I only offered because I was going his way and I wanted him out of the shop so I could do the delivery – he has an awful habit of hanging around when he calls.' The florist's face filled with panic. Her hands began to shake. 'He was in my car. He was sitting right next to me, and he was on his way to murder people!'

'Daisy, Daisy,' Annie once again brought her focus back. 'We're going to need a written statement from you because his movements that day are very important to us. Can you recall what he was wearing?'

'What he always wears – baggy, low-hanging jeans, a style I hear attributed to prison culture where inmates are not permitted to wear belts, and a T-shirt.' Another pause. 'Are you absolutely certain it's him?'

DC Connor gave her a quick nod. 'Absolutely. He was caught in the act, overpowered, and the weapon was recovered.'

Daisy shuddered. 'That's the last time I ever give anyone a lift.'

Annie chewed the side of her mouth. 'Did he speak to you or seem agitated at all?'

'Not that I noticed. He said, like he always did, that he was off to have a chat with his mum. I always got the impression that underneath that rough, tough exterior he was quite a sensitive soul at heart.'

Wilkie snorted. 'Well, I can honestly say that's a first.'

Daisy pointed to her hair. 'You know what they say about blondes?'

Annie looked at Daisy and shook her head. 'No, not stupid, just too trusting maybe,' she said.

–

Wilkie and Annie were back in the car and heading towards the police station in the midday sun, tarmac melting under the car's tyres, and by now both were sweating and hungry. It was incredibly busy and Annie was glad she wasn't driving. Although Wilkie pulled down his sun visor, it was still hard to see the sun-dazzled road ahead.

'Where are your sunglasses?' Annie scolded.

'Can't afford any. Our lass's just cost me £360.'

'So that's where you were the other day when we couldn't get hold of you. You weren't slacking at all – you'd taken Fran to the opticians. Why don't you tell someone and then we can cover things such as optician's appointments?'

Wilkie's eyes were focused on the people crossing the road in front of them. 'The optician didn't promise, but she said these new all-singing, all-dancing lenses might help, so… Her eyesight is failing. It's nothing we weren't expecting, but still…'

If Daisy Alice Wainwright wanted an example of a sensitive soul with a tough exterior, one who, despite working full-time in a demanding job, also took care of a disabled wife, then Wilkie Connor was it.

'Do you believe her?' Annie said.

'Who, the optician?' Wilkie asked.

Annie laughed. 'No, the florist, you numpty.'

'I knew who you meant. Yeah, she admitted straight up that she'd given him a lift. She's not involved.'

'It appears Patterson might have bided his time a while on Saturday by his mother's grave.'

'Maybe he was telling her what he was about to do? If only the dead could talk, eh?'

'The boss isn't going to be too happy that the BMW hasn't led to anything, is she? The line of enquiry looked so promising.'

Suddenly Wilkie swung the car to the kerb side. Ricky-Lee was walking into the sandwich shop where his girlfriend worked.

'I know, we'll get her a cake,' Wilkie said, nodding towards their colleague. 'I know for a fact he doesn't pay.'

Still smiling at his good fortune a few minutes later, Wilkie passed Annie a couple of paper bags through her open window. Inside one was a warm pie, in the other a piece of carrot cake.

'I think she might've expected flowers since we've been to a flower shop,' she called out to him as he walked round the front of the car towards the driver's door.

'Well, you know what thought did,' he said, popping the remains of a sausage roll into his mouth as he hurled himself into the driver's seat.

—

Charley met up with Neal Rylatt and Annie at St Cuthbert's graveyard. Maurice Gaunt from Ballistics had suggested the possible distance and direction of fire and Annie had identified the plot in which Edith May Patterson was buried, but there was no headstone. The area around the grave was tidy and there was a small bouquet of fresh flowers placed beneath a simple wooden cross laid upon the grass.

Charley stood at the graveside with the others. She pointed at the flowers. 'Photograph them, please,' Charley instructed Neal.

Then she turned to Annie. 'Can you show it to Ms Wainwright, to confirm that these were the ones that Benny Patterson bought from her for his mother's grave?'

Annie nodded towards Neal. 'Yes, as soon as he sends it to me.'

Leaving Neal in the graveyard taking pictures, the ladies walked together to the car as Charley chatted about the way forward.

'With the footage of the CCTV and the flowers on the grave, we have corroborated Ms Wainwright's account of her involvement on Saturday morning,' Charley said. The heat outside was such that the air conditioning was welcome. 'Can you recall what time was shown on the CCTV footage when Benny Patterson was dropped off at Argyle Street?'

'Just after ten o'clock,' replied Annie. Kicking her shoes off her hot, tired feet she instantly felt more comfortable.

Charley stopped and whirled round to face her. 'Then he sat up here for approximately an hour beforehand. That makes me think that maybe the person with the rifle would also be *in situ* for a similar period.'

'That gives us the opportunity for either, or both, to have been seen by others.'

Charley steered the car down the winding country road that led into the village. 'Exactly. I want a timeline for Benny Patterson from leaving Daisy's flower shop until the murders took place shortly after eleven a.m. We need to appeal for anyone who may have been in the graveyard at that time or who saw anyone acting suspiciously in this vicinity,' said Charley.

–

Sitting with the officers viewing CCTV, the SIO asked them to concentrate on anything and everything that had moved through the village between 9.30 and 11.30 on the previous Saturday morning.

'Our rifleman is no James Bond. We know he didn't skydive in, so, he is left with two options: he either walked or drove to his selected position from where he intended to fire his rifle at Sullivan. There is only one main route through the village. If he drove, would he have left his car in the village car park? Maybe so, but it's highly likely, as we discussed previously, that he is shrewd enough to know about CCTV and ANPR, and he had plenty of time to consider his route very carefully so as not to be seen. So maybe he parked further out of the village on one of the side streets and walked.'

Back in her office, Charley sat down and discussed with the team the possibility of the rifle user also being a hired gun like Patterson. Wilkie scratched his head. 'The million dollar question is: who is the mastermind of the operation?'

'God knows, but finding the rifleman is one step closer to catching our mastermind. Pre-planned, premeditated, and looking more like a vendetta than ever it seems?'

'What's next?' asked Annie.

'We continue to clear the ground beneath our feet. Pursue the tried and tested strategies in accordance with Home Office national guidelines. I am continually looking at what information is falling out of the wedding guest interviews, and I confess that's not a lot yet, but we are securing new lines of enquiry all the time, and all we can do is keep digging. If there's nothing, then we dig deeper, and we interview the wider family, friends, and associates. There has got to be a link to Sullivan somewhere, and we will find it.'

Another twelve-hour day had been and gone, and they were still no nearer to catching their rifleman. Charley knew that without an early breakthrough, the pressure from the bosses would start to build.

'One thing about Detective Inspector Charley,' she heard Ricky-Lee telling one of the officers drafted in from another division, 'is that she won't be bullied by anyone. She'll listen to the experts, but she'll make her own decisions.'

It was true. Experts, although they rarely did get things wrong, were only human. However, in the end, the SIO had sole responsibility for detecting the murders. No one else.

–

That evening, Charley was completing a report stating that they needed more resources and didn't finish until it was half past ten. Tired but wanting to flick through the HOLMES database before she left, she was delighted to see more information filtering through.

Her eyes were drawn to some intelligence showing that the bridegroom's best man, was called Jarvis Cooper.

He had no previous convictions but what was interesting to the SIO was that he had been stopped and checked, whilst in a car two weeks prior to the wedding. Mr Cooper was reportedly a backseat passenger in a black Mercedes EQ at 2300 hours and the car was flagged up on police records for drugs and firearms. Adrenaline rushed through Charley as she searched eagerly for intelligence about the other occupant. The owner and driver was an Oldham drug dealer known as Mad Mick Dawson. He was suspected of drug running and reinforcing county line distribution, according to Oldham CID. The front seat passenger was Patricia (Patsy) Henderson, Dawson's girlfriend. Patsy was a known user of heroin and cocaine, and described as an addict.

Charley tapped her feet as the computer changed screens. 'Come on, come on, anyone else?' Charley whispered urgently. 'Yes!'

The girl in the back seat next to Jarvis Cooper was someone by the name of Ellie Yates, but although the vehicle and occupants had been checked by uniform patrol, they had found nothing. *What's his connection with the known drug dealer Mad Mick Dawson?* Charley asked herself.

It would have to wait until tomorrow. Mr Sandman was hovering over her tired shoulders.

Chapter Twelve

Mike followed the voice of the SIO as she walked through the door with Annie. He stood to catch her attention as she passed by on her way to her office.

'Can we have a talk about the best man Jarvis Cooper and his associates?' he asked.

Charley stopped, rubbed a hand across her sweating forehead and knocked her sunglasses off her head. Mike bent down and retrieved them. She checked her watch and gave him a tight smile by way of a thank you, nodding her head in the direction of the coffee jar on his desk. 'My office, five minutes, and bring me one of those, will you?' she asked in a flat tone of voice.

Mike flashed her a weary but slightly mischievous grin. 'What, a decaf?'

A look of pure horror overcame Charley's face. 'Are you having a laugh?'

In her office, the SIO dumped her bag beside the desk and slid into her chair. The room felt stifling although the window was open. She turned on her computer as she leaned over the pile of paperwork in the middle of her desk to switch on the rotating fan.

Her thoughts turned to the old, faded newspaper cutting that had been pinned to the board on her wall by her predecessor. She considered the colossal amount of money that had been spent on a new custody suite at

Peel Street, a controversial decision at the time and the cost of which had wiped out the building's budget for the foreseeable future. She sighed heavily, accepting that the fan only blew the warm air around with very little cooling effect.

The upgrade had been presented to the Divisional Commander as a foregone conclusion by HQ to meet with new Health and Safety Regulations for those in police detention. There was no doubt then, as now, that it was to the detriment of those working in the rest of the crumbling building built in the 1800s.

Charley's eyes closed when Mike entered the room, her face towards the fan, obviously relishing the sparse air flow. He shut the door softly behind him and she did not move until he slid the welcome mug across her desk.

For a moment when he sat down, the peace and quiet was intoxicating to him, and Charley recognised the familiar feeling of her stomach knotting.

'I know you want me to make a decision, don't you?' she said.

He nodded his head, a smile tugging at his lips.

'Did you know that computers produce enough heat to make your workspace considerably warmer than the rest of the office?' he told her. He was in no rush to get back to his desk. Time away from phones ringing and people constantly wanting his attention was rare.

Charley's eyes were glued to her computer. 'I do now,' she quipped, tapping her fingers on her desk as she waited for the requested screens to load on her computer.

'Mad Max Dawson's personal numberplate is 5MAC 1. The number five has been made to look like an S, so it reads SMAC 1,' Mike said.

The SIO altered her sitting position and took a sip of her drink. 'Course he has. He knows that a plate like that is like a red rag to a bull for a copper, and he thinks he's untouchable these days with his minions that do all his dirty work for him.'

Mike's eyebrows furrowed deeper. 'He knows he's not carrying anything onboard, yet we have a duty of care to the public to stop him and check. Then why does he kick-off when he gets stopped and searched?'

Charley scowled. 'Because he's a twat and because he can. However tenuous Jarvis Cooper's link to Max Dawson, Patsy Henderson and Ellie Yates is, I think we've got to pursue it. Let's see who their associates are and where that line of enquiry takes us. Also, check Cooper's plus one at the wedding, will you?'

Mike slowly leaned back in his chair, entwined his fingers and stretched out his arms. 'Well, we know it wasn't Yates or Henderson because they aren't on the guest list,' he said on the back of a yawn.

'Never assume,' said Charley with a wink of an eye.

Mike's eyebrows knit together. 'What do you mean?'

'Nothing!' Her voice was lifted with surprise. 'We just need to check that those attending on the day were the people named on the guest list, that's all. After all, it was drawn up two years ago, as I understand it.'

Charley watched Mike lean forward with his elbows on his knees and bow his head to look down at the floor between his legs. His mouth followed in a full-blown yawn. Then he shook his head as if to help him think more clearly.

Charley looked across the desk. 'Keeping you up, am I?' She stifled a yawn of her own.

The detective sergeant stretched his back. 'I don't know about you but I'm not getting much sleep. This job, it just keeps going round and round in my head.'

Charley picked up her mug and raised it in the air. 'Tell me about it. What you need is a good strong coffee. Never mind that rubbish,' she scoffed, indicating his mug. 'That won't put hairs on your chest. And check whether Oldham Police have any recent pictures of Dawson, Henderson and Yates, will you? I'm wondering if any of these could be Patterson's supplier and if they have another link to Bob Sullivan that we don't know about yet.'

At the door, Mike turned to look over his shoulder. 'It might also be beneficial to let Oldham CID have a look at the wedding photos and see if they recognise any of the guests. What do you think?'

'I think that's a great idea,' Charley said with a smile. 'And Mike?'

'Yes?'

'We'll all sleep better once this investigation is brought to a successful conclusion.'

Mike shut the door behind him.

'Until the next,' she whispered softly.

Chapter Thirteen

The face of Abbie Norton, shown on the guest list as Jarvis Cooper's plus one, filled Charley's computer screen. She used a split screen to upload pictures of an Abbie Norton from the National Data Base to sit alongside it in the hope that Charley would find a match, along with further details about her. Drawing a blank, the SIO scrolled through the wedding photographs seized from several sources to discover any clue that the team could pursue.

Once again, she drew a blank. However, what she did identify was a story between the groom and his best man that was growing clearer. Cooper obviously took his role as best man very seriously. At all times, he was either standing alongside or close to Mark James. Charley considered the two of them. In style, stature, and appearance, they were complete opposites.

Jarvis Cooper was tall, skinny, and long-haired. He looked uncomfortable and overdressed in a suit, especially with the tattoo of a spider in a web peeping over his white shirt collar. Whereas Mark James, sporting an elegant suit, looked every bit the successful businessman who took pride in his appearance, and obviously took care of himself.

Charley pointed at Cooper's picture on the intelligence board that evening at the debrief and shared her thoughts and observations with the team.

'What are your thoughts on the best man?' she asked.

'He looks like he could do with a good wash,' remarked Wilkie.

'Yes, and a good meal,' said Annie.

Ricky-Lee waved a hand dismissively. 'That's what drugs do for you.'

Charley was thoughtful. 'I wonder how Cooper and James know each other?'

FLO Helen Weir surprised Charley by having the answer to her question at her fingertips. 'Jarvis Cooper went to school with Mark James. They've been best mates since junior school.'

Charley was impressed and told Helen so.

'I've just come off the phone with Oldham CID and they have identified our picture of Abbie Norton as being someone they know as Ellie Yates,' said Mike.

Charley couldn't resist a smile. 'That's interesting. She was the one sitting next to Cooper in the rear of Mad Max Dawson's car when it was stopped recently, wasn't she?'

Ricky-Lee cleared his throat. 'I'm going to play devil's advocate.' Everyone turned to look the detective's way. 'It could be innocent. Cooper might have recently broken up with Abbie Norton and just took Yates, whom he knew, as his plus one instead.'

Charley pondered his remark. 'That's true. However, I'd be interested to know if Yates gave her own name to the officers at the church after the shooting, or whether she used Abbie?'

Wilkie scratched his head. 'I don't know. I wasn't the one who spoke to her or that filled out the pro-forma, but I'll check with who did.'

Civilian support officer Bill Levine was at the debrief on behalf of the intelligence unit. 'We have a sighting of Jarvis Cooper at a Nationwide cashpoint machine in Slaithwaite on the morning of the wedding.'

Charley raised an eyebrow. 'This guy is starting to look interesting,' she said, glancing around the room. 'Do we have a current address for Ellie Yates? I'd like to see what she can tell us about Jarvis Cooper.'

'Yes, ma'am, it's on the system. How up to date that will be, only time will tell. It depends on if she gave her correct details when Mad Max Dawson's car was stopped.'

With the enquiry team instructed to pick up Jarvis Cooper and Ellie Yates early the next morning, Charley's priority tomorrow was to get the pair interviewed.

Stomach rumbling, Charley glanced at the clock. She hadn't eaten since she'd had a cookie with her coffee at lunchtime. Winding up the meeting, she thanked the team. Now all that was left to be done was write up her policy log before she went home.

It was a quarter to ten when Charley walked through the windowless corridors of the police station towards the exit. The divisional management team's doors had been locked hours before.

The night shift was arriving for duty when Charley reached the ground floor and the two-till-ten team was getting ready to leave. Scanning their faces, she recognised the signs of fatigue, which told her immediately which team they belonged to.

Marty Webb was standing at the front desk, handing over to his civilian colleague Marie-France when Charley passed through the enquiry office. On seeing her, he smiled and waved. 'Straight home now young'un, do you hear? I won't ask you to give us three rings like I used to.'

Charley raised her hand to her best friend Kristine's dad. Her and Kristine had applied to join the police together. But something held her back from telling her childhood sweetheart, now jail bird, Danny Ray, who when told was dead against it, which resulted in him making threats, and violence due to his possessiveness and jealousy.

'See ya, m'old fruitcake,' she replied, chuckling.

Outside, the night air seemed cool and fresh after the stuffy office, the smell of cut grass wafting from the embankment. On this, the last day of the old moon, the vault of sky above Huddersfield was jet-black with a myriad of stars shining down.

During the twenty-minute seven-mile journey home on the familiar roads, memories of her childhood flooded back. Harsh as the weather was in the winter, and short as the summer could be in the North, the seasons turned the moorland she knew into a wonderful welcoming terrain for picnicking, tree swings, jumping the stones on the waterfall, and swimming in the brook. Driving up the steep, narrow road, hugged by dry-stone walls from the main street in Marsden to the well-defined Victorian terrace house in the hillside that she had inherited from her parents when they died, she reflected that she would never get used to going home alone to the dark, cold house that had always been so welcoming in her youth.

When she reached Beatrice Street, she turned off the car engine and looked down the dark road. The silence in the vehicle was all-consuming. Through the windscreen from her elevated position, Charley could see the intermittent lights of emergency vehicles, the lightning flicker of car headlights, and the occasional flash of a shooting star. Once out of the car, the only noise was the wailing of cats and a whistle from a train in the village below. She paused for a moment, drinking in the tranquil atmosphere of the summer's evening before turning on her heels and walking briskly to her door.

-

The first rays of sun woke Charley the next morning. She yawned, rolled over onto her stomach, stuck her head beneath her pillow, and moaned loudly. She knew that once she was awake, she would not go back to sleep. Charley heard the ticking of the clock and, opening one eye, she could see that it was quarter to six. Bleary-eyed, she made her way to the bathroom. There, she washed and dressed, scraping her blonde locks back into a tight bun that sat at the base of her neck – a habit born in her uniform days.

It was a bright crisp morning with newly unfurled leaves glistening vividly in the summer sun. By seven o'clock, she was sitting at her desk enjoying the relative cool and calm of the office, despite Winnie fussing around her like a mother hen cleaning the nest, albeit with dusters, rags and lavender polish.

'Wet your bed, have you, girl?' the old lady grumbled as she vacuumed around her.

Ignoring Winnie whilst trying to keep a straight face at the old lady's mumblings, Charley picked up her mug of coffee and a thick slice of buttered toast from the tray that the old lady had put in front of her. 'Don't you know by now that breakfast is the most important meal of the day? And I bet you haven't eaten anything yet,' Winnie scolded her.

Unperturbed, Charley feasted her eyes on the overnight report from the night detective. She was well aware that it wouldn't be long before the team started to arrive, and hopefully Jarvis Cooper and Ellie Yates would be with the enquiry team.

–

With the noise coming from the incident room, Charley lifted her eyes from the computer screen and looked at the clock above her office door. It was twenty past seven and the quiet she had enjoyed was now gone for the day.

Wilkie Connor was the first to stick his head around her door. 'Morning, boss, you been up all night?' he asked. Before Charley had time to answer, his nose led him to Tattie's desk. The sandy-haired office manager was carrying a batch of her homemade cookies for the office to share.

Mike Blake was in her office next. 'Jarvis Cooper and Ellie Yates are en route. They were found together earlier this morning at Cooper's flat.'

'Any resistance by either to attend voluntarily?' she asked.

'None whatsoever,' he replied. 'The officers attending tell me that the two appeared somewhat bemused by the unexpected knock on the door, and judging by the smell, they suggest that the pair could still be under the influence of cannabis.'

'Anything else of note at the flat?'

'Apparently not. The lounge was hardly conventional – no settee or chairs but a mattress, a couple of guitars laid on top of a heap of clothing, a skateboard, a pair of girls' skates, and an electric scooter.'

Charley rolled her eyes. 'A sign of the times I guess. I remember when living rooms housed motorbikes and kitchen tables were covered with dismantled motorbike engines.' The SIO paused. 'Who's interviewing?'

'I'm speaking to Cooper with Wilkie, Annie and Ricky-Lee to Yates.'

When Mike got to the door, Charley called him back. 'Just a thought – did CCTV or ANPR pick up on an electric scooter, or a skateboard in the vicinity of the church during the relevant time, by any chance?'

Mike shook his head. 'Not that I know of. I'm sure the team would have let us know if they had. They pick up on anything that moves, even animals. However, I'll raise it to be on the safe side.'

Mike turned to leave for the second time.

'And Mike, we don't want to delay the pair longer than is necessary, but what's most important is to see if their response to the questions is corroborated by each other. Be nice. They're not arrested, so there is always the chance that they will get up and leave should they feel threatened or intimidated.'

An hour and a half later, there was news from the interviewers, and Charley couldn't wait to hear what Cooper and Yates had to say.

Chapter Fourteen

Bewilderment was written all over DC Ricky-Lee's face when he threw his notepad and pen down on his desk and sat down after speaking to Ellie Yates in an interview room at the police station.

'What planet is she on?'

'Hey man,' Annie said through a smile as she did her best impression of the young woman. 'Did you want to shake her? Because I did.'

'I did too, but that said, I also got the impression that she has nothing to hide.'

On hearing them return, Charley came to lean against her doorframe, arms crossed. 'No joy?'

Both detectives turned in the SIO's direction, but it was Annie who spoke. 'She openly admits to being a regular cannabis user, but it wouldn't surprise me if she also used harder drugs. She was still spaced out from last night. That said, she was able to tell us that she met Cooper at the Leeds festival and since then, they've spent most of their time together. He told her at the time that he'd just finished a relationship. When he invited her to a wedding, she agreed to go. "Free food and booze, what's not to like?" she said.'

Ricky-Lee was consulting his computer when he joined in. 'She also stated that she didn't know anyone else at the wedding nor did it bother her to sit in the place earmarked for his ex.'

'We asked if she had lied to the officers who spoke to her at the church by giving them a false name and she admitted it straight up. Apparently, in her mind, she didn't want to create problems, and she also said she was in shock after seeing someone shot,' continued Annie.

'Did you tell her that we knew she had been checked in a car with Dawson, Henderson and Cooper?' asked Charley.

Annie nodded. 'Yes, and she went to the defence of her Uncle Mick. Apparently, he was giving them a lift from a gig in Manchester.'

At that moment, the door to the corridor opened and caught Charley's eye. Mike walked into the room followed by Wilkie. The former went directly towards the restroom and Wilkie headed for his desk opposite Annie's.

'Well?' said Charley, expectantly.

Wilkie slumped into his chair, sweeping stray hairs from his sweaty forehead. He wrote something on his notepad, put his pen down and looked across at Charley.

'Tell ya what,' he said and let out a deep sigh. 'If that's the best Mark James could do for his best man, he can't have many friends.'

The SIO was eager to know more. 'Where did he say that he and James met?'

'Grew up on the same street, went to the same school, and both lifelong Town supporters.'

'And when you brought up the shooting?'

'He started crying. He admits he's got a little problem with the bottle and to taking recreational drugs, but says that since the shooting, he's sought help for his anxiety and depression.'

'Check that out with his doctor,' instructed Charley.

Smiling, Wilkie pointed to the note he had just made. 'I'm already on it.'

Mike joined them mid-conversation and handed one of two plastic cups of water to Wilkie, who drank it down in one.

'What did he have to say about Abbie Norton and Ellie Yates?' Charley asked.

Mike sipped his drink. 'He says he ditched Norton a while ago, apparently she had issues... He then took Yates... He never thought to update any guest list because the bride and groom knew that he and Abbie had split and Ellie and him were an item.'

'Did he know that Yates had given the police a false ID?'

'He did. They spoke about it afterwards, but they decided it was too late to do anything about it, and besides, she had told them what she saw,' said Wilkie.

'Did he say anything about how they met and how they both came to be in the car with Dawson and Henderson?'

'At Leeds Festival apparently. He says she appeared to him like an angel in a vision.'

Annie laughed. 'Course she did if he was high!'

'And Dawson?'

'He says he doesn't actually know him. He knows Dawson is Yates's uncle, and Dawson gave them a lift, which is when they got stopped and searched,' Mike continued.

'Do they know Benny Patterson?'

There was a collective shaking of heads.

'Mmm... I guess the general agreement is that they're not involved?'

There was a deafening chorus of, 'No!'

'Where are they now?' asked Charley.

'Yates was waiting for Cooper in the foyer when we escorted him from the building. They thanked us for the lift, then walked off hand in hand.'

Charley closed her eyes briefly and sighed. 'Well, let's look on the bright side. Another two eliminated. Now for our next priority line of enquiry.' She nodded towards her office. 'Bring a notepad and pen for a brainstorm. My office in five.'

A few moments later, feeling frustrated, Charley sank down in the chair behind her desk, and in one smooth movement, kicked off her shoes. She sat for a moment with her head in her hands. It was swimming with random potential lines of enquiry. Then it came to her. What changes had been made in the wedding planning over the last two years that could possibly significantly affect the day? She swiftly picked up her pen, eager to get her initial thoughts down. The guest list had already been highlighted and enquiries were ongoing.

- Venue

- Florist

- Photographer

- Caterer/staff

- Vicar

- Organist

- Bellringers

- Wedding car/Driver

The SIO still had her head down, busily writing, when the four detectives took their seats in her office without the usual chatter and banter. When she looked up from her notes, she saw that Ricky-Lee had removed his tie and Mike's top button was open, his tie askew. There were wet blotches on Wilkie's flannel shirt and half-moons of perspiration under each arm.

Aware that her cheeks were flushed with the heat, Annie handed out glasses of homemade lemonade and gave Winnie's apologies. 'You'll have to imagine it's cold. It's only been in the fridge five minutes.'

Nevertheless, Charley accepted the thirst-quenching nectar gratefully, as did the others, smacking their lips together when they'd finished. Her grandma's freshly squeezed lemons recipe tasted good. There was a lot to be said for Charley's Yorkshire heirloom recipes and the folklore she lived by.

'Moving forward. I've just been thinking. How would our killers know where and when this wedding ceremony was going to take place, and who would have had to be informed other than the guests?'

Charley's gaze was met by silent, thoughtful faces. 'I know it's a long shot, but I think that line of enquiry is worth pursuing.'

'Don't worry, I'm on it. However, you are aware that if Stacey and Mark announced it on social media, then possibly the world and his dog would know about it,' said Annie.

'Yeah, I know it's a long shot. However, somehow the information got to the killers, and if it's possible to find out how, it might lead us to them.'

At the conclusion of the meeting, mindful of Benny Patterson's custody clock coming to an end, and with no further questions to put to the prisoner, Charley asked Ricky-Lee to go down to the cells and charge him with Ralph Bateman's murder so that he could be put before the courts for a remand in custody until his trial on two counts of murder and the associated firearms offences.

'Tell him we'll see him in twelve months at Crown Court,' Wilkie called after him.

Charley nodded in his direction. 'I've got news for you. You'll be seeing him in seven days' time when he goes to court for arrangements to be made for the trial.'

'Do you reckon he'll plead guilty?'

'Caught at the scene of the crime in possession of the weapon and with video evidence? Not on your life. You and I know we still must prove within the prosecution file what took place beyond any doubt and to support it with evidence. What's he got to lose by going not guilty? The trial isn't going to cost him anything, it's not like he's got anything else to do, and who knows which way a jury is going to jump. To quote Robert Frost, "You've got twelve persons chosen to decide who has the better lawyer."'

Thirty minutes later, engrossed in the end of month returns, Charley jumped when she heard a knock at her door and saw Annie standing in front of her desk.

When she spoke, her words came out in a rush. 'Unable to get in touch with Stacey or Mark. I spoke to Helen, and she asked Josie Sullivan, who has Stacey's wedding journal. From that, the only thing that they can see has changed from the original arrangements is the photographer.'

When Charley replied, it was slowly and calmly. 'Do we know the reason why?'

'No, but according to the journal, the original photographer was a man by the name of Brandon Settle, which was crossed out and had been replaced by Chelsea Clough.'

Charley massaged the crick that she felt in her neck. 'I guess it could be no more sinister than Brandon Settle not being available for that date, or maybe he hasn't reinstated his business since the pandemic. However, the obvious place to start is by speaking to Chelsea Clough, and corroborating what she says by speaking to Brandon Settle, and the bride and groom.'

'Leave it with me,' Annie said, and raced out of the office with the shout, 'Wilkie, get your coat! We're off out.'

Chapter Fifteen

DC Annie Glover knew nothing more about Chelsea Clough before they arrived at her photographic studio than what she had read on social media.

With his hands at ten to two on the CID car's steering wheel, Wilkie Connor scoffed when he saw her scrolling through the woman's posts on Facebook. 'You do realise that people only put on there what they want you to see. It's not actually real life.'

Sitting in the passenger seat, Annie flashed him a look of annoyance. 'Maybe not, but you can learn a lot about a person if you take it in the context that it's written and consider their motivation.' Annie briefly turned the screen so he could see Chelsea's profile picture. However, she could see that the detective's focus was on locating the studio nearby.

'From reading this, I know that Chelsea is twenty-four years old, she's attractive – well, if you like skinny women with long dark hair, cute faces and large boobs,' she said grimacing.

'What's not to like?' he replied with a grin.

When Wilkie pulled up at the kerb in front of the big glass doors, Annie slid her mobile phone into her tunic pocket. First out of the car, she led Wilkie through the entrance where the sound of serene music greeted them.

When the young photographer walked towards them, china cup and saucer in hand, she was immediately aware that her womanly assets were appreciated by the older of the two.

'Close your mouth,' Annie whispered to Wilkie out of the corner of her own. Wilkie scowled at his colleague defensively. 'I don't know what you mean.'

Annie found her lips cracking a smile. 'Whatever!' she replied before showing Ms Clough her warrant card.

Dark plush carpets absorbed their footfall as they were shown to a luxurious seating area. Wilkie's eyes followed Chelsea Clough, and in turn, Ms Clough's eyes were focused on him. It was Wilkie to whom she spoke, seductively crossing her legs when she gracefully lowered herself onto the chaise longue, indicating they should sit opposite on the sofa. She appeared to be appreciative of his undivided attention. 'Tell me, Inspector, in what way do you think I can help you?' she asked, her voice taking on a velvet tone.

Perched on the edge of her seat, Annie had an overwhelming urge to challenge her. 'It's Detective Constable, Ms Clough. We're both detective constables. Our detective inspector is called Charley Mann.'

Mindful as Annie was not to sink into the middle of the temptingly soft cushions, they fully absorbed Wilkie's weight. Upon seeing Clough's unsuccessful attempt to stifle a giggle at his awkwardness, Annie saw red. When he had recovered, she noticed Wilkie regaining his composure. 'Just a few routine questions in relation to the shooting at the church,' he said.

Clough nodded. 'Please, go ahead,' she said, her smile showing off her perfectly white teeth.

However, it was Annie who answered, and Clough's eyes flipped from one to the other.

'We'd like to know who approached you to cover the photography for Stacey and Mark James's wedding, as it's our understanding that you weren't the couple's first choice?'

Clough pursed her lips, and before she answered, took a sip of her herbal tea. Being a seasoned interviewer, Annie suspected it was a delay tactic.

'That's true. The couple's original photographer was someone called Brandon Settle, whom I didn't know. Mr Settle telephoned me to ask if I was available on the day in question as he had another commitment. When I told him I was, he asked me if I'd give them a call, and I did.'

'And the rest, as they say, is history,' Wilkie said.

Clough's nodding head reminded Annie of the nodding dog on the rear shelf of her car. 'Has that ever happened to you before?'

'No, but it wouldn't make good business sense to turn down work if I'm available, would it? First choice or not.'

Suddenly Clough shuddered and stroked the goose-bumps that appeared on her arm. 'I must admit, when Bob Sullivan and Ralph Bateman were shot, I wished that I hadn't agreed to do it.'

Annie wasn't about to be diverted from her line of questioning. 'Do you happen to have Mr Settle's details by any chance?'

Clough stood with ease and glided the few paces to the ornate sideboard. She opened a small drawer, extracted something, and turned to face them. 'Yes, I kept this in case I could return the favour one day.' In her right hand, pinched between her thumb and index finger, she held a small scroll of paper. Bending down, she offered it to

Wilkie then stood up and looked at her watch, then back at him.

'Is there anything else that I can do for you, Inspector? I have a client due any minute.'

No sooner had the words left Chelsea Clough's lips than a dark-haired, middle-aged woman, who could only be described as mutton dressed as lamb, made a grand entrance.

Chelsea Clough lost out to her client. Annie stood up and offered a helping hand to Wilkie to help him get out of his chair. He scowled at his younger colleague, but after futile attempts to get himself up, he had no choice but to accept her hand.

'We'll need a written statement from you at some point, but it'll do another day,' Annie said to Chelsea as they passed her on their way out.

—

Wilkie Connor was quiet in the car heading to Brandon Settle's studio.

'What's up?' asked Annie after being given one or two one-word replies to her questions. Wilkie hadn't offered any arguments to her observations about the meeting with Clough.

'What did you have to go and show me up for?' he said eventually.

'I don't know what you mean,' Annie said haughtily, but she could feel the mischief hovering on her lips.

After a while of staring out the passenger seat window, Annie broke the silence. 'Do you think she was being straight with us?'

Wilkie didn't turn to look at her, but rather kept his eyes on the road ahead. 'Why wouldn't she?'

'I wondered whether it was possible that she was as fake as her boobs and as false as her lashes. It was without a shadow of a doubt she knew we would be calling to see her. Did you see the ease with which she found Settle's details?'

'Intuitive as well as attractive. I don't see any problem with that. You can put me down for the return visit to get a statement,' said Wilkie.

'I will not! I suggest that eyeing up young women is not good for you at your age.'

Wilkie's face crumpled in a wry smile and he started chuckling. 'I hadn't put you down for the jealous type.'

Annie pulled a face at him. 'As if! I was thinking more about your poor long-suffering wife!'

At Settle's studio, the detectives showed their warrant cards and asked to speak to Brandon Settle. Annie guessed that the photographer was in his mid-forties as his promotional banner in the foyer not only told her that he specialised in weddings and family portraits, but that he had been a photographer for over twenty years.

Within minutes, Settle welcomed them into his small office where Wilkie told him the reason for their visit.

'I wasn't able to accommodate Mr and Mrs James's latest wedding date, no,' he said in reply to their question.

'Why was that?' asked Wilkie.

Settle looked shifty. 'To be completely honest with you, the man who telephoned me requesting a family portrait insisted on that particular day and time. He made it crystal clear that I could name my price. When I told him that I was already pencilled in for a wedding, which had been postponed twice, he offered me double. At the time, in my defence, the wedding date still wasn't an absolute confirmation, although the dates were looking good for all concerned for the third attempt. I felt awful. However, I was worried that I wouldn't be able to resurrect the business after the ball-breaking pandemic, and I thought that a portrait sitting was more likely to go ahead than that wedding. How wrong could I be?'

'Was the person a regular client of yours?' asked Annie.

Settle hung his head. 'No, I have to confess that the man was someone I hadn't had any dealings with before.'

'A recommendation maybe?'

'Apparently a friend of a friend did, and he paid me a five hundred pound deposit the same day, which I can tell you was an absolute godsend.'

'You met him before the sitting?' asked Wilkie.

Settle looked uncomfortable. 'Well, not exactly. He posted five hundred pounds in my post box on the ground floor.'

'But then you met him on the day?'

'No, he cancelled the sitting the day before, owing to enforced family isolation, he said.'

'When did he book again?' asked Annie.

Settle's eyes rested on her face. He paused for a moment. His forehead showed her a frown. Then he began to shake his head slowly. 'He hasn't, at least not yet.'

'Have you rung him to ask why? After all, he paid you a handsome deposit.'

Settle licked his lips. 'I haven't got his number. He said he'd ring me when they had the all clear.'

Annie could feel her heart quicken. 'What was this man's name?'

'Mr Patterson, a Mr Benny Patterson.' Unaware of the impact of his revelation on the detectives, Settle carried on. 'To be fair, as much as I felt sorry for those involved, I am glad that I wasn't present at the wedding. I don't think my nerves would have stood it.'

'It was very fortunate that you knew Ms Clough and that she was available to cover for you that day, wasn't it? How well do you know her to be able to recommend her?' asked Wilkie.

Settle looked surprised. 'Oh, I don't know her at all, but Mr Patterson was very helpful in suggesting that she may be available to do it, as he had spoken to her. However, he said that he was looking for someone more experienced for his portrait than she. Hence the reason he contacted me.'

Annie looked taken aback. 'Did you not think that rather odd?'

Settle looked shocked. 'Well, no. I was rather flattered to be honest.' Again, Settle paused. 'Why? You don't think there is anything sinister gone on, do you?'

Annie shrugged her shoulders. 'I'm not sure, but there are a few loose ends that we need to tie up.'

Wilkie took his notebook and pen out of his shirt pocket and looked at Mr Settle. 'We'll need a brief statement from you, if it's convenient?'

He appeared flustered. 'Of course,' he said eventually, indicating the table and four chairs, and offering them a drink from the cold-water dispenser.

Wilkie penned the statement, Settle signed it, and Annie folded it neatly and put it in her pocket. 'I don't suppose you kept the envelope in which the money came?' she asked.

Once again Settle shook his head. 'No, sorry. I banked the money straight away, and it was immediately swallowed up to pay the rent. Do you think that this is connected to the shooting somehow?'

Again, Annie shrugged her shoulders. 'Who knows? However, I do know that we don't leave any stone unturned on a murder investigation.'

On the way back to the lift, Annie processed what had just happened. 'Good plan to take the statement from Settle straightaway,' she said to Wilkie. 'I know there is likely to be more than one Benny Patterson living around these parts, but it's too much of a coincidence for this not to be connected, don't you think?'

Wilkie indicated for her to step out of the lift before him when they got to the ground floor. 'I wonder why Chelsea Clough didn't mention it?'

'Why would she? She must have lots of enquiries that don't come to fruition,' said Annie, gathering her breath as they walked to the car. The hottest part of the day had passed, but the heat had not fully gone away, and the cool breeze, however slight, was much appreciated as they walked around the corner of the building towards the car park.

When the car came into view, Wilkie pressed the key fob, unlocking the doors. A blast of heat hit Annie when she got in and immediately wound down her window.

'Perhaps she didn't because she wasn't being totally honest with us?' admitted Wilkie.

Annie's eyes narrowed as she looked at his big, round, sweating face. 'It feels like there's a rabbit off, doesn't it? I wonder if the name Benny Patterson would mean anything to her?'

Wilkie's eyes glinted mischievously. 'Shall we go back and ask her?'

Annie shook her head. 'No, we shan't. We'll go back and see what the boss thinks.'

Chapter Sixteen

It was Thursday July 24th, and back at the station Detective Inspector Charley Mann and Detective Sergeant Mike Blake were familiarising themselves with the evidence in Charley's office when they heard loud noises coming from the CID office. Looking up, they saw Detective Constable Wilkie Connor scurrying across the room holding Tattie's cookie jar, which he had obviously snatched from her desk.

The office manager was pulling at her wild, frizzy hair. 'When're y'gonna grow up and stop lakin about?' she called after him.

The senior detectives gave each other a knowing look. Wilkie's large mischievous eyes met Charley's when he walked in her office with Annie a few moments later, nibbling on a homemade biscuit. The SIO's eyes flashed. 'If you weren't such a bloody good detective, you'd 'ave been out on your ear long ago. You do know that, don't you?' she said. The expression on her face, however, told him otherwise.

Nodding his head towards the outer office, Wilkie wrinkled his nose and winked at the SIO. 'She loves me really,' he said.

Charley sat with her legs crossed at the ankles and shook her head in his direction when Tattie knocked and entered with a tray of drinks. Notably, three cookies were on the plate, not four.

Tattie whispered to Annie. 'There's more than one way to skin a cat.'

When the office manager closed the door behind her, there was a distinct expression of satisfaction written on her face. Wilkie leaned back in his chair that was positioned around a low coffee table with the others for the meeting, and sighed, taking several biscuits out of his pocket. Without making a comment, he happily dunked them in his drink.

Charley sipped her tea. Listening to the detectives' news, several thoughts fought for supremacy. When they had finished recalling their interviews with the photographers, she was confused.

'Let me get this straight. Mr Settle is a professional photographer with over twenty years' experience and a reputation to uphold. However, he would have us believe that he'd ditch a long-term contract at the last minute for a smaller job that he accepted over the phone from a person he didn't know, and then went on to recommend another photographer to the bride that his new client had recommended?'

Wilkie nodded his head. 'He also admits that he's never met Chelsea Clough, nor does he know the quality of her work.'

Annie twisted her lips. 'That's about it in a nutshell. Not only that, as serendipity would have it, Chelsea Clough was available at short notice that day.'

Wilkie drained his mug and put it down heavily on the table in front of him. 'The name of that new client only happens to be Benny Patterson, and he paid a deposit, in cash, which he posted in Settle's post box. Yet more incredible is that Mr Patterson cancelled the day before it was due to take place.'

'Which just happens to be the name of one of our perpetrators,' said Charley thoughtfully.

Annie observed her face. 'Stinks, doesn't it?'

Mike was sitting quietly with his mug nestled in the palm of his hand. He too was thoughtful. 'Hold on. We've interviewed Patterson on a number of occasions, Annie. Do you really think that he's capable of that amount of planning and cunning tactics?'

Annie shrugged her shoulders. 'To be honest, I don't know what to think.'

Taking a deep breath, Charley spoke slowly. 'Okay, I want you to find out everything you can on Brandon Settle and Chelsea Clough, and let's see where that information takes us. We have their mobile phone numbers, so I think a good place to start would be with their service providers to see who they were calling around the time of the wedding.'

Annie looked up from writing down the SIO's instructions. 'Don't you think anyone with any salt would have used a burner phone?' she asked.

'Maybe, but it'd be neglectful of us not to rule out the line of enquiry, wouldn't it?' Charley gestured towards the younger woman's notepad. 'Make a note to find out if there's CCTV covering the place where Patterson is supposed to have posted Settle's deposit.' She paused for a moment. 'There has to be a link to our unidentified killer somewhere, and we need to find it. If it isn't here, then on the positive side, we will be eliminating another two people from the enquiry.'

Mike sat up straight and stiffened in his chair. 'Actually, the photographers are a really interesting potential link to our killer, because if you think about it, what they would know is the position that their subject would be in for official photographs, and when.'

'Exactly,' said Charley.

When the others had left, Charley felt motivated to call Ballistics to enquire if they had any update for her.

Maurice Gaunt informed her that he was just about to call. 'Having consulted our database, I can now tell you that neither of the weapons used in this incident have been catalogued as being used on previous jobs. I don't know whether that's good news for you or not.'

Charley then knew that the killer had no problem acquiring a gun and had not used a pool weapon.

'If you're about tomorrow,' Maurice asked, 'I'll come over and we'll go see if we can pinpoint the spot from which the rifle was fired.'

Having tried to locate where the shooting took place, and with several potential sites identified but none confirmed, it was important for Charley to have a professional report from someone with experience in the firearms arena. She was more than aware that, without evidence from the scene to confirm, this line of enquiry might always remain speculation. Nevertheless, it was worth a try.

–

When Gaunt arrived on site the following day, Charley was walking the church grounds with CSI Neal Rylatt. Gaunt quickly managed to identify the direction in which the shot was fired, pointing out a flat roof of a single-storey building in the distance as worthy of a look. It was much further away from the murder scene than Charley had anticipated.

The building was a takeaway that was well known to police officers, but it was closed now, boarded up, with graffiti tags sprayed on the metal shutters covering the windows and doors. The garden was neglected with waist-high weeds flourishing in the summer heat. Gaunt wandered through the grass around the exterior of the building. Charley stayed with Neal, who was photographing what appeared to be recent scuff marks they'd identified on the stone wall where, by standing on a refuse container, the roof was accessible.

Neal nodded his head in the direction of the old, tattered poster that was still pasted, in part, to the wall. 'Remember the kebabs we used to get after a shift night out?'

'God, just thinking about them makes me feel sick,' she shuddered.

'That'll be word association. Your body hears kebab and it thinks "hangover from hell"!'

The pair laughed together and she felt her mood lift a bit.

Maurice Gaunt never travelled anywhere without ladders on his roof rack, Charley knew, and within minutes, the specialist from Ballistics had them up against the wall of the building and was offering Charley a hand up on the roof. Shortly after, the pair were joined by Neal, who was eager to see what potential evidence might be waiting.

Unexpectedly, the roof was neatly paved with flag-stones and surrounded by a half-metre-high wall. All three instinctively stood still in the afternoon sun, facing the direction of the church, each alone with their thoughts.

Gaunt broke the silence. 'Well, you can see for yourself there's an uninterrupted view of the church from here. Just as I thought.'

Charley turned to Neal, who was fiddling with the camera around his neck. 'Take pictures to show where the deceased were standing in the grounds of the church, please,' she said, pointing in the direction of the church entrance.

Neal did as he was instructed, zooming in to show Charley how the killer might have seen his prey.

It was as though Gaunt had read Charley's thoughts. 'With a telescopic sight, it would be an easy shot for a trained firearms user,' he said, his eyes following Charley as she scanned the ground beneath her feet with a trained eye. However, the area appeared to be clean.

'Are you looking for anything in particular?' he asked.

Without looking up, Charley shook her head. 'No, not really. However, if our gunman was here, it would be good if we could find something that connects him to this place – anything from which we might get DNA, such as litter, chewing gum…' Charley stopped in her tracks. Her heart skipped a beat. She turned her head in the direction of the other two. 'A cigarette butt,' she said, pointing to a tab end in the gutter a few feet away that had wedged under a loose piece of mortar.

Charley signalled to Neal. 'Get a picture *in situ* and recover it.'

'Okay.' He nodded, going down on his knees to get a better shot. Neal lifted the tab end of a roll-up with gloved hands and placed it carefully in an evidence bag.

'The only thing that concerns me is that I'd have thought that the perpetrator would have been more careful, but we'll leave nothing to chance.'

With the pictures taken and one piece of potential evidence sealed in a bag for the lab, they went back down to the ground and Gaunt carried the ladder to his vehicle. At the car, Charley thanked him for his assistance and asked him to submit a statement to the incident room with his professional opinion of the site as a possible location for the gunman.

When he had left, she asked Neal to arrange for some aerial photographs to be taken that would show any future court the proximity of the locations. For a brief moment, the thought of using a drone took her back to the loss of her police horse Eddie, who had been spooked so badly at her ex-fiancé's hands that it had caused his death. Quickly, she pushed the thought to the back of her mind. She would never get over the loss of her beloved Eddie, but she was more than happy that Danny Ray was languishing in a prison cell for his crimes.

As Charley drove back to the station, she considered the situation. The enquiry was heading in the right direction, but they had yet to find a motive or a suspect, and as the SIO of the enquiry, she knew that as the days passed, there would need to be a formal review of Operation Danube, the name that Headquarters had given to the murder of Bob Sullivan and Ralph Bateman.

An in-force review would require the team to put together a presentation detailing the circumstances of the incident, priority lines of enquiry, as well as what point they were at in the investigation, what had been achieved so far, and where their focus was. This would be headed by an Assistant Chief Constable, accompanied by another Senior Investigative Officer, Crime Scene Investigator and HOLMES office manager. The extra work was not what she needed right now, but a duplicate management team might suggest other possible lines of enquiry, which might assist her. Extra minds and bodies reviewing what they knew so far could help. She welcomed a review because it was a safety net to ensure nothing had been missed.

Charley pulled up in the station car park and watched the family liaison officer Helen Weir heading towards the building. She was on her way to see the SIO and Charley was eager to hear what she had to tell her. Walking into the CID office, Charley learnt that there had been independent second post-mortems successfully carried out that morning on behalf of any future defence. This would allow the coroner, if he was satisfied, to release the bodies for burial if they were no longer needed.

'The coroner has released the bodies for funeral purposes,' Helen said. 'Bob Sullivan's funeral has been arranged for a week on Thursday. The family want his cremation to be a family affair, a time to reflect and say farewell.'

Clenching her teeth in her lower lip, Charley felt a hint of rage coursing through her veins. 'We must be prepared for whoever is responsible for his murder turning up.'

Helen nodded. 'True. I wouldn't put anything past them.'

Charley scowled. 'It's possible that they may want to cause more mayhem, too, should this be a vengeance attack.'

'Yet no one has done, have they?'

'What concerns me is whether these killings are the end of something or just the beginning,' said Charley.

Chapter Seventeen

On the day of Bob Sullivan's funeral, when the curtains closed on his flower-laden coffin, Charley felt a chill in her bones. The lives of his family and friends had changed forever and with the person responsible not yet found, and no further developments in the case, she felt sick to her stomach.

For a moment she stood still, eyes closed. The noises that washed over her were full of grief and she was grateful that the service had not been interrupted by those who had caused his death as they feared might happen. All had passed peacefully and the service had been a suitable testament to a pillar of the community – the loving husband, father, brother, uncle, and friend.

'Why does it have to be so sunny?' the SIO heard Stacey ask her new husband as they walked out of the crematorium and into the garden of remembrance. Mark tried to comfort her, but there were no words to take away her pain. As he held her in his arms, Charley witnessed the apology in his eyes, and she swallowed hard to prevent her tears from spilling onto her cheeks.

Driving back to the station, Charley passed the stable where she knew Wilson the retired police horse would be. She was sorely tempted to turn down the driveway to Kristine's yard to see him. However, after what she had just witnessed, her motivation to solve this case was stronger than ever, and there was no time to lose. As she continued along the country lanes she knew so well, by association more memories of Eddie, Wilson's one-time stable mate at the mounted section came flooding back. Once again, she immediately blocked them because they were too painful to bear. As his handler, the valiant beast had been her protector in so many difficult and sometimes dangerous situations, riding alongside Kristine and Wilson, before Charley had been sent on secondment to the Metropolitan Police force.

Within minutes, Charley received a call from the incident room that sent goosebumps down her spine.

'A prison officer from the intelligence unit at HMP Manchester would like to speak to you. He wouldn't say what it was about. He said he would prefer to see speak directly to the person in charge of the enquiry,' said Tattie.

When she returned to the office, Charley gave Mike an enquiring look. 'What do you know about the phone call?'

'No more than you,' Mike shrugged, his folded arms across his chest.

Annie was sitting at her computer listening in. 'HMP Manchester is commonly known as Strangeways, isn't it?'

Mike nodded. 'It's a Cat. A high security.'

'I haven't been there yet, but I've heard about it.'

'A prison that had its own gallows until the abolition of hanging in the 1960s, and the executed prisoners were buried in unmarked graves within the prison walls, as was the custom back then,' Wilkie said in a low growl.

'A deterrent or a practical solution, I wonder?' Annie mused.

'Probably a bit of both,' said Charley.

Five minutes later, Charley picked up the phone and dialled the number that Tattie had left for her on a Post-it note stuck to her computer keyboard.

When she heard the ringing tone, she considered again what the call might be about. Benny Patterson was on remand in Armley Prison, Leeds, so it was highly unlikely that this was anything to do with him.

The officer who answered identified himself as Prison Officer Patrick Fowler. Charley listened intently as Fowler told her that he worked with male offenders sentenced to life imprisonment and added that he had been a prison officer for over eighteen years. He had some information for her.

'Would it be possible to call in to see you to discuss? I finish work at six, so I'll be with you by seven this evening, if that suits?' he said.

Replacing the receiver, Charley was intrigued. 'What could the information be, and how could it move the investigation forward?' she asked Mike.

'Whatever it is it will need to be corroborated, but we should be thankful that he hasn't just sat on it,' he replied.

At seven o'clock, Fowler arrived at the police station and asked to speak to Detective Inspector Charley Mann. Once introductions had been made and coffee was brought into Charley's office, she and Mike settled down with Fowler to listen to what he had to say.

It quickly became evident from his direct approach that Fowler was used to giving concise, succinct reports on the inmates.

'We have an inmate doing a minimum term of thirty-four years for a double murder. After sentencing at Newcastle Crown Court eighteen months ago, Tyrone Wade was sent to us at HMP Manchester. Within days, he had taken a violent beating when he received life-changing injuries, so he was moved into solitary confinement for his own protection. Since then, he's had his head down and we've had no more trouble. However, despite this quiet, controlled, disciplined man that we have come to know, the intelligence tells us that at twenty-five years old, he was one of the biggest players on the drug scene in Manchester and the instigator of the most violent feud in recent British history. However, despite his keeping himself physically fit, inside he is a nobody. All his assets were seized by the authorities as proceeds of crime and the gang have reportedly distanced themselves from him.'

'What did he do?' asked Charley.

'The background to his conviction tells a story of a fatal bad-on-bad attack in the city. Several rival gangs were each taking ownership of a patch. It is alleged that Tyrone Wade started that feud by shooting two men allegedly dealing in his area. One of those was Shane Dooley, the son of Malcolm Dooley, the kingpin of one of Manchester's most violent drugs cartels.'

Charley looked from Patrick to Mike. 'Can't say I've heard of him, have you?'

Mike shook his head. 'There's no reason why we should unless they come into play on us though.'

'According to my sources, Malcolm Dooley is said to be untouchable, but the rumour on the landing is that he's offered up a twenty-five-grand price on Wade's head.'

Mike whistled through his teeth.

'I guess they couldn't get to him before he was nicked then?'

'Apparently not, but what puzzles me is that they don't want him dead, they want him to suffer. You see, Shane Dooley was an only son and, most importantly as far as you're concerned, he was due to be married within a few days of him being murdered.'

'I see the loose connection, but how is Wade related to the victims?'

Fowler fumbled in his pocket and handed Charley a copy of the intercepted anonymous letter addressed to Tyrone Wade.

'The original is at the prison,' he said, sounding apologetic.

Charley and Mike could see that the letter was handwritten and brief.

> *I want to cause you and your family as much pain as you have me and mine. Uncle Bob might have only been a distant relative of yours, but you ruined our wedding day and vengeance was still sweet. Be aware that as you sit alone in your cell unable to do anything about it, ALL of your family and friends are targets, and this is just the beginning...*

'Well that couldn't be any clearer, could it? Whoever has written this has not only named one of our victims, but they've also given us a motive. We will need the original letter and the envelope. Please tell me your governor still has it?'

Fowler nodded. 'Of course, I understand, I'll clear it with the Governor. Tyrone Wade will be shown the letter as it was addressed to him, but he will also be told that the original has been passed to the investigation team dealing with the murder of his uncle, etcetera.'

Charley turned to Mike. 'We need to speak to Bob Sullivan's wife and ask her about Tyrone Wade, and it goes without saying that we need to identify the person who wrote the letter.' Her attention turned back to Fowler. 'It's all relevant to our enquiries but from what you have told us, it's unlikely that Malcolm Dooley would dirty his own hands by pulling the trigger.' She paused for a moment and the faintest of smiles crossed her face. 'However, it would be good to connect him to the murders in some way,' she said.

Charley and Mike thanked the prison officer and they exchanged business cards before Mike showed him out of the station. Returning to the office, the detective sergeant saw that Charley's smile was wide as she sat at her desk, holding the new information in her hands. It might be the evidence they needed to bring the murderer down.

Mike flopped into the visitor's chair in front of her desk. 'Well, it seems we have a clear motive for the murders if his son Shane Dooley was due to be married when Tyrone Wade shot him dead. I wonder if Wade will speak to us knowing that it might be down to him that his uncle was murdered?'

Charley screwed up her face in thought. 'He doesn't sound like the sort of person that would care about anyone other than himself, to be honest. Although I guess we don't know what relationship, if any, they had, do we? First thing tomorrow we need to liaise with the National Crime Agency and Manchester Intelligence Unit to see what they can tell us about the Dooleys.'

Mike left Charley sitting at her desk. She watched him pick up his jacket from the back of his chair and head for the door.

'You should go home and get some rest,' he called before he left.

Once the CID office door had closed, the office seemed eerily still. All of a sudden she felt cold and pulled her cardigan around her. She turned on her computer and started typing up a report for the Divisional Commander and HOLMES before completing her policy log.

Chapter Eighteen

Charley woke up the next morning to the windowpanes rattling slightly in their frames in a light wind that preceded the rain. Replacing them was on her to-do list and had been since she returned to the fold three years ago, but she still found it difficult to change things in her childhood home she'd inherited as an only child when her parents died. Soon the faint, soothing, rhythmic sound of soft, gentle rain followed. It felt slightly cooler than of late in her bedroom, and she felt she owed her good night's sleep to the change in the weather, coupled with the fact that she had gained a plausible motive for the murders. She would have fresh lines of enquiries to put into action.

The hands on the clock showed five-thirty, and unable to go back to sleep, she got up, showered, and as soon as she was dressed, headed out of the door. The pavement was damp and her footsteps resounded on the stone flags, the sharp smell of rain infiltrating her nose.

The wind picked up, the darkening clouds rolled in, and as she drove down into the village with her window slightly open, she inhaled the sweet, pungent zing of petrichor. Without doubt, the team had an uphill struggle ahead of them. They would need sufficient evidence to secure a conviction and she had no idea if anyone would dare to incriminate the likes of Malcolm Dooley.

The SIO was the first in the office and saw the night detective just leaving, his night report showing no new information. Charley was eager to get the day-to-day stuff out of the way so she could learn about the Dooley family, their associates, and their feuds, which she hoped would show her further links to Tyrone Wade.

Murder investigations were always about the past, the present, and the future. Nothing could be ignored. They needed to get a full picture of the lives of those involved, which would hopefully result in an understanding of why it had happened.

Eagerly she switched on her computer and found her hands trembling from anticipation when she requested a copy of the file appertaining to the murders of Shane Dooley and Reece Brown. She wrote down the telephone number for the Manchester Homicide Team who had dealt with the investigation to obtain firsthand knowledge of the enquiry.

With the others starting to arrive, she knew she had to update them on the new intelligence as a matter of urgency, but in a cautionary way, because the last thing she wanted was for other lines of enquiry to be neglected or sidetracked by association. However, the morning's briefing contained some massive intelligence from a reliable source, which involved another police force, and linked major criminals, and it was difficult for her to keep a lid on her feelings when this new information could be the lucky break, which could open the door, to crack the case.

Annie and Ricky-Lee followed her out of the team briefing. Her eyes were bright and optimistic. 'That's what I love about this job. There's never a dull moment, is there?'

'Doesn't suit everyone's lifestyle,' said Ricky-Lee grumpily.

Annie showed him her bottom lip. 'Early mornings, late nights and weekend working not going down well with the girlfriend?' She shrugged her shoulders. 'What d'ya say, Wilkie? It'll be reight. You can allus get another girlfriend but you won't get another chance in CID?'

'Tis true,' he said.

Ricky-Lee showed her his middle finger and Mike rolled his eyes.

Charley was in no mood for frivolity this morning, though, and as she walked back to her office, a mixture of adrenaline and anticipation ran through her veins. She was oblivious to the others' banter as she refreshed her computer.

Wilkie peered around his computer screen and nodded his head in Charley's direction for Annie to see. 'I also say the most dangerous animal in the world is a silent, smiling Yorkshirewoman. The boss is on a mission.'

When she input Tyrone Wade's name, the SIO came across Reece Brown, the second man who had been slaughtered by Tyrone Wade, along with his friend Shane Dooley. Brown was twenty years of age at the time of his death. Suspended from school at an early age, he was known to the police as a career criminal.

Brown's antecedent history gave her a list of convictions in his short career ranging from burglary to robbery, wounding, illegal possession of a firearm, and drug possession. He was also flagged up to the authorities as a carrier of weapons.

Prison Officer Patrick Fowler was correct in his rendition of the incident in which Brown and Shane Dooley had died. There were no innocent parties involved or hurt in the shooting. It was deemed as brutal criminal rivals seeking the upper hand.

Having digested all there was to know about the Dooleys from the computer, she picked up the phone to speak with the intelligence unit at GMP CID to ascertain more information, and whilst she waited for them to answer she watched the staff, buzzing in the incident room. The new information could be just the motivation they needed to find the rifleman. His identification would be a huge step forward in the enquiry, and when taken to court and convicted, he would be looking at a whole life term.

When no one answered, she left a voicemail and wondered if the rifleman would roll over for a deal of some kind or whether he'd be loyal to his fellow criminals. Would he remain silent from his arrest to sentencing and thereafter?

'Misguided loyalty, or survival, not just for themselves but for their families,' she said out loud.

–

The priority enquiry for DS Mike Blake and DC Annie Glover that morning was to speak with Bob Sullivan's widow about her knowledge of Tyrone Wade.

Briefed about the detectives' visit, Helen the family liaison officer opened the door when they arrived at Josie Sullivan's home and showed them out into the back garden where Bob Sullivan's widow was deadheading geraniums in the rockery. On seeing them, she smiled weakly and put her secateurs down.

'I don't really know what I'm doing,' she confessed. 'Bob was the gardener and he always said that it directs energy into stronger growth and more flowers. Not that it matters anymore because he won't see them, will he?' she said.

'What can you tell me about your nephew Tyrone Wade?' asked Mike.

Josie looked surprised but not put out. 'He's Bob's dead brother's son. I know of him, but we haven't seen him since he was little. When his parents divorced, he went to live with his mum, and then sadly his dad died shortly after. Last we heard, he had been sent to prison.'

'Would you know if Bob had contacted Tyrone or vice versa?'

Josie frowned and shook her head at Mike. 'No, he'd have told me. Bob and I, we didn't have secrets.' Her face paled and her expression became devoid of emotion. 'Why? You don't think he had anything to do with his murder, do you?'

Mike shrugged his shoulders and sighed loudly. 'He's in prison like you say, so we know it wasn't him.'

Josie looked sideways in Helen's direction, and upon a gentle nod, turned to face Mike once more.

'I've just had a thought. A couple of years ago, might be three, I've lost all sense of time what with the pandemic and the wedding, and then...' There was a short pause. 'Out of the blue, Tyrone rang Bob one evening. Bob said he was in a right state, asking for a lift, and stating it was urgent. Bob didn't swear often, but I remember him standing in the hallway and cursing his nephew. When he came home, I was tucked up in bed. He slept in the spare room that night. He said that he hadn't wanted to wake me, so I don't know what time he got in. Bob was quiet the next day. He said he was tired, but I knew Bob was angry about something. He told me that when he picked

Tyrone up, he thought that his nephew was under the influence of something, whether that be drink or drugs, he didn't know. Tyrone asked him to take him to a mate's house, and en route admitted that someone was after him and had threatened to kill him. Then Bob stopped the car and told him to get out. Bob wanted nothing to do with whatever trouble he had got himself into. After that, Bob said he didn't want to talk about it. To be honest, I'd enough on with Stacey, the wedding and Bob folding up the business. We didn't speak about that night again.'

Mike looked more deeply into Josie's eyes. 'I know this is difficult for you, but did something else significant happen that day that might help you remember what date this was?'

Josie looked uncomfortable at being asked the question, and sad she couldn't be of more help. 'Sorry, no I don't.'

'Do you know where Tyrone asked Bob to pick him up from?' asked Annie.

Josie's eyes were hooded. Again, she shook her head. 'No, but I do know it was somewhere in Manchester. But I don't understand. If Tyrone is in prison, he can't be guilty of killing Bob, can he?'

It was Mike's turn to shake his head. 'No, like I said, we know it wasn't Tyrone. He's definitely behind bars and there is no given date for his release. We are just checking anyone on our system that knew Bob and Tyrone Wade's name cropped up, that's all.'

'Would Stacey be in contact with Tyrone?' asked Annie.

Josie frowned. 'Oh, no. She knows nothing about that side of the family, nor her wayward cousin.'

Mike, sensing that Josie was getting upset, told her that he just had one more question for her before they left her and Helen alone.

'I know you said that you hadn't seen Tyrone since he was a child. But do you think it's possible that because the business has been in the family for three generations, and Tyrone knowing where his uncle was, he might have visited Bob in the shop if he was in trouble? Maybe Bob just didn't tell you because he didn't want to worry you?'

Josie looked tired with all the questioning. 'Like I said, Bob and I had no secrets, and I am sure if our nephew had visited the shop, Bob would have told me.'

Thanking her for her time, Mike and Annie left the house and made their way to see Jerry Campbell to question him about visitors to the shop.

Could there be more to Bob Sullivan than they first thought?

Chapter Nineteen

Back at the police station, Mike found Charley drinking soup from a mug for her lunch. She pushed the box of powdered sachets across her desk towards him.

'Be my guest,' she said. When he declined, she picked up the box, looked at it more closely and pulled a face. 'I don't blame you. It tastes like dishwater. I should sue the manufacturers for false advertising, that's never seen a mushroom.'

The SIO indicated for her deputy to sit down and share his news. Eating a half-eaten bar of chocolate she found in her bag, she said, 'Am I right in thinking that Jerry Campbell has no recollection of any incidents whilst he was in Sullivan's employ that caused him any concern?'

Mike shook his head. 'No, nothing. He talks of Sullivan being a mild-mannered family man who impressed on him that the customer was always right. He says he went out of his way to make his customers feel valued.'

Charley was thoughtful. 'In relation to Josie Sullivan's memories of the night that her husband went to Tyrone Wade's aid, this might be my mind working overtime, but I wonder if it was the same night that Shane Dooley and Reece Brown were killed?'

Mike shrugged his shoulders. 'If it was, Wade used Sullivan to get away from the murder scene aware that his uncle's car wouldn't be connected to him or the area.'

'Then you think Wade confessed to his uncle about the murder?'

'Could've been why Sullivan abandoned him? Let's face it, being involved in a gangland murder is not something anyone would want to be associated with.'

'I wonder why Sullivan didn't come and confide in us, though, if he was totally innocent?'

Once again Mike shrugged his shoulders. 'Like most people who don't consider contacting us, they don't want to get involved. Would you?' He paused. 'His daughter was planning her wedding. Then shortly afterwards, the pandemic struck and his business was in financial difficulty, and ultimately closed. To be fair to him, although Tyrone is said to have told Bob Sullivan that he was on the run, and someone had threatened to kill him, he might not have shared with him the extent of the shit he had got himself in.'

'But then you think that perhaps the Dooleys might have heard about Sullivan's involvement somehow, and that brought about the reprisal?'

'Maybe Tyrone told someone.'

'I wonder if Tyrone will speak to us?' said Charley. She looked doubtful. 'Could these senseless murders really be nothing more than an eye for an eye?'

'If you ask me, Sullivan made an easy target, and as we have always suspected Bateman was simply in the wrong place at the wrong time.'

Charley was thoughtful. 'I want you to get me Sullivan's mobile service provider to see who he was in contact with around that time. And find out what phone number Wade was using at the time of his arrest. This may give us the confirmation of where Sullivan went that night to Wade's aid.'

'You think that there may be no other connection to these murders except that Sullivan and Wade are distant relatives?'

Charley nodded her head. 'Yes, I do, and let's not forget the family of Reece Brown. Who are they? Are they involved? They might have also wanted revenge for their son's death and were happy to support any reprisals, including Sullivan's murder. Trouble is, right now we don't know which gang is in bed with which, and this enquiry is leading us right into the world of drug cartels. Above all else we need to remain focused on our murder enquiries, whatever we discover along the way.'

—

The file R. V. Wade, which appertained to the murder of Shane Dooley and Reece Brown, made for interesting reading. There was a lot to digest, but what jumped out at Charley was that the double murder had been a premeditated revenge attack for the hospitalisation of two of Wade's drug runners. She scrutinised the content and intelligence in the file, and, where relevant, the information was added to the Operation Danube database.

Charley was looking for any other connection with the wedding party other than Bob Sullivan and anyone that had come into the enquiry since the murders.

'I want to find a link between members of Malcolm Dooley's gang and West Yorkshire, if there is one,' the SIO told the team at the debrief that night.

'Whoever they are, they made a big mistake when they encroached on our patch for the revenge murders,' she heard Annie say to Helen. 'The boss doesn't care who they are, or their notoriety, she'll bring them to justice.'

Charley was pleased to hear that someone had faith in her – more faith than she had in herself at times.

Before he left that night, Divisional Commander Bobbie Stokes informed her that they cancelled the requirements for the internal formal review that had been looming. He told her, 'I appreciate that you've a lot of work to do yet, but at least now there is a focus.'

The Greater Manchester Homicide Team were most accommodating, promising to speak to their contacts to find out if there had been any whispers on the streets of Manchester about the shooting in West Yorkshire. Annie Glover was happy to share the news that she had been able to make arrangements for them to visit HMP Manchester to see Tyrone Wade, who had agreed to see them.

'I almost wonder if it's just a fishing expedition on his part to find out what we know about his uncle's murder, though,' Annie said to Charley. 'After all, by now he's bound to have seen the letter.'

'Well, whatever his reason for agreeing to speak to us, it's a positive development,' she replied, reading a note left on her desk. 'This says Prison Officer Fowler passed the original letter and its envelope on to an officer from the WYP traffic unit. It's now on its way to Eira White the forensic officer in the case. Let's see what she can do for us.'

'I do hope that the letter's author has been a bit careful in his approach and has left something of a trace,' said Annie.

'If there's evidence to be found, then Eira will find it,' Charley said confidently.

They had four days to prepare themselves to visit Tyrone Wade, and Charley found herself looking out for the folklorist signs, concentrating on the ones that promised good luck and dismissing the others with a 'pinch of salt'. She prayed that further information would come in prior to the visit.

The next morning, in a conversation with Annie, Charley voiced her fears that, although Wade had agreed to see them, it didn't mean he would speak to them.

'If he doesn't speak to us, we might still get a reaction when we confirm that, because of the murders he committed, his innocent uncle was gunned down,' Annie assured her.

Charley's mind was taken off the visit entirely, however, when Mike delivered the news that Tyrone Wade was linked to a family by the name of Musgrove, who were allegedly the main opposing drug dealers of the Dooleys.

'These two families have been at war for a decade. It seemed neither was ever satisfied with what territory they had, so their feud grew,' said Mike.

Later, DC Annie Glover showed up at Charley's office door when Charley was on the phone. The younger detective was hopping from one foot to another, reminding Charley of a child desperate for the toilet. Eager to hear what Annie had to say, she ended the call to finance regarding the enquiry budget.

'What is it?' she asked as she replaced the receiver.

'It's Eira at Forensics. She wants you to give her a call now!'

Chapter Twenty

'I guess you'd say flippin 'eck in Yorkshire,' said Annie when she heard that the remnants of the roll-up found on the flat roof contained a mixture of cannabis and tobacco. The smoker, traced through the saliva on the cigarette butt, had given Forensics a DNA profile with which to search the national database. It came up with the name of Grace Westbrook.

'I think I used stronger language when Eira shared the news,' confessed Charley.

'How did Westbrook come to be on the national data-base?' asked Mike.

Annie was already on her computer checking her out. 'Drink-driving offence five years ago.'

'Can you inform the HOLMES team and get the report from Forensics on the system as soon as it comes in?'

Charley pulled a chair up alongside Annie, and saw Mike was speaking with the HOLMES office manager Sergeant Steven Taylor. Leaning in to read Annie's computer screen, she asked her, 'What else do we have on her, anything?'

'Not a lot. She's twenty-seven years old. Originates from the Longsight area of Manchester. Positive breath test at that time, stating to the arresting officers that she had been to a function at the Territorial Army Drill Hall.'

Charley was thoughtful. 'I wonder what link she has to the Territorial Army?'

'Maybe nothing,' said Wilkie, leaning back in his chair. 'She might have been to some function.'

'Maybe something,' said Charley, flashing him an irritated look. 'Haven't you somewhere you need to be?'

Wilkie fell silent, got out of his chair, picked up his jacket and left the room with a wave of his hand. 'The boss is right. Places to go, people to see. Catch y'later.'

Eagerly, Charley and Annie scanned the intelligence screen. 'Can you see a connection to Bob Sullivan?'

Annie shook her head.

Charley sat back in her chair. 'Nevertheless, I want her housing as soon as possible.'

Charley caught Ricky-Lee rolling his eyes.

'Don't be bloody negative. It's not a red herring, and if we can't find a link, then we'll put it to bed. Go find out if there were speeding tickets or parking tickets issued in the village on the day of the wedding,' she ordered. 'Or if there are any pedestrians yet to be identified on the CCTV.'

Ricky-Lee slid out of his chair and headed for the desks where the HOLMES team were located at the far end of the room.

Annie concentrated on the computer as she flicked through the information screens. 'Seems very strange that everything we are turning up has a Manchester connection, don't you think?'

'It might be another county, but we are only a few miles away, over t'ill, so not as strange as it might seem.'

Mike Blake appeared to still be a little shocked when he returned from speaking to Steven. 'I honestly never gave it a thought that the person using the rifle could be a woman.'

'Don't beat yourself up. Neither did I,' said Charley. 'It only reinforces that we should never assume anything; but, if Grace Westbrook is or was a member of the Territorial Army, my way of thinking is that she has likely learnt how to use a weapon.'

'Apparently, Steven's been told that she is now a care worker.'

Charley stood. 'I'll go and start typing up some priority lines of enquiry that we need to get on with. Check and see if she's a registered firearms holder, will you?'

''Ey 'up it appears she was riding a motorcycle at the time. It'll be interesting to see if there's a connection to the Dooleys,' said Annie.

'She'll have some explaining to do once we catch up with her. We'll be able to ask what she was doing in Marsden on the roof of a derelict building where we believe a rifle was fired and killed someone.'

'Let's hope that if she is the culprit, she's still in possession of the weapon.'

Charley's eyes lit up. 'That'd be a turn up for the books, wouldn't it?'

Within half an hour, Sergeant Steve Taylor was knocking at her door. His eyes were bright and his voice teasing. 'I've just been going over the information that we've been sent from GMP. Guess who identified the body of Reece Brown in the Manchester pub killings?' He paused.

The SIO found herself holding her breath. 'Go on,' she said.

'Chelsea Clough.'

Charley's jaw dropped. 'Really?'

Steven nodded. 'I've done some digging. Would you believe that Clough is, or rather was, Reece Brown's half-sister? Same mother, different fathers.'

Charley could feel her heart start to beat at a rate of knots. 'You're joking.' Within seconds, her eyes had narrowed. 'She's got to be more involved than she's letting on. We know for a fact that her role as wedding photographer on that fateful day was manipulated. If not by her, then by another. This revelation could give us the connection that we are looking for.'

'We don't know the extent of her involvement yet. However, we do know she isn't one of the people with a gun.'

'But she was on site at the venue, and probably knows who the person is that shot the rifle.'

'Exactly. It seems naïve now not to think that somehow, she is party to the shooting.'

Charley sighed. 'The debrief tonight will be interesting to say the least,' she said. 'And there's no denying we're making progress.'

Steve had a spring in his step as he left Charley's office. Progress at last.

Charley sat quietly for a moment taking the new information in, and connecting it to what she already knew before she started to reread the priority line of enquiries.

Pen in hand, she stopped to muse. What was the connection between Grace Westbrook and Chelsea Clough? Was it Clough that kept Westbrook abreast of the arrangements for the day? It seemed highly likely that the photographer had purposely positioned the bride's father at the front in the centre of the line-up of important men, knowing that he was about to be shot. The thought sent a shiver down the SIO's spine.

Unsurprisingly, Grace Westbrook wasn't listed on the firearms register in either Force area, which left them no alternative but to think that the rifle was illegal.

At the debrief, Charley made the team aware that their focus was not only on Grace Westbrook, but also Tyrone Wells, and Chelsea Clough was back in the frame. Mike Blake brought up that perhaps none of them would open up to detectives, but that wouldn't deter them from being questioned.

That evening, when everyone else had left, Charley sat in her office watching the seized video footage from the fateful day. This time, however, she focused on Chelsea Clough's reaction to the shooting. Unfortunately, she was the one behind the camera and took the only footage that showed the entirety of Benny Patterson's shooting. This would become the damning evidence for the prosecution's case, confirming Patterson's guilt for the murders of Sullivan and Bateman.

She was greatly tempted to immediately move in on Chelsea Clough and Grace Westbrook, but first they had to find Westbrook. Apparently, the information they had been given was that she had gone to ground. Who was Grace Westbrook and what connection did she have to the Dooleys?

In the meantime, Charley wanted to know everything there was to know about the pair. She now believed somewhere amongst the intelligence they would have links to the Dooley family, and it was important to find that connection, and link those involved.

-

The next morning, Mike was playing devil's advocate in the SIO's meeting with his boss.

'To be fair, we still can't rule out the fact that the killings were a joint enterprise,' he said.

'Come on, how likely would it be for two or more gangs to be after the same target, at the same time, and wait so long until the target's daughter's wedding date to pounce?' she argued. 'Nonetheless, I agree that we can't rule anything out at this stage.'

The intelligence unit in the incident room was busy, and further liaison with Greater Manchester Police and the National Crime Agency was active.

Charley was speaking to Tattie about the overtime budget and expenses that were being questioned by HQ when Mike entered her office with a purpose. Both of the women sensed the urgency.

'I'm being told that Grace Westbrook has a younger sister called Sinead, and what we've not picked up on is that she is, or should I say was, the fiancée of Shane Dooley,' he said.

'How've we missed that?' exclaimed Charley.

'I guess it's because we've been concentrating on the whereabouts of Grace?'

'I'll be having words with our intelligence unit. We can't afford to let stuff like that pass through our net.' Charley paused for a moment as if a thought had just come to her. 'When Grace Westbrook was breathalysed she was riding a motorbike. I wonder if she now drives a car, and if so what?' said Charley.

Chapter Twenty-One

Detective Constable Annie Glover stood alone in the car park, transfixed by the atmosphere created by the tall ominous building. Strangeways' iconic landmark watchtower, along with its sixteen-foot-high walls, cast an almighty shadow as shoppers headed into the nearby popular shopping area of Deansgate. There was a queue at the prison entrance waiting to pass through security.

Standing in the queue with Charley, Annie, new to GMP, considered its Category A prison visitors who came in all shapes, size, and ages.

Her reverie was broken by word coming down the line that the hold-up was owing to a very loud, red-faced woman, whom Annie thought could have been anywhere between twenty and thirty-five, trying to cadge a pound off someone, anyone at all to pay for a locker to safeguard her pram whilst she was inside. By the look of it, she was having no joy. She had a baby in her arms and a toddler that she had turned out of her pram onto the floor, who was now at her feet, screaming hysterically. Charley Mann left Annie's side, and as she walked towards the woman, she pulled something out of her pocket and gave it to her. The woman stopped begging, the child stopped crying, and the relieved woman smiled at Charley through painful looking sores on her lips. There was soot on her fingertips and her long-sleeved top pulled up to her elbow attempted to cover the track marks on her arms — signs to the detective of substance abuse.

Nearing the entrance, posters informed the visitors that the pandemic rules were still in force and the play area for children was closed. Annie wondered if that was what had upset the toddler further, or something else. For surely no one would choose to be going inside on such a sunny day, apart from herself.

As the people moaned and groaned at the time-consuming rigmarole, all hot and bothered, mostly due to the heat, Charley was more than aware how important security was in an establishment that housed potentially violent male criminals, prisoners who, if they were to escape, posed the most threat to the public, the police, or national security.

A handsome dark-skinned man with pearly white teeth, and smelling faintly of aftershave, observed Annie's ongoing interest in the tower. 'Don't be fooled. It's not the lookout point people think,' he said, in a low well-educated voice.

Annie looked over her shoulder, slightly taken aback. 'What is it then?' she asked.

'Ventilation, but it adds to the gloomy Gothic menace, especially when it rains,' he replied.

Annie turned back to raise her eyes up into the Manchester sky, to take in its height and concentrate on the building as a whole. It was part red-brick castle, part Alcatraz. 'If only those bricks could speak,' she whispered.

'If they did, they'd have a story or two to tell, without doubt,' the man said, with a sly smile and a wink of the eye.

On hearing the exchange, Charley tugged at the younger woman's arm, pulling her forward to stand alongside her. She frowned as a mother would when catching a child talking to a stranger and frowned at the man behind them.

'What's wrong?' asked Annie.

They took a step forward under the shade of the canopy at the door, and instantly, the world was in shadow. Annie shivered.

'You don't know who you're talking to,' she scolded.

'He looks nice,' she said out of the corner of her mouth.

'And yet he might well be an inmate's accomplice,' Charley replied through her teeth. 'Don't tell me that you haven't clocked his saggy pants?'

Annie glanced over her shoulder and the man smiled cheekily at her. 'And?'

'Let's say that they identify an inmate to more masculine prisoners as available for sexual action, and what better way to display their buttocks prouder in a manner reminiscent of the peacock displaying his tail feathers to attract a mate,' Charley whispered back.

As the significance of Charley's words became clear to Annie she involuntarily gasped, and crossed herself out of habit. 'Holy Mother of God. When I think I've heard it all.'

'Hypocrite,' said Charley.

'Fair play,' she agreed, looking at her watch.

–

The entrance to this Category A prison was in some respect no different from going into the Crown Court for a hearing or trial, Annie realised. No one, apart from the judges, was exempt from being searched.

Emptying pockets, checking hand luggage, showing ID, being party to a pat-down search, and being sniffed by the security dogs was all part and parcel of getting through security. However, Annie felt a knot in her stomach. She couldn't tell if it was nerves, excitement, or the fear of the unknown.

After being screened, the detectives were taken by uniformed personnel along a stifling, clinical-looking corridor that had a distinctive scent, not unlike pine needles.

Annie gagged. 'It smells like the green sawdust that the nuns at my school used to throw down on the floor when someone vom'd.'

Charley turned to the younger woman as they walked. 'Do you think that olfactory memory operates by recalling smells we associate with certain environments, which then gives us the extraordinary capacity to call up very specific memories?' she asked.

Annie nodded. 'I guess so. The nunnery was very much like a prison to me.'

When they came to a central hall from which four corridors were linked, the three left the area behind the hall where the prison visitors had congregated.

'It sounds like a giant beehive in there,' observed Annie.

'And one that can sting you if you're not careful, too,' said the prison officer without turning round. Just then he stopped and indicated that they should go into a room not much bigger than a cell, where moments later they could see Tyrone Wade making his way towards them.

The first things Charley noticed about him as he neared the doorway were his size and his muscles. His muscles were so big that it seemed his arms couldn't hang normally. He certainly looked as if he could handle himself in a scrap. However, when the light enabled her to make out his features, it was the results of his beating that made Charley cringe inwardly. The scars that the gym-head had been left with after the sugar and boiling water attack were horrific. Guided to his seat by his guard, he lowered himself down to sit on the grey plastic dining chair at the other end of the table. It was clear to the detectives that Wade's eyeballs were still there, but the damage to his eyes was so bad that his vision was severely impaired. The prison officer, in military fashion, took a step back from his ward and stood silently, back to the wall, a few feet away.

Detective Inspector Charley Mann introduced herself and Annie to Wade, and explained the reason for their visit, before thanking him for agreeing to see them.

'Our understanding is that Bob Sullivan was your uncle, is that right?' she asked.

The skin on his face was so badly damaged and tight that it was apparent that it was impossible for him to reveal any emotion. However, a muscle on Wade's neck twitched. There were beads of sweat glistening on his face. 'Yeah, but we didn't 'ave owt to do with each other. So why've you come to see me?'

'Because we're seeing anyone that he had a connection with to see if there's anything they can tell us about his murder. So, although you might not have had anything to do with each other, how well did you know him?' continued Charley.

Wade flinched. 'I knew him as well as I know you.'

'When did you last speak to him or see him? Can you remember?'

Wade slowly moved his head side to side. 'Can't remember. I was sent a letter telling me he had died.'

'Yes, we've also seen the letter.'

Wade attempted to shrug his shoulders, but there was little movement, potentially due to the size of his muscles, but also maybe due to his scarring.

Charley paused and Annie took a deep breath. She knew the SIO was ready to share some of what they knew with him and she also knew how important his replies could be.

'Do you think the Dooley family are behind it?' Charley asked.

The low croak of his voice added menace. 'What makes you think that?'

'The letter. It suggests to me that because you killed Shane Dooley and Reece Brown, not only was your uncle murdered, but your family are still at risk.'

For a moment, without being able to read his body language, it appeared to Charley that he might clam up. Was he using the time to try to take control over the situation? Give himself extra time to think about what he would say, or to think about how he would deliver his answer? Charley wondered. Then he spoke.

'The Dooleys are trying to get back at me for killing that big gobby twat and his mate. However, if they've killed my uncle to get back at me, the truth is that they've wasted their time, because I don't give a shit about him.'

'Do you have no feelings at all for the devastation it caused? Killing your uncle, and your cousin Ralph, on the day of Stacey's wedding?' Charley asked.

'Hadn't you heard, hardened criminals don't have hearts they have swinging bricks.' Wade smirked.

If Tyrone Wade thought that he was going to intimidate Charley Mann, he would be left disappointed.

'When you killed Shane Dooley, did you know that he was engaged to be married? Do you think that's why the

Dooleys chose your cousin's wedding day to shoot your uncle and Ralph?'

'How would I know? I don't know whether he was engaged to be married or not. I'm hardly likely to get an invite, am I? Look, I killed 'em to let them know that they don't come onto my patch, and they can't beat the shit out of folk without retribution.'

Charley pushed on. 'You said that you can't remember the last time you spoke to your uncle. How do you account for the fact that his wife says you phoned him one night, about three years ago, pleading for his help?'

Wade didn't respond, though Charley gave him a few moments to do so.

'Was that the night that you killed Dooley and Brown? Your uncle told your Auntie Josie that he stopped the car and told you to get out when you told him that someone was trying to kill you. At that point, you got out of the vehicle and ran off. Why would he tell her that if it wasn't true?'

Wade's unseeing eyes stared at Charley, his lips and tongue moving but no intelligible sound emerged, just garbled mumblings.

'Tyrone, your uncle was no criminal. He didn't belong in your world, but even though you didn't have anything to do with each other, when you asked him for his help, he came without question. The result is that he paid with his life. He was executed in cold blood on what should have been one of the happiest, proudest days of his life – his daughter's wedding. I'm being straight with you. We think his murder is a reprisal killing because they can't get to you in here,' Charley told him.

Wade pointed to his scarred head, his face, his throat, his chest. 'They tried.'

'But you'd expect that, wouldn't you? That's no different from being on the outside, an eye for an eye, a tooth for a tooth. That's your chosen world, not his. I get it. You killed Shane and Reece and their families no doubt want you to hurt like they're hurting. The prison officers will protect you the best they can in here. All we are asking is for you to confirm what we already know. We want the people responsible for this. You owe your uncle that much, don't you? Isn't that the very least you can do after he removed you from danger that could have led to your death that night?'

Wade raised his voice. 'I owe nobody nothing. He came, yes, then he dumped me, just like people have done all my fucking life. People don't tell me what to do anymore. Understand?' Getting to his feet, she could see that he was angry.

The prison officer moved towards him.

Wade turned in his direction. 'I'm done here,' he said. 'Take me back to my cell.'

Without further ado the two vacated the room.

The interview was over.

The women collected their belongings. 'We got more than we expected, didn't we?' asked Annie.

'I guess so. He confirmed what Josie Sullivan told us, including that Bob Sullivan turned out for him.' Charley pushed her chair back abruptly and stood up. 'Let's get out of this place. It's depressing.'

Walking out into the heat of the midday sun, Annie took a deep breath, enjoying the fresh air even though it was still stifling. 'I think deep down Tyrone Wade is scared they'll get to him, don't you?'

'Well, he isn't going anywhere, so there will be opportunities as time goes by. However, he's still living a life, whatever that may be. His victims aren't.'

Driving home, Annie was unusually quiet, watching the countryside go by.

'Penny for your thoughts?' Charley asked.

'If my husband took up bodybuilding and looked like Tyrone Wade, I think I'd divorce him,' she said.

Charley started laughing. 'You've got to find someone daft enough to marry you and the job first.'

Annie nodded, opened a bag of jellies and offered Charley a sweet. 'This is true.'

Chapter Twenty-Two

Annie was eating her sandwich at her desk at the same time as she was typing up her notes from the prison visit.

Charley was in her office with Mike, talking through the strategy for her next priority line of enquiry. It was the SIO's job, and her job alone, to make the decisions that she believed would continue to move the investigation forward and bring it to a successful conclusion. Nursing a cup of coffee, she shared her thoughts on Grace Westbrook with her deputy and listened to his. Mike had his pen poised, waiting for her instructions.

'I want to know which branch of the Territorial Army Grace Westbrook was attached to. I also want to know if she is trained to carry and use firearms, and if so, find out to what level and if she is upskilled with any additional qualification, including rifles. We need to know exactly what we're dealing with.'

Mike looked up from his writing. 'For what it's worth, I think your gut instinct to pursue the Grace Westbrook line of enquiry is on the money,' he said, picking up his mug and taking a sip of his drink before putting it back down on her desk so he could continue.

Charley smiled. 'I'm glad you agree with me. I'm sure others will have their opinions about the way forward, but we have to work with the facts, the evidence and what the intelligence tells us. There's no place for speculation.'

The SIO pointed to Mike's notes. 'While you're at it, speak to Patterson's solicitor and ask him to make contact with his client to see if he's willing to see us.'

Mike cocked an eyebrow. 'You think it's worth the man hours? He didn't co-operate in interview.'

'I know what you're thinking: "snitches get stitches."' The tension in Charley's face relaxed into a smile when Mike looked puzzled.

She explained that the old saying had regularly been on her friend Kristine's police officer father Marty's lips when she was a kid. She and Kristine had often warranted her dad's interrogation after returning home after dark, when they had been climbing trees, rolling down hills and generally larkin' about in the river, resulting in them, and their clothes, being much the worse for wear.

As quickly as Charley's detective mask had lifted, it fell, and Mike could sense by the change in her demeanour that her focus was clearly back on the task in hand.

'I'm hoping that Patterson might talk to us now that he has had time to reflect that he's been used as the fall guy by others trying to cover their own arses, and that the shit has well and truly fallen at his feet.'

Without waiting for a reply, having satisfactorily quantified her reasoning in her own mind, she looked down at her notes. When she raised her head a moment later, she moved straight onto the next point. 'Were any fingerprints found on the money that Patterson had on him at the time of his arrest?'

'I've not heard, but I'll find out,' said Mike.

'If so, get me the names of those now linked to the enquiry with previous convictions. We need to pass the likes of Malcolm Dooley and his associates onto the fingerprint department to get them ruled in or out.'

Charley sat back, took a deep breath and folded her arms. In a determined voice she expressed her aim. 'Stating the obvious, we need good solid, unequivocal evidence to connect those involved in the shootings that's good enough to put before the courts.'

As Mike stood to leave, Wilkie tapped at the open door and walked in, his face redder than usual and obviously excited about something.

The senior officers gave him a questioning look.

'We've got an update as to the whereabouts of Grace Westbrook. She flew to France on a one-way ticket the day after Sullivan and Bateman were shot.'

Mike turned to Charley. 'Surely that can't be a coincidence, can it?'

Charley shook her head. 'I wouldn't think so. I'm presuming we don't know where she is now?'

'No,' replied Wilkie.

The SIO frowned. 'I wonder if GMP can tell us if the Dooleys have a place in France.'

'I'll put a call in,' Wilkie told her before returning to his desk.

Mike stood by the door. 'Is there anything else that we can be doing?'

Charley's jaw tightened and Mike could see that she was thinking. He waited for her to express her thoughts, but they were not what he expected.

'Truth be known, I'm still itching to pull Chelsea Clough in and see what she'll tell us, but I'm holding off until we know beyond doubt that she's involved. That way, we'll have the upper hand. Because the last thing I want is to alert them to the fact that we believe we know what happened until we have more evidence.'

Mike agreed but looked apprehensive. 'I understand. We still don't know a lot about Westbrook, do we? Let's face it, the only reason she's on the police system is because of a drink-driving offence some years ago. All the rest is currently circumstantial.'

Charley hesitated. 'If Wilkie doesn't get any joy with Grace Westbrook's whereabouts, then I think we need to put out an all-ports warning. We need to interview her in connection with the murders.'

After Mike left, Charley briskly walked into the main office to give Wilkie further instructions. He was otherwise engaged on the telephone and when he eventually put down the receiver, she looked at him questioningly.

'GMP are on it,' he said reassuringly.

Charley pulled up a chair alongside the old-timer. 'I want you to find out how Westbrook paid for her ticket to France if you can, along with when she booked her flight, what airport she flew from, and if she was travelling with anyone. While you're speaking to airport security, maybe you could ask them if they have CCTV that covers the car park and the departure lounge at that date and time available for us to view. That way, we can see for ourselves how Westbrook arrived at the airport and with whom.'

Annie peered around her computer screen. 'I don't suppose you have any results from Forensics yet in connection to Chelsea Clough? I seem to be hitting a lot of brick walls.'

'No, nothing we haven't shared already. Have you the details of Clough's vehicle, and do you know if she has a residential address or does she live at the studio?' asked Charley. 'I'm considering putting surveillance on her to see if that assists us in obtaining any connections with the likes of Dooley.'

Annie pulled a blank piece of paper from her printer and started to write down the details Charley had requested. When she had finished, she pushed the paper across the desk for the SIO to see.

Thanking Annie, she turned back to face Wilkie. 'I wonder what sort of relationship Westbrook and Clough have? Did they only come together to avenge the death?' Charley stopped and paused for a moment. 'I wonder if there could be a connection between Clough and Sinead Westbrook for us to pursue?'

There was no reason for Charley to feel deflated, but she did. If only they could turn up the weapon that Westbrook had used. Then her thoughts turned to how someone would pay for a weapon because they knew from their enquiries that it hadn't been used in previous crimes and weapons didn't come cheap. She wondered who could help her with this line of enquiry. The financial investigation team could look into Westbrook's and Clough's bank transactions, but only when the women's bank details had been obtained. Ultimately, Charley hoped that at this stage, it might also reveal if one or both had been paid for their part in the murders. However, she was more than aware that, as the enquiry progressed, it was perfectly plausible that they were both, maybe all three were willing participants who were intent on seeking revenge.

Head in a shed, as Annie would say. Charley was on her way to the office cold water dispenser when Steve Taylor called her over.

'Boss, you might be interested to see this CCTV footage of a furtive, dark-haired woman pushing a push-chair more briskly than I would expect along the main road about an hour before the wedding.'

Steve pointed to the moving image on his screen. 'The same woman is seen walking rapidly in the opposite direction shortly after the shooting.'

Charley leaned in closer to look at the footage.

Steve zoomed in. 'Could this be Grace Westbrook?'

Charley's voice dropped an octave. 'We won't know that until we get a recent photograph, will we?'

Steve turned his head towards Charley. 'You don't think that she may be using the pushchair to conceal the weapon?'

Together, they watched the footage several times. There was no doubt about it – the way the woman was acting made her look highly suspicious.

'How far can we track her movements?'

Steve pulled a face. 'Not far enough. Sadly, this CCTV is privately owned and only covers the main road in front of the owner's shop premises. We can't see where she has come from, where she goes, or if there is a baby in the pram.'

Charley looked downcast.

'The still from the footage is also blurred, but that's because she's moving. If she had been standing still, it would be clearer.'

'Can it be enhanced?'

'I doubt it. Think of the grainy image you see here as a photograph when the shutter speed is too slow for the action. When there is bright light in the lens, as in this case because it was a bright sunny day, this can also smear the image. This is caused by a phenomenon called 'lag' or 'smear'. Higher scan rate CCTV cameras are readily available that don't do this – but sadly, this is not one of those.'

Charley stood up straight and stretched her back, but her eyes stayed on the image. 'On a positive note, we will know if it's Westbrook once she's traced, and we can use facial mapping to help us should we need it.'

Not wanting to lose momentum, and knowing that an investigation meant keeping more than one plate spinning at a time, when the debrief was over that evening, Charley sat alone in the office and switched her attention to the intelligence on the murder of Shane Dooley and Reece Brown.

Eyes tired, the SIO flipped systematically through the computer screens until her eyes started to close. She was just about to turn it off when she saw Grace Westbrook's name on a list of those who had been present in the public house at the time of Dooley and Brown's murder.

Tiredness forgotten, she sat bolt upright, and for some unknown, unrelated reason, her mind jumped to Benny Patterson. Had he had any visits from anyone else other than his legal representative whilst on remand?

The telephone ringing made her jump. It was the duty officer at Leeds prison, seeking the night detective to pass information onto the SIO. Benny Patterson had been attacked by another inmate, and was on his way to hospital by ambulance. They were trying to save his life, but his throat had been slashed with a homemade sharp object, so it wasn't looking good.

The attempted murder had been referred to the local police.

How bizarre that she had been just thinking about him.

Chapter Twenty-Three

Half-expecting a call from the night detective to report on Patterson's demise, Charley had slept with one ear cocked for the phone. The night seemed to last an eternity and, while driving to work, she felt irritable and less tolerant than usual with other road users.

At the station, the team started to arrive in the incident room. The faint murmur of voices filtered into the kitchen. Winnie was brewing up. Charley put an arm around her and gave her a warm squeeze. Winnie pulled back and looked at her, her old grey watery eyes gazing directly into the younger woman's, the blue accentuated by the signs of exhaustion in the shadows beneath.

'You look tired, lass,' she said with a frown. 'You can't run an engine on an empty tank, you know. I hope you had a bite to eat before setting off. Yer dad would have a fit if he thought I wasn't looking after you.'

Charley indulged Winnie's watchful look as a child would a parent, with a smile that told her not to worry and that she was okay. She felt grateful for Winnie's presence and her kindness, for Charley had no one else in the world who looked out for her as Winnie did.

Charley, however, ignored Winnie's observation and instead inhaled the aroma of her coffee, wishing it tasted half as good as it smelled.

The news of the prison attack was on everyone's lips for the moment, but the SIO knew they'd probably move onto something else very soon. One of the best parts of being a cop was not knowing what was going to happen next. It was also, however, one of the downsides, because it was a labour of love and impacted their personal lives. It was perhaps just one of the reasons why Charley was single.

Charley poured herself another coffee, finally feeling more alert as the caffeine was injected into her system, when Mike entered the kitchen.

'He's still with us then?' he said whilst trying to pinch a slice of dripping on toast that Annie was holding aloft from Wilkie, but she whipped it out of their reach.

'Apparently so. He's on a ventilator in intensive care. He lost a lot of blood.' She looked at her watch. The next few hours were crucial.

Toast eaten, Annie licked her fingers. 'Do you think someone is trying to silence him?' she asked.

'I know this sounds selfish, but I'd just like to know if there's a possibility that the attack is connected to the murders at the wedding,' Charley replied.

'How did the attack come about? Have you any ideas?' asked Mike.

'According to Detective Inspector Graham Thaxter from Holbeck, who is in charge of the police enquiry, the motive remains unknown, and the initial interviews with the offender Terry Morris have failed to get a response.'

'What do we know about Morris?'

'Thirty-five years old, apparently on remand for wounding. He's got four previous convictions for assault. The rumours are that Patterson had been bad-mouthing Morris earlier in the day.'

Mike screwed up his nose. 'Looks like he met his match this time, though that doesn't assist us, does it?'

Charley shook her head morosely. 'No.'

Ten minutes later in the briefing, Annie confirmed that her enquiries had resulted in the information that Chelsea Clough lived in a flat above her studio. Downstairs, there were two rooms at the front where she and Wilkie had met with the photographer. She had also discovered that the lease on the property had only been running for eighteen months.

'I think, as a matter of urgency, we need to take the bull by the horns and visit Chelsea Clough,' Charley said.

Next, Ricky-Lee shared the information that a rival gang by the name of Musgrove had been mentioned on several occasions by local intelligence at Manchester police when he had made enquiries about the Dooleys. The Musgroves were allegedly involved in all aspects of criminality. Like the Dooleys, their primary source of money was thought to be from the drugs scene, including the hidden world of 'county lines'. What appeared to be unique about the Musgroves, however, was that they owned several handwash car cleaning companies in Longsight that were currently under investigation for labour trafficking. Was this Tyrone Wade's gang?

Wilkie brought the news that Grace Westbrook had travelled via EasyJet to Charles de Gaulle airport in Paris. Unfortunately, from the investigation's point of view, her one-way ticket had been paid for with cash, which meant that there was no paper trail and therefore the financial investigation department was unable to help.

Charley reassured a morose-looking Wilkie. 'Although I think it's pretty obvious that Westbrook had planned her exit after the shooting, she is only human, and she will no doubt have made other mistakes just like she did with the carelessly discarded cigarette butt that led us to her in the first place. You mark my words.'

The vibrant hum in the room quietened as Ian Chamberlain from the fingerprint bureau indicated to Charley that he had something to say. The tall, slender, quietly spoken man stood up quickly, his glasses slipping down his moist nose and a sheaf of well-thumbed paperwork in his hand. 'I have an interim report regarding the banknotes seized from Benny Patterson's house that have been processed to date.'

The look in the SIO's eyes told him to continue.

'We have found three sets of prints. Like you would expect, Patterson's are there. The other two are smaller, and in my experience, look very much like they belong to women, or children. Sadly, there is nothing on the system that confirms or identifies whom these belong to.'

Chamberlain feared that the SIO might be disappointed, but Charley looked at him, intrigued by what she was hearing. 'That's interesting. We have three women who have come into the frame, and are becoming a priority for our attention.'

Before Charley closed the meeting she updated the others in respect of the ongoing enquiry into the attack upon Benny Patterson in prison, and afterwards they all dispersed with a renewed hope of success. There were times in an enquiry when things needed a nudge to keep things moving forward and keep morale high. This was one of those times.

With the news that the result of Clough's mobile data was imminent, and the fact that Charley had been told that nothing had occurred from static observations on Clough's address, Charley chased up the results of the financial investigation enquiry into the photographer, informing those involved that these were urgently required to make an arrest.

'We need to know if there are any anomalies to talk to her about in interview,' Charley told Mike.

That afternoon, Charley called a meeting to discuss the arrest of Chelsea Clough for conspiracy to murder.

'This will give us access to Clough's premises,' she told Annie. 'I want you to arrange for specialist search teams to be present.'

'What will they be specifically looking for?' asked the younger detective.

'Anything that connects her to the deceased, whether that's in Manchester or here, and also to the likes of Grace and Sinead Westbrook, Benny Patterson, the Dooleys and the Musgroves.'

'I want to make sure that she's in when we call,' she told Mike.

'I'll put a call in asking her availability,' said Wilkie.

DC Wilkie Connor's phone call was met with a pre-recorded message that stated Chelsea Clough was away from the office.

On discussing the arrest at the debrief, Charley shared her thoughts. 'Whilst we wait for DC Connor to confirm a date on which Chelsea Clough is available, I want us to review what evidence we have. I'm hoping that her phone data shows the connection between her and Grace Westbrook,' she said.

It was early evening when the intelligence unit in Manchester rang to update Charley on their enquiries, and to assure her that although they had been unable to find a recent address for Sinead Westbrook, their enquiries were ongoing. Apart from Mike the others had gone home, so when she put the receiver down she went to stand at her open door, quite still. Mike looked up from his desk questioningly. The top button of his shirt open, and his tie pulled down, he looked all but done in.

'GMP...' she said, referring to the telephone call. 'They tell me that at the time of the Manchester shootings, the sisters were at loggerheads because Shane Dooley had recently been found to be shagging them both.'

'What? Even though he was marrying Sinead?'

'Apparently so.'

Mike arched a brow. 'And she forgave him?'

Charley nodded. 'Looks that way. It'll be interesting to see what contact, if any, she had with Grace recently, won't it? We'll need her fingerprints and DNA when Sinead's traced.'

Head back, Mike stretched out his arms above his head and yawned.

For a moment neither of them spoke, and yet it was a comfortable silence. Then a glance at her watch brought Charley back to the present and the fact that neither of them had eaten.

'I don't fancy going home to an empty house, not just yet. Do you want to go for a drink and something to eat?' Charley asked him.

Mike didn't need asking twice. He grabbed his jacket, made sure his keys were in his pocket, and waited for Charley to gather her things.

Chapter Twenty-Four

There was no denying that Charley had drunk far too much red wine, and was grateful that Mike, having read her mood the previous evening, had suggested that she drop her car off at home before they went to the pub. Despite her hangover, the SIO still arrived at the station before the others the next morning. Winnie, however, was standing with her back to the door and hands on her hips looking at the piles of papers and files on the desk when Charley walked into her office.

The poster on the door felt somewhat significant: If you can't do the time, don't do the crime.

'Since I can't actually see your desk to dust it this morning, I've just blown on it,' she said. Winnie turned to see that Charley's face was green around the gills. 'You're hungover,' she said with no sympathy in her eyes.

When Charley sat down, Winnie turned on the vacuum cleaner. To the SIO, it sounded like a pneumatic drill, but trying to explain the waves of nausea and that the noise made it worse was impossible. Winnie was not going to switch the device off, so Charley unplugged the Hoover, resulting in precious silence.

When she remembered how the evening ended, she let out a groan. 'Did I really ask if he wanted to stay the night?'

'Who?' asked Winnie.

Charley put her head in her hands. 'Mike.'

Winnie shook her head and was silent on the matter, which somehow made it worse.

On hearing the door, and suspecting Winnie had left her to stew in her own juices, Charley ventured to look up, only to see Mike standing at her door carrying a bag of fresh fruit. He was grinning from ear to ear.

'Hair of the dog?' he joked, stepping forward to slide the fruit across her desk. 'I thought you might need a vitamin boost.'

Charley grinned back. She couldn't stop herself. Mike was the best deputy anyone could ask for. 'Why do all the good guys have to be gay?' she asked him.

'Not all,' he laughed.

She really needed to do something to keep her mind busy, so she worked systematically through the papers on her desk and piled them up in order of priority. This morning organisation was key.

At the top of the pile, the update from the night detective informed her that Benny Patterson was not responding as had been hoped, and the news that he wasn't out of danger irked her. The least he could do for the victims and their families was to serve the sentence befitting the crime.

On the other hand, his attacker, Terry Morris, had been charged with attempted murder and subsequently moved to another Cat. A prison. He had chosen not to make any comment about the attack on his fellow inmate. It wasn't surprising, but it also wasn't helpful to her enquiry. She was pleased to see that those investigating the attempted murder were confident of a conviction, owing to the evidence that had been secured at the scene.

If only every enquiry was so easily solved.

Feeling tired and frustrated – she hated waiting for results – Charley was reluctantly drinking the peppermint tea Winnie had made for her when a call came in from Stacey James, née Sullivan. Charley was surprised to hear that, when helping her mother with her financial situation, Stacey had uncovered what seemed to be irregularity in her father's business affairs.

'I don't want Mum to think I'm being disloyal to her, or Dad, but I'm starting to think that Dad might have been in some sort of trouble,' she said.

Charley tried to reassure her. 'If there is anything untoward, then we'll deal with it, together. Can you bring the paperwork into the station this afternoon about three o'clock?'

'Well, yes, I suppose I could...' Stacey sounded surprised at the urgency.

Charley wasn't about to admit that was because of the inference of money laundering to Bob Sullivan's daughter. However, immediately she had put the phone down on the young woman she requested the attendance of Des Ryder from the Financial Investigation Unit at the meeting. Des Ryder was the stereotype of an accountant, and he had a proven ability for achieving solutions to complex problems.

Mike brought her a coffee and sat down opposite her to eat his lunch. Embarrassed by the fact that she couldn't remember how he had declined her offer to stay over, but that she knew he hadn't because he wasn't at the house when she had woken up, Charley purposefully avoided making eye contact by consulting both her notes and her computer screen as they discussed the case.

'What's your thoughts Mike?' she asked after telling him about Stacey's call. 'Did Bob Sullivan have a hidden secret, a secret that he had kept from even his nearest and dearest?'

'It might explain his sudden rush to go help his nephew,' he replied.

'Maybe the story he told Josie of chucking Wade out of the car was one that they agreed on to try and keep Sullivan's involvement to a minimum?' she continued.

'Once he got involved, he may have felt that there was no way out,' he said.

Charley glanced briefly at her colleague to find his eyes already upon her. On his face was a frankness of interest that caused her to quickly turn back to her computer, unwilling to see the disappointment in his eyes due to her outrageous behaviour, that she'd observed earlier that day.

Charley adjusted her sitting position and tone of voice. 'We need to deal with Clough and the Westbrook sisters and try to find out who is linked to Benny Patterson,' she said brusquely.

'Maybe if Patterson believes that he was attacked to keep him quiet, and whoever was behind it won't stop until he is dead, he might not feel quite so loyal to those who employed him and decide to talk to us.'

Charley inhaled deeply and her stomach rumbled. 'There's certainly nothing to lose in trying. If we go via his solicitor, he might be the one to persuade him to open up.'

Mike offered her a sandwich.

Charley shook her head. She still felt nauseous. 'That's if he pulls through.'

'Sometimes things happen that make you reassess your life. Let's hope this is a life-defining moment for him.'

What a funny thing to say, Charley thought, but then Tattie brought in some of her homemade lemonade.

Charley thanked her, then referred back to her paper-work. 'We need to know where Sinead Westbrook was at the time of the shootings.'

'If she is involved, and she's got owt about her, she was probably ensuring that she had an alibi, knowing that she could potentially be a suspect in a murder enquiry.'

Charley's eyes narrowed. 'We need her to be inter-viewed as a matter of urgency and her fingerprints to eliminate her from those found on the notes in Benny Patterson's possession at the time of his arrest. We also need her DNA.'

Finishing his dinner, Mike stood, screwed up his napkin into a ball and then aimed it at the wastepaper bin. 'We have a couple of detectives in Manchester today attempting to find out her whereabouts,' he said. 'Have we done here?'

Charley swept her paperwork to the side and pulled another pile towards her.

'For now,' she replied, dismissively turning towards her computer screen.

–

When Stacey James arrived at the station to speak to Charley, as requested, she had brought with her a very old, battered case containing her father's accounts. The SIO's office had been set up to ensure that Stacey felt at ease. The comfortable chairs were around the low coffee table, on which there were three glasses and a jug of cold water. The blinds were pulled up to let the light in, the window was open, and the cooling fan was on. Joined by Des Ryder from FIU, Charley made the introductions and took the lead.

'Whatever it is, it can't have been easy for you, so thank you Stacey,' Charley said.

Stacey emptied the case of the paperwork onto the table in an orderly fashion.

'These are the shop accounts for the last three years. As you know, because of Covid, the business was closed for a while, which resulted in Dad's having to close it, or so we thought. However, as you will see, there was money – a lot of money – still passing through the business during the pandemic.'

'Did Mr Sullivan do the accounts?' asked Charley.

Stacey nodded. 'Yes, Mum said that he never even let anyone bank the takings at the end of the working day. I guess Jerry will confirm that for you.'

Ryder cleared his throat and took a sip of his coffee before he spoke to Mrs James. 'I don't want to speculate. First impressions. There seem to be anomalies,' he said with a frown. 'I will need to look these over in more detail and make some enquiries before I can give you any definitive answer.' He gave Stacey a laboured smile. 'This is where accountants get a bad reputation for being dull, boring and spineless,' he said with self-deprecating humour. 'I'm sorry I can't give you the instant solution that I guess you were hoping for, but I'd rather be that than be dishonest with you.'

Charley leaned forward and nodded her head reassuringly towards Stacey. 'As soon as we have anything to tell you, we will.'

It was an ordeal for Stacey to leave the station without knowing whether her father was involved in criminality or not, still wondering if it might be the reason he was killed. However, it wasn't a total shock that Des Ryder needed to do further work, considering the complexity of the accounting.

In Charley's office, the SIO nodded to the papers in Ryder's hands. 'What are your initial thoughts?'

'Like I said to Mrs James, I'm not going to speculate until I have had more time to digest the accounts, and like you said to her, I will get back to you as soon as I have something to tell you.'

When he closed the door behind him, Charley groaned and rubbed her hands over her face. She tipped her head back and closed her eyes. It was true that the tighter you kept something to yourself, the less chance there was of someone finding out. Was Sullivan involved with his nephew and the young man's cronies all along? If so, when Wade got sent to prison and someone else took over, did they get greedy or cross the line? Could that have ultimately cost Sullivan his life?

The news from the debrief that night told Charley that Sinead Westbrook was believed to have gone on holiday, destination unknown.

Charley voiced her thoughts. 'Could it be that the three women were acting together?'

Annie shrugged her shoulders. 'Could be. Chelsea Clough's rent has been paid up for another three months.'

Wilkie informed the others that there was no change in Benny Patterson, according to his medical team, and they were reluctant to bring him out of his coma anytime soon because the shock might kill him.

Ricky-Lee had interesting news from his enquiries at the Territorial Army base, where he had obtained photographs of Grace Westbrook. Her records showed that on leaving the TA two years previously, her conduct was said to be exemplary, and she had been awarded a distinction for Rifle and Pistol Shooting.

Ricky-Lee pointed to the photograph of Grace West-brook, and then to the next. 'I have also been sent this photograph of Sinead Westbrook with her deceased fiancé Shane Dooley by GMP. We know, for obvious reasons, that this is approximately three years old.'

Charley was immediately struck by the sisters' similarity.

'Can we also share a picture of Chelsea Clough, please?' Charley asked. 'I know Wilkie and Annie have met her, but no one else has, as far as I am aware.'

The SIO's question was met with a sea of shaking heads. Mike cleared his throat. 'On the topic of their contact with each other. Mobile phone data is trickling in, which is being charted by our analyst. We would expect sisters and friends to be in contact daily, which is evident, but the two-dimensional representation of the mass data on the Anacapa chart will clearly show these links.'

It was Charley's turn to speak and conclude the meeting. 'Whilst we now believe we know who was involved in the church murders, and we are beginning to unravel the complexity of the case, we still don't have a location for the suspects or evidence to prove their involvement beyond doubt. Can we please speak to Clough's landlord? I assume that he will have a key, and after explaining what we know, he might give us access, which saves us time having to get a warrant.'

Wilkie Connor raised his hand. 'The landlord is a David Saxby. I'll give him a call. When are you thinking of going in?'

The SIO's tone was determined and decisive. 'Tomorrow morning. We will need the help of a POLSA search team. Let's get this done and move things forward.'

Chapter Twenty-Five

The SIO was aware that a large group of officers lined up outside drew attention, so at the seven o'clock briefing with all those involved in the operation, she told them to remain in their vehicles until further instruction.

The search team's brief included looking for women's clothing and a push chair like the image of interest captured on CCTV on the day of the murders, as well as anything that appertained to a firearm, or the murder enquiry, with the caveat that anything of interest must be photographed *in situ* before being seized.

An hour later at Chelsea Clough's photographic studio, there was no response to the police knock on the door. After a few moments, and with a determined look on his face, DC Wilkie Connor knocked louder. Still no response. Wilkie tried the door, but it was locked.

The landlord and keyholder, David Saxby, was standing to the side by a large bush entwined in weeds and was then asked to come forward to help gain access. Unbeknown to him, there was a lot riding on what was inside the premises. Charley's heart raced. All eyes were on Saxby and he too looked as if he could sense the import-ance of the operation, as well as the danger potentially involved with firearms. His hands were shaking, but the turning of the key and the unlocking of the door was swift.

Then he was immediately whisked off to the CSI van to take elimination fingerprints.

Detective Wilkie Connor opened the door, and he and DC Annie Glover entered the premises with a certain amount of trepidation. They had been trained to expect the unexpected and to check that there was no one at home. Since they had both previously been inside the studio, it gave them the advantage of being able to report any changes since their last visit. Charley had instructed CSI supervisor Neal Rylatt and his team to go in when the detectives had finished the visual checks and to fingerprint the interior before the search team were admitted.

Within minutes, Wilkie emerged from the building. Charley's heart rate began to creep up again. She looked at him enquiringly.

'There's no doubt that she's done a flit,' he said. 'We've checked every room. The photographic equipment has gone.'

Annie followed him out two minutes later. 'I've checked behind the door. There's no post other than junk mail.'

'Sounds like someone's made a good job of covering their tracks,' said Charley. She turned to speak to Neal Rylatt. 'Let's get some fingerprints lifted. Hopefully, we'll be able to secure Chelsea Clough's and anyone else that has been here.'

Charley was left alone with Annie. 'My hope is that we'll be able to show that Sinead and Grace Westbrook have both been here, and therefore not only prove the connection between the three, but just as importantly, show that the sisters have been in the Kirklees area.'

After updating David Saxby on their findings, Charley thanked him for his assistance and told him that they would return his keys once CSI had finished and the police search team had done a thorough search of the building.

Looking over his shoulder towards the open door, Saxby looked relieved. 'I'm just thankful to hear that the tenant hasn't trashed the place. There's no rush with the keys. The rent's paid. However, she's not left her keys.'

'Then, it might be a good idea to change the locks,' Charley advised.

Back at the incident room, all Charley could do was wait for the professionals to complete their part in the operation. Not wanting to leave her office in case there should be a notification of a significant find along the way, with one eye on the clock, she focused on the paperwork that needed her attention because nothing could be filed without her, or her deputy's signature.

An hour and a half later, the call came. What was initially thought to be a camera lens cap was now suspected to be from a telescopic sight. It was clean, and in the opinion of the ex-firearms officer who had seen it, it hadn't been on the floor in the storeroom for long.

Charley felt a thrill of delight. 'Can you send me a picture for me to forward to Maurice at Ballistics to confirm?' she asked. 'If it is what you think, that suggests that a firearm has been on the premises.'

For a few minutes after Charley had forwarded the photograph of the round, black cover to Maurice, she studied it. Mike stepped forward with an outstretched hand to take a quick look and then passed her mobile back. He liked to see the flush of excitement on her face and wished that he didn't have to dampen it.

'There is no doubt that's a cap to protect a lens from scratches and minor collisions, but it looks pretty generic to me. I think we might have trouble proving where it came from. Do you not think we might be jumping to conclusions?' he said.

Taking another look, Charley pondered for a moment. 'That's true. Let's wait to see what Maurice says.' However, calm she appeared she felt the butterflies in her stomach in anticipation of a positive result, and when Charley took a call a few minutes later, Mike witnessed a look of elation on her face. Telling Maurice to repeat what he had told her, she put her phone on speaker so Mike could hear.

'I'm one hundred percent satisfied that the exhibit is the flip-up cap lens cover that can be found on a telescopic sight. There are several types, but it is very clear to me when the comparison is made.'

'Chelsea Clough has a lot to explain away when we get to speak to her,' said Mike.

'She certainly does,' replied Charley.

The clock said it was four o'clock when Charley heard loud, jovial voices entering the incident room.

The search had proven fruitful despite a good attempt, it appeared, by Chelsea Clough to cover her tracks. Refuse bins had been removed from the premises, all personal items taken, and cupboards and drawers emptied and cleaned. However, the team was eager to share the news of their find in the attic, where a pushchair had been discovered, abandoned to the side of the hatch. It wasn't dusty nor did it show signs of mould, which suggested that this piece of seized evidence hadn't been there long.

Charley was excited by the possibility of DNA and gunshot residue being found on the pram. 'GSR usually stays on a living person's hands for anywhere from four to six hours, and on other materials perhaps up to four days,' Eira at Forensics told Charley.

'I want a statement from Mr Saxby as to who the previous tenant was, along with if there have been any children at the address and when he last checked the attic,' she told Annie.

By the six o'clock debrief, Saxby's statement was done, and he had stated that at no time had there been a tenant with a child at the property, and before Clough, the premises had been emptied, and a full inventory taken, with no mention of a pushchair.

Before the team dispersed that evening, the items seized from Chelsea Clough's rented property were prepared to go to Forensics, and the fingerprints lifted by CSU were ready to be put through the system.

It was clear that the enquiry was being fuelled by adrenalin after a fourteen-hour day for the team, knowing that they were getting closer to the killers and gaining evidence to prove their guilt.

Had Grace Westbrook and her sister Sinead been at Clough's place? And if so, would their fingerprints have been lifted? Charley wondered. Before she left, Charley created a list of priority enquiries to be carried out the following day, including obtaining the whereabouts of private CCTV cameras or facilities that might give the team evidence of Grace, Sinead, or both, visiting Clough.

- Was there a local food store where they might shop?

- Where was the nearest garage that she and those visiting her might use for fuel?

- What was the origin of the pushchair – new or secondhand?

- When were they going to locate the three women, and where were they now? An intelligence bulletin needed to be created and circulated with regards to the women being connected to the murders of Sullivan and Bateman, including a contact number for the incident room and for herself.

- A marker needed to be attached to Grace West-brook's file, as she was known to be a firearms user.

For a moment Charley thought about where each team were at in their enquiries and the evidence showed that the admin team had been researching phone data, looking at who was calling whom to prove their connection, and also GPS mapping which would show them where they had been at the time of the call. Her hope being that before long this line of enquiry would result in giving her an indication of where the women might be now.

–

Daylight was fading as Charley travelled home. She anticipated that sleep would not come easily that night, and she was correct. When her head hit the pillow, her brain went from park into drive. She wondered if Chelsea Clough had set up the photography business just so she could be at the wedding and to arrange the guests for their photographs. Did she know the link between Bob Sullivan and Tyrone Wells? Had they planned everything since the murder of Dooley and Brown? They had plenty of time and were in no doubt hoping that they had covered every angle of their criminal activity. As she finally drifted off to sleep, she rode the peaks and troughs of the investigations like riding a horse across the moors. She was prepared for the jumps as much as possible and she was ready to respond when they came. Tomorrow was another day.

Chapter Twenty-Six

Charley Mann slipped from her bed at six-thirty the next morning. She checked her phone and saw a text from the night detective at six o'clock to say that he had checked in with the hospital before leaving the station. Benny Patterson was breathing independently and had a good chance of survival, although the road to rehabilitation would be a long one. Charley fist-pumped the air. It was going to be a good day. She could feel it in her bones.

Mike's jacket was draped over the back of his chair when she arrived in the office. She found him sitting at the kitchen table drinking coffee and eating a bowl of cereal. He smiled and pointed to his mug. 'Do you want some?' When Charley sat down opposite him, he added, 'Good news about Patterson.'

'Absolutely, although I'm not sure everyone would agree.'

'Yes, well, I can understand that. If someone had killed my nearest and dearest, I can't say that I'd not want them dead too.' He looked at his watch, then picked up his crockery and carried it to the sink.

'You going somewhere?' asked Charley.

Mike stopped washing his pots, and when he spoke again, Charley could hear the smile in his voice. 'No, I'm expecting a call from the intelligence unit. There'll be nobody there until eight.'

'Good news or bad?'

'No idea, just a text asking me to call. I wanted to do it before the briefing, just in case there was something that we needed to follow up today.'

'Will you let me know what it is?' asked Charley as he headed towards the door.

'Of course.'

Less than ten minutes later Mike entered her office with a smile on his face.

'It's confirmed. Sinead Westbrook travelled out of the country a week ago, on Eurostar, with an adult passenger in her vehicle.'

'Do we have a return date?'

'We do.'

'Details of her vehicle?'

'Yes, she's driving a white VW T-Roc with a personalised numberplate SW 1717.'

Charley wrote down the details. When she looked up from her notepad, she had further instructions for her deputy. 'Get a marker put on the Police National Computer System affirming that the driver of the vehicle is wanted for interview in connection with Operation Danube.'

'On it,' Mike said over his shoulder as he headed for the door when Annie walked into the office.

Annie threw him a questioning look at his haste. Charley shared his update and considered the news with a thoughtful look on her face. 'We've a few days to arrange how we are going to approach her if she returns as her ticket states.'

The phone rang and already adrenaline-fuelled, Charley grabbed the receiver. On hearing that the call was from Forensics, she switched to speaker and informed Eira that DC Annie Glover was with her.

'There's DNA on the pushchair and the lens cap found at Clough's photographic studio. We've run it through the national database,' Eira told them.

Charley liked the flush of excitement on Annie's face and the SIO felt the thrill of things moving in the right direction. The team had a lot to work with already, but she could always do with more.

'And?' asked Annie.

Hearing the eagerness in Annie's voice, Eira wished she didn't have to douse it. 'The DNA doesn't belong to Grace Westbrook.'

The two detectives looked at each other. 'I wasn't expecting that,' Charley said.

'I know it doesn't sound like good news,' said Eira, 'but it's good news in that now we have the DNA, we can check any fingerprints that you send to us straight away.'

'What about firearms residue on the pram?' enquired Charley. There was hope in her voice.

Eira sighed. 'Nothing so far.'

—

It had been a few weeks since the murders at the wedding. The investigation was moving at pace and now they were in pursuit of known suspects. Mobile phone data input by the enquiry's analyst to create the Anacapa chart showed the team there had been little communication between the three wanted women. However, there had been some contact, and that was just before the wedding.

The GPS also showed that Grace Westbrook had sent a message from her mobile phone whilst in Slaithwaite on that fateful day. This, along with the cigarette butt that had been found on the roof of the building, put her in the area at the time of the shootings. It was a positive result.

Half an hour later, Charley carried a bundle of papers through the incident room, heading for the door to the corridor.

'Where you off?' asked Annie.

'It's half-past nine. Morning prayers,' said Charley, referencing the divisional meeting that the senior officers had every morning.

Annie grimaced. 'Have uniform asked us to return the staff they loaned us for the enquiry?'

'No, but it's coming,' Charley replied. 'You can bet your life on it.'

Mike looked up from his desk. He handed her a pack of printouts. 'Proof for you that the workload of all the officers on the enquiry remains high. We still have suspects to trace and to arrest. We can't afford to lose anyone just yet.'

Charley was grateful to him for giving her the ammunition to update the command team to reinforce the need for them to maintain manpower and justify expenditure, and she told him so.

It was mid-morning, and Charley was sitting with Mike discussing the logistics for the return of Sinead West-brook on the Eurostar, when a telephone call came into the incident room from a Police Road Traffic Unit on the M1 motorway. They had stopped the white Volkswagen, registered SW 1717, on the northbound carriageway in the Cheshire area.

'They've arrested one female occupant, believed to be Sinead Westbrook, on our behalf. Headquarters' control room have arranged with our motorway unit to liaise and bring Sinead Westbrook back to our cells and recover her vehicle. ETA approximately three hours, but they will update us on their arrival at the bridewell,' Ricky-Lee told them.

Mike raised his eyebrows at Charley and put a strike through the notes he had been making. 'That solves one problem. We don't have to plan for her return,' he said, turning to a clean page. 'Looks like the circulation of the three has paid off.'

'I want you and Annie to do the initial interview with her,' Charley said to Mike.

Mike stood. 'I'll go find her. We've got time to look at our approach together before she arrives.'

—

It was four o'clock in the Peel Street custody suite when the newly arrested, short, skinny woman appeared in front of the custody sergeant to be booked into the cells. One of the uniformed officers accompanying her placed her insurance certificate and other vehicle documentation on the counter.

Annie was down in the cell area watching the process, interested to see what Sinead looked like, and her attitude towards her arrest. The detective's senses were heightened. There was a mixture of smells emanating from the kitchenette where microwave meals were no doubt being heated up for the prisoners. It was in sharp contrast to the stench of excrement, vomit, and disinfectant which often greeted her here.

A prisoner down the far end of the corridor was loudly reciting words from the Bible, repeatedly. '"Do not judge, and you will not be judged. Do not condemn, and you will not be condemned. Forgive, and you will be forgiven."'

'Luke 6:37,' whispered Annie. There were some things that a child schooled by nuns would never forget and significant Bible quotes were certainly included.

Late afternoon to early evening was usually a quiet shift before the drunks were brought in singing, crying, shouting, and even trying to fight anyone they came into contact with.

The female prisoner was carrying a brown wig and sporting a short, spiky, bleached blonde haircut. Annie's gut instinct told her that something was not quite as it should be, and she was proved right because when she was asked her name by the custody sergeant, she replied, 'Patricia Henderson, but feel free to call me Patsy, cock. Everyone else does.'

Annie put her hand to her mouth at the confession. The custody sergeant looked puzzled. He leaned forward, his chin jutting out. 'I don't understand. You told the arresting officers that your name was Sinead Westbrook.'

The prisoner rolled her eyes and sighed. 'What it is, right. The car is in me mucker's name, cock. I swear down, I thought it was a routine stop and it would be quicker to say that I was her.'

The custody sergeant gave Henderson a look of which only police officers were capable.

'But you were arrested for conspiracy to murder! Didn't you think to tell them who you really were at that point?'

Henderson lifted her hand in the air, along with the wig. 'The Dibble had already cuffed me and they never gave me a chance to speak. I'm not involved in no murders. I swear down it's a case of mistaken identity.'

The custody sergeant was looking at the wig. 'Or is that what you want us to think? Let's get you booked in, and your fingerprints taken, then we might get confirmation of who you really are.'

Henderson pointed to the computer. 'Yer wot? You still don't believe that I'm who I say I am? Well, you'll soon see because I'm on the system, cock, more than once.'

—

Back in the incident room, Annie shared the latest revelation with Charley and Mike. 'The automatic fingerprint retrieval system confirmed her identity as Patsy Henderson,' she told them.

Charley put her hand to her forehead. 'She's the girlfriend of Mad Mick Dawson, so what in God's name is she doing driving Shane Dooley's fiancée's car?'

At that moment an alert came through from HQ Control that GMP road police were waiting for the marked police vehicles to do an armed stop on a vehicle registered to, and believed to be driven by, Mick Dawson.

Mike's eyes widened. 'I wonder what the crack is?'

Charley was reading from the computer screen. 'According to the inspector, they've had an anonymous tip-off regarding 5 MAC 1's location, and it's that they are transporting drugs. The information also names the passenger as Grace Westbrook. Maybe now we'll get some answers.'

'The interceptors are using armed response because Grace Westbrook is flagged on the system as a user of firearms and is wanted in connection with our operation,' said Mike.

Charley nodded. 'Exactly, and rightly so.' Picking up the phone to ask control for an open radio link to enable them to hear the live commentary from TPAC, the tactical pursuit and containment vehicles, she continued, 'We wouldn't want anyone taking any chances.'

Moments later the three detectives sat in silence, listening intently, and eagerly awaiting further updates with bated breath.

'The black Mercedes EQ is failing to stop at our requests,' an officer said. The excitement of the voices belonging to the commentators of the vehicles in the high-speed chase rose in intensity and pitch, precipitated by the sudden action on the part of the perpetrators. 'The female passenger has thrown a bag out of her window. Location recorded for later collection. The vehicle continues to travel at speed. The vehicle is now heading onto the M62 in the direction of West Yorkshire. The present speed is one hundred and five miles per hour...'

The vehicle would not out run the interceptors, Charley thought as, nails digging into the palms of her hands, she visualised the events taking place. Her thoughts turned to how the pursuit would end.

West Yorkshire were in liaison with GMP and NPAS, the national police air support helicopter, was airborne for the eye in the sky.

Next came the news that a rolling block of police vehicles was in place on the motorway to bring the dangerous driver to a controlled stop to prevent injury or harm to others, and notification was shared that other traffic units in the area were now holding back vehicles on the motorway and the slip roads.

The marked cars were in position to box the Mercedes, 5 MAC 1 in, and the call was made that everyone was waiting for.

'Strike!'

With no way forward, the driver slowed the vehicle down and was brought to an immediate standstill by the interceptors.

Charley felt her heart beating in her chest, and heard her pulse racing in her ears. Then came the roaring in her ears that was Annie, fist bumping the air. 'YES!' she cheered.

Armed officers quickly had the two occupants of 5 MAC 1 out of the vehicle and laid face down on the tarmac, both immediately handcuffed. With the ease of professionals who had done the act a thousand times before, the detainees were pulled back to their feet and subjected to a quick search before they were taken to separate awaiting police vehicles.

In the background, Mick Dawson could be heard shouting and swearing at the officers. His phone must have hit the floor, and he raged even more whilst stamping on the device, but there was no sound from the female passenger, although it was relayed for those listening in that she was crying when she identified herself as Grace Westbrook.

A search was started to see what the female passenger had thrown from the vehicle. With the dash-cam footage, and the police commentators dialogue recorded on the incident log it wouldn't be long before it was located and seized. The detectives heard arrangements being made for both prisoners and the vehicle to be transported off the motorway to the nearest DHQ, Peel Street Police Station.

'Will you speak to the custody sergeant, to make sure that neither of them gets anywhere near Henderson when they arrive,' Charley instructed Annie. 'And I want confirmation as soon as possible that the female is Grace Westbrook.'

—

Forty minutes later, down in the bridewell, Annie was witnessing both prisoners being booked in from the same position in the custody suite that she had earlier seen Henderson going through the same process. Confirmation quickly followed that this time the woman professing to be Grace Westbrook was definitely her.

Charley and Mike were discussing the operation in Charley's office and she asked him, 'Do you think that they had been travelling together, with Henderson in the VW, on the M1, and saw what had taken place when she was stopped and arrested?'

'We could check the motorway cameras,' he suggested. 'It seems too much of a coincidence that they were both on the M1, travelling in the same direction at the same time. Don't you think?'

The live feed was still open, and it was confirmed that the package thrown from Dawson's vehicle had been found. The haversack contained a large parcel of white powder believed to be cocaine.

Mike whistled through his teeth. 'That possibly has a street value of thousands of pounds.'

Annie joined them, shaking her head. 'Henderson continues to be disruptive. She's made an allegation of a sexual assault against the officer who brought her into custody.'

'Denied by the officer I presume?' asked Mike.

Annie nodded. 'Of course. It's just delaying tactics. She's asked for her solicitor and they're waiting for them to make contact. I've seen Mick Dawson's phone. It's smashed to smithereens.'

Mike cocked an eyebrow. 'Very naïve of him to think that we won't be able to retrieve the information from the SIM card. Maybe it'll contain some numbers of interest?'

Charley was pragmatic and focused. 'Looking ahead to Henderson's interview: I want her to be told that Dawson and Grace Westbrook have been arrested and are in custody.'

'It might change her mind about talking to us,' said Annie.

'My thoughts exactly, and that's what I'm hoping,' said Charley.

Mike looked thoughtful. 'Do you think Dawson and Henderson had been to meet Grace Westbrook off the Eurostar?'

Annie looked confused. 'Wait up. If Grace Westbrook was Sinead Westbrook's passenger, then where's Sinead? Still in France?'

Mike shrugged his shoulders. 'Who knows?'

'I think that Grace Westbrook was Sinead's passenger and they brought the drugs back into the country in Sinead's car, and Dawson thought that both Grace and the drugs were probably safer in his car than Sinead's, because as we know, his car has been the subject of many stops in the past. Coppers in the Manchester area have stopped pulling it over for fear of further complaints by Dawson,' said Charley.

'But, if Henderson drove Sinead's car, possibly pretending to be Sinead, then where is Sinead now?'

'Knowing she was circulated maybe she went into hiding on her return to this country? What he might not have known however, is that Grace Westbrook's details had been circulated as also wanted in connection with the murders, otherwise surely he wouldn't have gone anywhere near Grace,' replied Annie.

Mike shrugged his shoulders. 'Once a drug dealer, always a drug dealer. They can't help themselves. Maybe he thought that Grace Westbrook couldn't possibly be connected to the murder, being so far removed from the action,' said Mike.

Charley was smiling. 'A lesson learnt: never underestimate the investigators. He ought to know by now that we never give up...'

Grace Westbrook was incarcerated in a cell, under arrest for murder and possession of Class A drugs with intent to supply.

Mick Dawson was under arrest on suspicion of assisting an offender, along with drugs possession, and with intent to supply.

'There are going to be some interesting interviews soon. I wonder who the informant against Dawson is?' Charley said to the others.

Ian Chamberlain from the fingerprint department telephoned through to the incident room with Ricky-Lee, who had just returned from other enquiries with Wilkie Connor, who picked up the call.

He stuck his head around the SIO's door. 'Apparently, the prints of Jerry Campbell, Bob Sullivan's shop assistant, have been identified on the notes that were in Benny Patterson's possession.'

'What about Grace Westbrook's fingerprints?' Charley asked.

Ricky-Lee shook his head. 'No, there was no mention of hers.'

Chapter Twenty-Seven

The prisoners were bedded down for the evening. Telephone calls had been denied to all three, owing to the enquiries that were ongoing and other enquiries which were pending. Despite the hour, the detectives were in good humour, and they continued in their quest to research those detained. There was still much to be done before they could clock off because they needed to begin interviewing first thing the following morning.

Members of the team who were required to remain on duty were sitting at desks in the incident room eating fish and chips out of the paper with their little wooden forks. Wilkie finished his first and started to lick the salt and vinegar from his greasy fingers.

'Looks like Jerry Campbell might not be innocent after all,' he said to Charley.

The SIO sighed, her stomach now satisfactorily refuelled. 'Let's deal with those we have in the traps first, then we'll get Campbell locked up and see what he has to say for himself. First, we need to decide on the three interview teams. The prisoners' phones need to be sent for examination, and the drugs to Forensics for analysis. Have we heard how the vehicle searches are going?' she asked no one in particular.

Just then her mobile phone pinged. She held it between her finger and thumb, glanced at the screen, and read the text.

'It's from the search team. They've found a cannabis spliff in the glove compartment of the VW T-Roc, and an ashtray with a number of tab ends, all seized.' Charley paused. Her eyes widened as she continued to read. 'They've also found a rifle with ammo secreted in the boot. Could it be the one used to shoot and kill Bob Sullivan?'

Everyone stopped eating and drinking for the moment, forks and mugs suspended in mid-air. Charley sensed the tension in the room as they continued to look at her whilst she texted Neal, instructing the CSI to swab the weapon and ammunition for DNA and lift fingerprints.

Mike broke the silence. 'What of 5 MAC 1?'

Charley looked up. 'Apparently, it's clean.'

Charley turned away from Mike and spoke to Annie who was sitting next to her.

'I want you to go down to the bridewell and have Henderson brought out of her cell, to the charge desk, and inform her in front of the custody sergeant so he can endorse her detention sheet, that she is now also under arrest for possession of a firearm and ammunition. She might want to speak to her solicitor again. If so, let the custody sergeant arrange that.'

Annie pushed back her chair, screwed up her greasy paper, and threw it in the waste bin. Having finished off her can of fizzy drink, she headed for the restroom to wash her hands whilst Charley continued giving orders.

'Before we leave tonight, the respective addresses that they have given need to be thoroughly searched, so we will get a POLSA search team to assist.' She turned to Ricky-Lee for his input.

'Patsy Henderson and Mick Dawson have given the same address in Oldham, and as I understand it, they have house keys in their personal possession when they were arrested, so Oldham CID, who are assisting us in this matter, will not have to put the door through. What you might find interesting is that Grace Westbrook gave an address in Marsden. Again, house keys were among her belongings when she was arrested so access should be straightforward.'

Annie returned to the incident room before the others had left to put their individual instructions into action. All eyes were upon her.

'Well?' Charley asked, though it was on everyone's minds.

'She never blinked an eyelid, boss. Just a simple acceptance of her predicaments it appeared, almost like she was expecting it.'

—

As much work that could be done, had been done that day and Charley suggested a change of scenery and calling into The Railway Inn before last orders, where work continued. For the next hour or so, the five detectives discussed how best to approach the interviews. There was no doubt in Charley's mind that the arrests had raised the team's morale.

'I think we'll start with Patsy and Mick Dawson. If he knows she's locked up, as is suggested, could it be that they were driving in convoy and that he drove past her when she was stopped by the police?'

'Who knows. Let's hope that at least one of them talks to us. I'm sure we'll have given Henderson something to think about whilst she's languishing in her cell tonight,' said Mike.

Annie shook her head. 'I don't know about you, but I can't for the life of me figure out who's done what. Can anyone?'

Charley laughed. 'If it was straightforward, Annie, you'd be bored. I admit, I expected the DNA on the silencer lens cap and the pushchair to have Grace Westbrook's fingerprints and DNA all over them, and they haven't, so whose DNA and fingerprints are they?'

'The discovery of the rifle in Sinead's car. That surprised me, and it's a definite bonus,' said Wilkie.

Annie put her hands together in prayer and looked up to the ceiling. 'Someone up there must like us.'

Wilkie eyed her suspiciously. 'I thought you'd done with all that God stuff?'

'Habit,' she said, raising her pint glass in his direction.

'Once the rifle has been swabbed for DNA, then Ballistics will be able to tell us if it is the one that was used in our incident. On another matter, has anyone heard more about how Patterson is doing today?'

Charley's mobile ringing interrupted the conversation. The SIO listened and thanked the caller. 'It was the control room. The search team at Dawson's address have found an old photograph that links him to the Dooleys.'

Mike drained his pint. 'Not much of a surprise there, then.' He stood to leave. 'I'd like to know where Sinead Westbrook and Chelsea Clough are.'

'I had this notion at one time that Grace Westbrook and Chelsea Clough were in a relationship, but you know what thought did. I'm counting on their phone data to help us with a location,' Charley said and finished her drink. When she also stood to leave, she lightened the mood. 'I bid you goodnight and in the words of our Yorkshire champion, Sir Captain Tom, "Tomorrow will be a good day."'

As soon as her head hit the pillow, Charley was asleep, only to open her eyes at daybreak to escape the dream that had rudely interrupted her slumber. The big fat ugly bastard that she knew as Mick Dawson stepped towards her menacingly. When she didn't back away, he shouted at her. His eyes burnt like blue gas flames. His huge bulbous fists threatened to smack her in the face. She shouted a warning to him, but softly.

For a moment, she savoured the irony of it. The big man was locked in a cell, and she knew that even her colleagues wouldn't want to be on the end of her right hook. She had been taught everything she knew by her father Jack, whose boxing career was curtailed when he was called upon to run the family farm when her grandfather died. He had wanted a boy, not a girl – hence her name. He taught her so well that she was more of a fighter than Dawson would ever be.

Chapter Twenty-Eight

For a moment longer, Charley stared at the bedroom wall. The familiarity of this space, filled with bright yellow warmth, gave her a feeling of peace and security that she couldn't imagine feeling anywhere else in the world. Routine soothed her. It gave her a buffer between what she could and could not control. Showered, dressed, and hair tied up in a bun at the nape of her neck – before she knew it, she was sitting at her desk looking at the clock above her office door. It was six-forty-five. Charley had forgotten how the smell of fish and chips lingered.

Winnie had brewed up, bread was in the toaster, and the older woman was asking the other early birds why they were at work at that time of day. She suggested they couldn't have all wet the bed so there must be a job on. The older lady had the innate ability to brighten Charley's day. Sitting with the others in the incident room, Charley hugged her cup of coffee close to her chest, and they instantly reverted to the discussion of the previous evening.

By a quarter to nine, DS Mike Blake and DC Annie Glover were prepared for the interview with Patsy Henderson in the presence of her solicitor Philip Nutbrown.

'Wish us luck,' said Annie.

'You won't need it,' Charley replied.

Sitting around the sparsely furnished interview room, in which the table was bolted to the floor, DC Annie Glover pressed the green button at the top of the recording device. The necessary introductions were swiftly made by Mike Blake, who reminded Patsy Henderson that she was still under caution.

Charley watched the interview from the livestream in her office. Patsy looked pale and decidedly fragile, and in that moment, the SIO wondered what must be going on in the woman's head.

Annie opened the questioning. 'Yesterday, you were stopped whilst driving a white VW, registration number SW 1717 on the northbound carriageway of the M1. Our understanding is that this vehicle doesn't belong to you, is that correct?'

Henderson nodded.

Annie spoke. 'For the purpose of the recording equipment, could you please say yes or no?'

Henderson's reply in the affirmative was barely audible and her solicitor indicated yes.

'Who does the car belong to?' asked Mike.

'It belongs to our kid.'

'Whose our kid, a relative?'

'No, Sinead Westbrook is my bessie.'

'Just to clarify, a bessie is a good friend?'

'Yes,' she replied looking a little confused.

'Why were you driving her car?'

Henderson suddenly appeared to have found her voice. 'I didn't nick it, if that's what you think. Look, Sinead and Grace had a falling-out about something, I don't know what. Grace flew to France, and Sinead drove over after her. Mick had a bit of business down Kent, so when Sinead told him what time they were arriving back on the

Eurostar, we arranged to meet up. He's still very protective of Shane's fiancée. We went for a drink, and before long Sinead, as always, was off her face – alcohol and drugs, although she swore she'd only taken travel sickness pills, are not good together, are they? When she gets off her face, she can be, let's say, difficult. She hooked up with a group in the pub, who said they knew her and would look after her, I don't know how, but they looked off their faces too. The next thing we knew she was heading off with them. Mick asked me if I'd drive her car back north as Grace was in no fit state. He said Grace would be better in his car. I wasn't going to argue.'

Charley allowed herself a faint smile. The prisoner was talking.

'Is your partner Mick Dawson?'

'Yes, you know he is.' Henderson scowled.

Mike looked thoughtful. 'Why would you be wearing a brown wig, Patsy? Was it to make you look like someone else, Sinead maybe?'

Henderson looked down at her hands, and shuffling in her seat mumbled a barely audible, 'No. I was wearing a wig that day. Is that against the law?'

The detective sergeant continued. 'Can you tell us where you collected Sinead's car from and where you were going?'

'In the pub car park where Sinead had parked it, and I was driving it home. I already told you. Don't you listen?'

When it became obvious that she was not going to respond to further questioning by Mike, Annie took over the reins. 'How do we know you had Sinead's permission to drive the car?'

Henderson looked up and frowned at her.

Good, she's regained her attention, thought Charley. Henderson, however, failed to reply.

Whilst Annie still had eye contact with the prisoner, she quickly moved on. 'Do you have a contact number for Sinead, so that we can confirm what you've told us?'

Just as quickly, Henderson replied, 'No comment.'

'Why did you tell the officers who stopped you on the M1 that you were Sinead?'

'I told 'em. I thought it was easier to say I was her, not me, as it was her car.'

It was time for the detectives to up the ante. Mike took over the questioning.

'You were further arrested last night because a firearm and ammunition were discovered in the vehicle you were driving. Can you explain that?'

Henderson appeared to have been struck dumb, but there was no suggestion in her body language to indicate to either detective that the question had come as a surprise.

Mike leaned forward over the table, his voice softer. 'Patsy, you need to think about the situation that you find yourself in. When you were arrested, officers thought you were Sinead Westbrook, and you confirmed that to them. You do know that conspiracy to murder is a very serious offence, which could result in a life sentence, don't you?'

Charley's eyes narrowed. *Was that a flash of panic crossing Henderson's face?*

The detective sergeant sat back, rolling his pen through his fingers and looked directly at Henderson. 'The rifle and ammunition that were discovered inside the vehicle are being forensically examined. Very shortly, we will have the results. It could be that the rifle was used in the murders of Bob Sullivan and Ralph Bateman.'

There was no doubt in Charley's mind that what Mike was telling her was sinking in because she looked like a rabbit caught in headlights.

'Is your partner Mick Dawson?' asked Annie.

Henderson nodded. 'Yes, he is,' she said. She looked puzzled.

Mike leaned forward again, as if sharing a secret with a friend. 'You won't know this, but yesterday, not long after you were arrested, your partner's vehicle was also stopped on the M1 northbound. He was arrested, along with a woman passenger. Why? He had failed to stop for the police, and they saw a bag containing a large amount of cocaine being thrown from the vehicle, which has since been recovered. What do you know about that?'

Mike looked at Henderson. Henderson shrugged, but he could tell that she was shocked.

Her solicitor, his eyes upon her, sensed this by the change in her demeanour and so requested a break to speak with his client. The interview was terminated to allow for the consultation and arrangements were made for the interview to resume in thirty minutes.

In another interview room, DC Wilkie Connor and DC Ricky-Lee were interviewing Mick Dawson. Dishevelled, unshaven, and sitting in a crumpled, nondescript outfit given to him when his clothing was seized, he looked anything but the smart, slick, hard-boiled leader of a drug cartel.

Dawson tried to weigh up the interviewing detectives.

Wilkie Connor's eyes told him that he wasn't a soft touch.

'Why didn't you stop for the police?'

'Because every time I get behind the fucking wheel, I get stopped, and I'm sick and tired of it. This time I thought bollocks!'

'You were travelling in excess of one hundred miles an hour. That's dangerous, don't you think?'

Dawson's eyes were as black as granite and just as hard, but the detectives saw something else in them too, fear. Dawson put his hands up in the air as if in surrender. 'Okay! I admit it, I shouldn't have, but I was so fucking annoyed.'

'Why do you think that the firearms officers stopped you?'

Dawson shrugged. 'Fuck knows. I can only assume that they've bugger all else to do.'

'What did your passenger throw out of the car?' asked Ricky-Lee.

Dawson eyed the younger detective with contempt. 'How the fuck should I know?'

Ricky-Lee cocked his head to one side. 'You know exactly what it was. It was a large amount of cocaine, and that's why you didn't stop for the police, isn't it?'

Dawson glanced at his solicitor. He was in a tough spot and he knew it. 'I've no idea what you're talking about.'

'So your DNA won't be on the bag or the cocaine?' Ricky-Lee pushed him.

With no intervention from his solicitor, Dawson felt that his only defence was to clam up, so he did.

Ricky-Lee stared Dawson straight in the eyes. 'How well do you know your passenger, Grace Westbrook?'

Dawson stared back. He began to sweat. By nature, he was stubborn and his usual rule of thumb was never to give an inch.

Wilkie sensed this and changed the line of questioning.

'Yesterday, we know you were travelling in convoy with your partner Patsy Henderson, who was driving another vehicle northbound on the M1. You drove past her when she was pulled over by the police, and a firearm and ammunition was found in the vehicle she was driving.'

Dawson flinched as if a sharp injection of acid had hit him in the stomach, and he tried once again to distance himself from the act. 'You don't know what you're talking about,' he said with bravado in his tone. 'I want to speak to my solicitor alone,' he demanded. DC Connor indicated for the termination of the interview to allow him to do so.

At the same time, DC Helen Weir and DC Lisa Bayliss were in an interview room with a notably anxious-looking Grace Westbrook, who, after introductions and caution, asked if her solicitor could be changed, much to their surprise.

The detectives had no objection, and when asked why, Westbrook told them that she knew that he worked for the same firm representing Mick Dawson. 'I prefer to be represented by someone with my interest at heart,' she told them.

Half an hour later, the three were back in the same room, in the same seats, but this time with a duty solicitor. After the necessary caution had been made, the detectives began the interview.

Grace Westbrook looked calmer, although still nervous. Her face was red and her swollen eyes sore from crying. She had started the interview by wiping the beads of sweat from her upper lip, but was clearly eager to talk.

'I want to say from the outset that I have not killed anyone, and never would, and as for yesterday, I had no choice but to do what I did because I was being threatened with violence.' She hesitated and took a deep breath. 'It's not the first time I have suffered violence at the hands of Mick Dawson.' Westbrook started shaking, her eyes filled with tears, and she wiped away those that escaped and rolled down her cheeks with her fingertips.

Her solicitor offered her a tissue.

Helen smiled at her, hoping to ease her tension, although she thought it probably wouldn't help. 'Can I get you some water?' she asked and made sure she was okay to carry on.

Grace Westbrook, head down, swallowed loudly. However, through her sobs, she assured the detective that she just needed an occasional moment, but was adamant she wanted to go on.

Plucking at the damp tissue, it seemed Grace was oblivious to the bits and pieces falling onto her knee. 'A night in a cell, with my shoes sitting outside the door and my belongings taken away, was not only terrifying but humiliating. I had time to think very hard about my life from now on.' Indicating the door with a pointed finger, she said, 'That other solicitor – he told me that I mustn't say anything until he had spoken to his colleague, who is representing Mick, and I knew that it wouldn't be the best thing for me.' Westbrook paused. The detectives waited patiently. 'The last three years of my life have been sheer hell,' she said. 'My sister turned against me. I had no idea that she had got herself so deep into the drugs scene. Although, I'm ashamed to admit that there were signs that I ignored, because I didn't want to believe she'd succumbed.'

Helen interjected. 'I'm sorry for interrupting. However, it would be best for everyone if you start from the beginning, and tell us your story slowly, and in your own time. We are in no rush,' she assured Grace. 'We've got all day.'

Grace nodded and took a deep breath before she went on. 'It all started about three years ago. My younger sister Sinead fell head over heels for a man who, to my horror, turned out to be a drug dealer. No matter what I said, it didn't matter to her, he was her world.' Grace paused. 'Gradually, I saw a change in her personality and behaviour. She'd often be agitated, irritable and irrational.' When she continued her voice raised octave after octave with each word. 'She became paranoid, accusing me, her only sister, of all manner of things. I guess it was naïve of me to think that it wouldn't happen, eventually. I tried my best to show her the error of her ways. Her fiancée, he retaliated by asking her to marry him. I tried to speak to him – no, to be totally honest with you, I begged him to leave her alone. He didn't care about her. He was just a control freak, like his father. One night, he beat me up and then raped me. I told her what he had done to me, but she called me a liar, and said that he had told her that I had come on to him, which was absolute rubbish. This sounds awful, but when I was told he had been killed, I was actually pleased. At least they hadn't got to the altar. However, as you can imagine, my sister was devastated. The person that killed him was caught and sent to prison, and I really thought that would be the end of it. But my sister's future father-in-law and some of her fiancé's friends had other ideas. They wanted revenge. I know that it is only a matter of time before they kill me because I know too much.'

Her solicitor asked if they could take a break for her client to compose herself.

'Can I just ask, Grace. These men you talk about, are their names Shane and Malcolm Dooley?'

Chapter Twenty-Nine

When the fifteen-minute break was over, and DC Helen Weir and DC Lisa Bayliss had taken further instruction from Charley Mann, Grace Westbrook would feel that, for the best part of the next forty-five minutes, she had made two new best friends in the detectives.

Knowing that the SIO was watching the interview, the detectives made themselves comfortable and Helen reminded Grace Westbrook, in the presence of her solicitor, that she was still under caution. The interview room was not only sparse of furniture, but everything from the walls to the chairs and the carpet tiles was in various shades of grey; the reason for the bland decor was to avoid giving the person being interviewed something to distract them. That way, they'd stay focused on the reason they were there.

This time round, Grace looked more at ease.

'Just for clarification, are you sure that you feel up to continuing?' Helen asked her.

Westbrook smiled. 'Yes, thank you,' she replied.

'Do you want to carry on from where you left off? You were telling us about your sister, Sinead?'

Grace Westbrook appeared more than happy to do so.

'After what had happened, my sister and I hardly spoke. I tried to support her from a distance, but she enjoyed being under Malcolm Dooley's wing. Sinead became unreachable, and money appeared to be no object for her. He treated her like a princess. When I did speak to her, all she wanted to talk about was getting revenge for Shane's killer.'

Helen's questions continued. She asked about the kind of help Grace attempted to get for her sister, but talking about it appeared to upset her, so the detective moved on.

'Shane was killed in the pub alongside another lad, Reece Brown, wasn't he?' probed Helen.

Grace bowed her head for an instant, but there were none of the usual physical signs of sorrow.

'He was, and after Tyrone Wells was sentenced and Sinead gave her evidence in court, I hoped that would be the end of it. I hoped my sister would eventually see Malcolm Dooley as the manipulating bastard that he was and come back home. Then life would go back to how it was between me and her before Shane Dooley came into our lives.'

Lisa shuffled to the front of her seat and referred to the notes in her spiral-bound book on the table. Helen sat back in her chair.

'Let's talk about the murder of Bob Sullivan at the wedding of his daughter. What do you know about that, Grace?' Lisa asked.

Charley noticed that Grace Westbrook didn't make eye contact with the detective, a sign that she was uncomfortable with the question. She wondered why, while Westbrook fidgeted in her chair. She sniffed and rubbed her nose before answering.

'I didn't have anything to do with it,' she replied eventually.

Lisa paused. Her forehead wrinkled when she looked up from her notes and she tapped them with her pen.

'You are firearms trained, aren't you? In fact, I see that you won an award for rifle target shooting in the Territorial Army.'

Charley could almost feel the tension in the interview room. This interview was about to become increasingly more confrontational.

'You see, we know for a fact that there were two shooters that day – one was a man by the name of Benny Patterson who used a handgun and was detained at the scene and another who used a rifle that was fired into the church grounds from a distance. We have identified the location as being the roof of a disused building,' Lisa told her.

Again, Westbrook sniffed and rubbed her nose.

'Have you ever been on a rooftop of a building in the vicinity of the church?'

Westbrook looked puzzled. 'No, why would I?'

'Then how do you account for your DNA being on a cigarette butt found at that location?'

Westbrook shook her head. 'That can't be right.'

'You see, we also recovered a rifle and ammunition secreted in your sister's car. Tell me, are they yours?'

'Absolutely not!' she snapped back.

'Well, we are aware that your sister doesn't have the experience with weapons that you have.'

Westbrook was indignant. 'I've told you, it's not mine.'

Lisa lifted her eyebrows. 'Okay, so you say that's not your weapon. Let's go back to the roof of the building where the cigarette butt with your DNA on it was found. Did you fire a weapon from the roof of that building on the day of the wedding?'

The question appeared to take Westbrook's breath.

'Do you admit that you were in the area on the day of the wedding?'

Charley could almost see Grace Westbrook's mind ticking over.

'Well?' Lisa pushed after a moment or two. She waited for a response now that she had dropped the evidence on her toes.

Charley bit her lip. If only her rank didn't prohibit her from interviewing a prisoner in case it was considered oppressive. She'd give anything to be in that interview room right now.

Then the silence came. The moment when a good interviewer feels the time is right to give a suspect that extra moment to reflect, and hopefully respond, and Charley found herself holding her breath. Could Grace Westbrook hold out?

Charley felt a thrill when she heard Grace Westbrook speak. For the first time in the interview, she looked Lisa in the eye.

'Yes. Okay. I was there. I went to see Chelsea.'

'Can you tell me why?' asked Lisa.

'Reece Brown, who was killed at the same time as Shane Dooley by Tyrone Wells, was Chelsea Clough's stepbrother. I heard that Sinead was putting pressure on Chelsea to be involved in a revenge attack. Chelsea isn't into drugs, so the Dooleys had no leverage with her.'

'And you had?'

'No, I wanted to warn Chelsea not to get involved.'

'How was Sinead able to put pressure on her?'

Ignoring Lisa's question, Westbrook carried on. 'I spoke to Chelsea. I thought she had listened to me, and we didn't talk about it again.'

'You are in contact with Chelsea then?'

Westbrook nodded. 'Yes. Then just before the shooting, Chelsea went silent on me, and I got the impression something was mitherin' her, so I went to see her that day.'

Lisa encouraged her to continue. 'And?'

Westbrook looked confused. 'By the way, I don't smoke either.'

It was Lisa's turn to looked confused. 'Have you ever smoked? Because there is no doubt that your DNA is on the cigarette butt found on the rooftop where the person used the rifle to kill Bob Sullivan.'

Westbrook opened her mouth as if to reply, then stopped herself. Perhaps she thought better of it. She looked up to the ceiling. Was she considering her reply? Charley wondered.

Her shoulders were slumped when she looked back at Lisa. 'There's no point in lying to you, is there? I have to admit to having an occasional drag on my sister's ciggie once in a while.'

Lisa frowned. 'Are you trying to imply that Sinead set you up by planting the cigarette butt?'

She shrugged. 'Well, let's face it, there's no love lost between us these days, is there? Although I think it's a bit much, even for her, to try to frame me for a murder I didn't commit, don't you?'

'So, let's just clarify what you are saying. You now admit to being in the area on the day of the wedding, but say the rifle and ammunition found in your sister's car aren't yours? You also admit that you occasionally have a drag of your sister's cigs, but you can't explain your DNA being on a cigarette butt where the person used a rifle to kill Bob Sullivan on that day?'

It was time for Helen to take over the questioning.

Westbrook's eyebrows furrowed. 'Err… yeah, I suppose I am.'

'My problem is that your account doesn't match the evidence, Grace, and now you're expecting us to believe that you went to see Chelsea, who had a wedding to photograph, and at a place where the murders incidentally happened on the same day. All this because you say that your sister Sinead was pressuring Chelsea to take part in a revenge attack on her dead fiancé's murderer?'

Grace Westbrook blinked at Helen. 'I'm not saying Chelsea is the murderer. I know Chelsea and, believe me, she wouldn't hurt a fly.'

'What did you say to her when you saw her that Saturday?'

'I invited her to come abroad with me the next day.'

'What did she say?'

'She told me that she couldn't.'

Lisa stared at her. 'Are you in a relationship with Chelsea Clough?'

'We are, but it's complicated. Sinead is desperate to ruin that for me too.'

'Where is Chelsea now?'

Grace looked down. 'It looks like she's with Sinead somewhere,' she said.

'I don't understand. Why would Chelsea be with Sinead if she's in a relationship with you?'

Westbrook stumbled over her words. 'Well, because, I mean…' All of a sudden Grace threw her hands in the air and her voice got louder. 'Okay! But, I'm frightened that if I tell you it could put Chelsea in more danger. Sinead told me that Chelsea was with her, and she'd be fine as long as I did the drug run with Mick Dawson. I swear that's the only reason I agreed to do it.'

Lisa interrupted. 'Sinead told you that, did she, and that's why you were involved in the transport of a massive amount of cocaine?'

Grace Westbrook's voice sank. 'I know it sounds bizarre. I know you won't believe me, but yes. She says she's got Chelsea, and Chelsea is not answering my calls, and I'm worried what she might do to her.'

'Mmm... You're that worried that you haven't thought to mention this before? I think it's about time you were straight with us,' said Helen. 'Especially if you think that your girlfriend is in some sort of danger.'

Grace Westbrook took another deep breath. 'Sinead phoned me. She said that Chelsea was with her, and I had to do as she said if I wanted to see her alive again. I was told to meet Mick Dawson, and he took me to a place in London. He parked up, and he indicated a black Range Rover with tinted windows. The male passenger handed me a bag. We left the car park and headed to the motorway. You know the rest.'

'You knew that the bag contained the drugs didn't you?'

Westbrook shook her head. 'No, well, I couldn't be certain, I didn't check what was inside. But, like I said I didn't have a choice, I did what I was told.'

'Why did you throw it out of the window on the M1 when the police officers were signalling Mick Dawson to stop and it was obvious that he had no intention of doing that?'

'He threatened me. He said if I didn't do it, he'd kill me. I tried to hang onto the bag for as long as I could, hoping that the police would catch up.'

Helen looked taken aback but pushed on. 'You expect us to believe that you were in fear for your life?'

Another sniff. Another rub of the nose and another deep breath. These seemed to be a regular reaction when she appeared to be lying or was uncomfortable with the questions.

'It's the absolute truth,' she declared.

'Where are Chelsea and Sinead now? Do you know?' Helen asked.

'No. I told you. Dawson told me that when the bag was delivered, then Chelsea would be freed.'

'Do you have telephone numbers for Chelsea or Sinead?'

Grace Westbrook shook her head. 'No, he took my mobile off of me, and I can't remember their numbers offhand.'

Charley was eager for them to move on, and as if Helen was telepathic, she asked Grace, 'Do you know Benny Patterson?'

Another sniff and another touch of the nose. 'Never heard of him.'

Helen's eyes narrowed. 'Do you know what I think? I think your earlier tears were crocodile tears, and that you have been talking an absolute load of bollocks, to put it mildly. You're as much involved as the rest of them, aren't you?'

In her eyes, Charley could see that Westbrook was debating her next move, but there was nowhere for her to go with her lies.

'Throughout the interview, you have lied. You know full well that on that particular day you were in the area. You were there to do one thing and that was to shoot Bob Sullivan dead. However, unbeknown to you, you left evidence behind, and so now you have to tell lie after lie in an attempt to cover your tracks. We believe that Sinead was with you on the day of the murders. She went to Chelsea Clough's home, and also she drove out to France to see you, and bring you home. The truth is that you and your sister are as close as ever, aren't you?'

Grace Westbrook's head bowed and she chose not to respond.

DC Weir glanced at DC Bayliss and indicated the termination of the interview.

Fifteen minutes later, all three interview teams were sitting around a table in the incident room, hot drinks in hand, ready to discuss the outcome of the interviews and the strategy going forward.

Charley joined them. 'I'm glad to see all that positive body language,' she said with a smile. 'I'm looking forward to hearing you share your thoughts about what they had to say.'

Annie was eager to start the ball rolling. 'I think Patsy Henderson is completely out of her depth. She's either nervous, frightened or both. Once she's spoken to her solicitor, we'll be speaking to her again,' she said.

Lisa was not surprised that Grace Westbrook had ditched the solicitor that Dawson had requested for her. 'It's always seemed kind of unethical to me to have two suspects for the same crime being represented by solicitors from the same practice. Just doesn't seem right.'

'Sounds to me, listening in, as if she's not as green as she's cabbage-looking, as Winnie would say,' chuckled Charley. 'Could it be that Grace and Sinead brought the drugs into the country in Sinead's car?'

'Then how did Grace end up in Dawson's car, and why did Henderson end up in Sinead's car?' asked Mike.

'Maybe it was because Sinead had been circulated as wanted and Dawson was trying to protect her?' replied Charley.

All of a sudden Annie's eyes were bright as a thought came to her. 'And, that's why Henderson wore the wig to look like Sinead to hopefully distract us?'

'The likelihood of her car being stopped being greater than Mick Dawson's because of the tag tying up the motorway cops?' said Ricky-Lee.

'I don't know... But, I'm satisfied that Grace Westbrook is the killer, and she's just making stuff up to make herself look like she's a victim. It's okay us pontificating but we have to prove it to be the case. That's the hard bit.'

'Dawson is reconsidering his position after we dropped the lot on him. I think we're looking at a no-reply interview next,' said Wilkie.

'Nobody suggested where Sinead or Chelsea might be?' Charley asked.

'Grace Westbrook suggested that Sinead has Clough with her until the drugs arrive at their destination in Manchester, which implies that she is possibly in Manchester, or at least in the north of England. That's if they are together at all. We have no proof either way.'

'Yeah, I heard her say that,' said Charley. 'It appears to me, from dipping in and out of the interviews, that everyone is covering their own back. I'd like to know if the seized weapon and ammunition are a match to the murder weapon and its ammo. We need an update on the samples lifted from the property Chelsea Clough rented. Every step is a step closer, but it's frustrating not knowing who did what. Or even if we have a sound case for joint enterprise.'

Mike was thoughtful. 'Surely, it is too much of a coincidence that Chelsea Clough opened the photographic studio in the same village as Bob Sullivan, and then she got the gig for his daughter's wedding by proxy. We know that she's linked to the people that are involved in his murder. We'll only know whether she was in on it when we find her, but it seems highly likely.'

Charley took a moment. 'I'm going to have a word with the Divisional Commander, Bobbie Stokes, about getting a further twelve-hour extension that I think we are going to need for all three. I'm also going to arrange for Jerry Campbell to be pulled in to see if he can explain to us why his fingerprints were on some of the notes paid to Benny Patterson, along with whatever else he might be able to enlighten us about.'

Charley stood to leave. 'Let's keep on at them. We are definitely in the driving seat, and I'll update you all as soon as I have any further updates or anything else of significance to tell you.'

Chapter Thirty

Charley tapped on the office door of the Divisional Commander's secretary. There was no need to announce her arrival as Ruth's guide dog Flora heard her coming. Flora's tail wagged furiously against the metal filing cabinet, alerting the secretary to the fact that it was her friend.

Ruth swivelled round in her chair and smiled. 'I'd recognise that knock any day of the week, Charley Mann. It's exactly the same one you used when you called for me to come out and play when we were little.'

Charley smiled broadly and looked towards Bobbie Stokes' door. 'Is he in?'

Ruth nodded. 'I'm just about to make his elevenses,' she said. 'Fancy a coffee?'

'Yes please, and make it a posh one, as I'm in the command suite,' she chuckled.

The Commander's office was on the top floor on a quiet corridor with a countryside outlook, and was south-facing. Bobbie Stokes was sitting behind his desk, his hands hovering hesitantly over his computer keyboard when she entered.

'Sit down, I won't keep you a minute,' he said. He appeared to be a little distracted.

The office that Stokes had inherited from Divisional Commander Roper was cosy and carpeted, with wood-panelled walls and ornate furnishings, the paintings more suited to a gallery than an office in Peel Street Police Station. Charley sat down on a leather chair that smelled of a saddle. The minutes passed, and she found herself gazing longingly out of the window at the great outdoors, at the rolling hills of the Pennines that made her ever hungrier to take herself off riding. It had been too long.

Ruth broke Charley's reverie when she entered the room, and Stokes rose from his chair to take the tray of drinks from his secretary.

Sitting quietly drinking his coffee, the Divisional Commander listened intently to the SIO's update, including details of the recent arrests and the time remaining on each prisoner's detention clock, the position of the enquiry and the reason Charley was there: to request the twelve-hour extended detention period on top of the twenty-four automatically given under the Police and Criminal Evidence Act. This wasn't a certainty. Stokes would need to be assured that she and her team were acting expeditiously because he would be recording those details on the detention sheet of each prisoner if he chose to support the application.

'Do you think we'll need the full twelve hours?' he asked, his lips still touching the cup.

Charley shrugged. 'Only time will tell, but it's looking that way. We aren't in a position to charge anyone at the moment.'

Stokes made to stand. 'Shall we go down to the cells and see if they want their legal representation present when I inform them of my reasons for granting the extended time in custody without charge?'

Charley stood up, lifting her cup to her mouth as she did so to drain her latte. 'Waste not want not,' she said with a grin.

On the way back from the cells, the officers discussed the prisoners' reactions to Divisional Commander Stokes' explanation and reasoning for the extended detention, and the fact that none of their legal representatives had objected.

'With people still outstanding, and considering the serious nature of the crimes, it's hardly surprising that we didn't get any hassle,' said Charley.

'I think it was pretty obvious that it was a complete waste of their time, and ours to go through the process of recording their objections verbatim with the custody sergeant,' said Stokes. The extra time meant breathing room for Charley. Twelve hours more in which to facilitate not only more interviews, but also more enquiries. Within the new parameters, more decisions would be made in relation to the relevant charges, and Charley was eager to liaise with Caroline at the Crown Prosecution Service to discuss them.

When she parted company with the Divisional Commander in the stairwell at the second floor, the walk down the corridor to the office took only two minutes, but in that short space of time, she had made the decision to swap the interview teams around.

'The reason for this is that at least one of you in the interview will have firsthand knowledge of what another prisoner has said in previous interviews,' she told them.

DC Annie Glover and Ricky-Lee would interview Patsy Henderson while DS Mike Blake with Wilkie Connor would interview Mick Dawson. DCs Helen Weir and Lisa Bayliss would stay with Grace Westbrook, as she had freely talked to them so far and they appeared to have a good rapport. Charley was now going to observe the interview with Patsy Henderson.

'She might be a weak link if her solicitor hasn't instructed her to make no comment, so keep at her,' Charley said to Annie.

Whilst the detectives prepared, Charley spoke to Intelligence Officer Levine to chase up outstanding results for the priority enquiries they required answers for whilst the prisoners remained in custody. The SIO was informed that Jerry Campbell was about to be arrested for assisting an offender in connection with his fingerprints being found on some of the notes in possession of the killer, Benny Patterson, and as luck would have it, Detective Ania Kierczynska knew Jerry Campbell and agreed to team up with Detective Constable Sarah Blackburn to interview him.

It was a busy afternoon, however everything was moving in the right direction. Maurice at Ballistics rang Charley, sounding quite upbeat. 'It appears that you have found both of the weapons used in the murders.'

Charley, otherwise engaged in interview strategies, was distracted at the time. Her heart skipped a beat. 'I hope you're confirming that the rifle discovered in Sinead's car, which was being driven by Patsy Henderson, was the outstanding weapon used at the wedding murders?'

Maurice was smiling. She could hear it in his voice. 'I most certainly am.'

Charley felt a little breathless. 'Well, we still have a way to go to confirm who pulled the trigger on the rifle, but we have three in custody, two circulated as wanted, and we are hopeful that we will get to the bottom of this enigma soon. But, we couldn't have hoped for better.'

'Good luck,' he said. 'It's a bit of a bugger when you can't be safe going to a wedding, isn't it?'

'Nowhere is safe these days, Maurice, with all the drugs that are about. You should know that more than most,' she said.

-

Charley passed on the evidence to Annie and Ricky-Lee so that they could disclose it to Henderson's solicitor prior to one of their impending interviews with the prisoner.

'That's going to put her under more pressure knowing that we know that the weapon concealed in the vehicle she was driving was used in the murder of Bob Sullivan,' she said with a hint of challenge in her voice.

On returning from updating the detectives, Charley's phone was ringing. Still standing, she snapped the receiver from its cradle. When she heard Eira at the other end, she knew by her tone that there was more good news. Charley sat down.

'I thought you might like to know straightaway that the fingerprints lifted from the bag containing the ammunition discovered in Sinead Westbrook's car have now been identified as Patsy Henderson's.'

Charley was eager to know more. 'What about the firearm?' she asked with urgency.

'We're still waiting for results on the weapon,' Eira replied.

Putting down the phone, she spoke to Annie, who had joined her. 'Henderson's going to struggle to keep coming up with excuses, isn't she?' Charley said, imparting the latest news that would also be revealed to Henderson's solicitor.

There was no doubt about it. The pressure was mounting as the evidence stacked up against her. Discussing the interview strategy with Annie and Ricky-Lee, Charley suggested that, on reflection, they shouldn't disclose the full details of what they knew to her until their second interview with Henderson. 'Let her tie herself up in knots with her lies if that's what she wants to do, for now,' Charley said.

–

At the same time, in another interview room at Peel Street Police Station, the first interview with Jerry Campbell was about to take place. On his arrest Charley was reliably informed that he had burst into tears.

However, from her office Charley was watching with interest as Annie and Ricky-Lee reminded Patsy Henderson that she was still under caution before the start of the next interview with her. As agreed, the officers hadn't disclosed the new information prior to this and Henderson maintained she knew nothing of the weapon or ammunition and that she was just driving the car back to Manchester for her friend Sinead Westbrook. She also denied knowing that her boyfriend Mick Dawson was travelling on the M1 at the same time as her with Grace Westbrook. Charley afforded herself a smile. Henderson was playing right into the interviewers' hands.

The first interview was terminated for a short break, at which time they told Henderson's solicitor that Henderson's DNA was on the ammunition bag, which had been secreted in the vehicle with the rifle, and the weapon had been confirmed as the second one used in the double killing. More specifically, the shot from the recovered rifle had fatally wounded Bob Sullivan.

Fifteen minutes had elapsed since the first interview, and back in the interview room, after being reminded she was still under caution, DC Annie Glover broke the news of their update from Ballistics and Forensics to Henderson.

'Previously, you told us that you had nothing to do with any weapon or ammunition linked to the murders of Bob Sullivan or Ralph Bateman, and that you didn't know that the car you were driving had weapons and ammunition concealed inside it. You are not the car owner, yet you told officers that you are Sinead Westbrook, and at the time were wearing a wig perhaps intending to look like her. However, you know she is wanted in connection with murder. You have had time with your solicitor to consider the position you find yourself in, so is there anything you want to tell us?' Annie asked her.

'I'm not a grass, okay?' she replied.

Annie was indifferent. 'Nobody is saying that you are. However, the evidence shows us that you have lied.'

For a moment, both Annie and Ricky-Lee remained silent, their eyes focused on Henderson.

'I've killed nobody. I wasn't near that church that day. I wasn't there and I have never fired a gun ever!'

It appeared to Charley that at times like these, when Henderson felt she was cornered, she took cover behind a whiny denial with no reasoning in her defence.

'By the sound of it, you knew it was going to happen?' suggested Annie.

'I had a feeling something bad was going to happen. I always have a feeling that something bad is going to happen because shit happens to me on a daily basis. I just do as I'm told. I'm not important enough in the grand scheme of things to be told all the details.'

'Am I to believe that you stayed away from the scene of the murder, but were quite happy to help a friend who was involved hide a weapon and ammunition? In other words, did you assist Sinead, knowing what had happened?' Annie continued to push her.

It appeared Henderson, apparently, had a gift for crying on cue. 'I swear that I only knew what had happened when I heard it on the news.'

Annie was puzzled. 'Yet you still helped your friends, knowing what they had done?'

Ricky-Lee pushed a box of tissues across the table towards Patsy, his face held no emotion.

Plucking one from the box, she blew her nose with unselfconscious vigour, then sighed. Her voice wobbled. 'Don't you understand? I didn't have a choice. If you don't want a good kicking, or worse… and you're a drug addict who needs her fix, you do what you're told, don't ask questions. That's exactly what I did.'

Annie showed her disbelief. 'Even when that involves murder?'

An innocent woman would not need to make the point so emphatically, thought Charley. Henderson's story had already changed from not knowing what the officers were talking about to admitting she helped someone because she felt she had no alternative, although she unknowingly knew all the facts. Several times, the detectives had seen her drop the ingenuous routing and reveal flashes of a more cunning personality.

Annie looked thoughtful. 'You did have a choice.'

Henderson shook her head.

'If it was as bad as you make out, then when the police stopped you, and you knew that you were safe, why did you not take the opportunity to tell them about it?'

Henderson remained silent.

It was time for Annie to shake her head. 'No. You lied. You wanted the arresting officers to think you were Sinead Westbrook. You chose to help your friends deal drugs, and to cover up the organising, and on top of that, you are now trying to cover up murder.'

Henderson's straight lips remained sealed.

'Tell me, which would be worse for you, Patsy? Not getting your fix of drugs or getting a beating from Mick Dawson?' asked Ricky-Lee.

Henderson looked taken aback. 'He's never hit me. He loves me. He looks after me.'

Ricky-Lee continued to pressure Henderson. 'In that case, it should have been easy for you to tell the police. If he really loved you, then he wouldn't let anyone beat you up, or want you to be framed for something that you didn't do. We've told you that he's locked up for possession of drugs with intent to supply, so he's not getting out any time soon, is he? You knew he had drugs in his car. You need to think seriously about it. We are still awaiting the results of telephone analysis from the mobile phones we seized, including yours. What's that analysis going to tell us? Because I think you were always in contact with Mick Dawson, and I also think you know very well how to contact Chelsea and Sinead, as well as where they are now.' Henderson remained silent. Ricky-Lee continued in earnest. 'We know you knew about the wedding of Stacey Sullivan and Mark James because you and Mick Dawson were stopped in the car a short time before with their best man Jarvis Cooper, along with Ellie Yates. It's time to be honest with us, Patsy.'

Henderson nibbled at her bottom lip. 'I think I need to speak with my solicitor.'

Ricky-Lee nodded. 'In that case, we'll terminate the interview, and once again give you time to reflect and decide where we go next.'

On the way to Charley's office, Ricky-Lee asked Annie what she thought.

'She's got to be the worst liar I've ever interviewed,' she said. 'What about you?'

'Same.'

The detectives agonised over how a third interview might pan out.

'We can't afford to make assumptions or to miss out on any important details. Keep at her,' said Charley.

In the third interview, Patsy Henderson told the officers, 'I knew Mick was collecting drugs, and he told me to drive Sinead's car.'

'Why did it have to be you who drove the car back?' Annie continued.

'Mick said he didn't trust her, so he wanted to keep her with him.'

'I understand,' Annie said gently. 'When did you see, and, more importantly, touch the rifle?'

'I held it whilst Mick took off the panel where he concealed it. Grace watched.'

'Do you know who the rifle belonged to?'

'I think I may have heard someone say it was Sinead's, maybe Grace, but I can't be sure.'

'How well do you know Chelsea Clough?' asked Ricky-Lee.

Henderson flushed and lifted both hands to her face. 'I don't know her at all. She hangs out with Grace, I heard.'

'We understand that the murder of Bob Sullivan was planned after Tyrone Wells was convicted of Shane Dooley's and Reece Brown's murders, so you have had plenty of time to walk away, but you chose not to, didn't you, Patsy?' asked Ricky-Lee.

Henderson's voice was hushed and sounded afraid. 'You don't walk away from the Dooleys.'

'Neither do you deal drugs or murder people and get away with it. You made your choice, and you chose who to help,' Ricky-Lee fired back at her.

There were no more replies, and the interview was terminated.

Annie stopped at the door to the cell area and breathed in the smell of currant buns and sausages hungrily. Dinner was being served to the prisoners.

In the incident room, the others were found sitting around the table drinking coffee and trying to eat dough-nuts without licking the sugar from their fingers whilst waiting for Charley to come off the phone to discuss the next round of interviews. Annie and Ricky-Lee joined them. Annie looked gutted.

'Dinner?' she asked, picking an iced doughnut from the large square box.

Mike rolled his eyes. 'I gave him a tenner to go get us some nourishment, and he came back with them.'

Wilkie's mouth was full. 'What's up with ya? Better than nowt, aren't they? The doughnut shop was nearest.'

At that moment, the SIO came bustling out of her office, and the team instantly quietened the banter.

'Dawson's DNA has been found on the material that was wrapped around the rifle, as well as on the ammuni-tion discovered secreted in Sinead Westbrook's car,' she said as she sat down, took a sip of her coffee, and grimaced.

'Mine's cold too,' Annie said, nibbling at the doughnut's icing, savouring the taste in her mouth before taking a bite so big that jam dribbled down her chin.

'Which corroborates what Patsy Henderson has just been telling us,' she mumbled, her mouth full of doughnut.

Charley nodded. Her eyes turned towards Mike who was sitting next to Wilkie. 'You'll need to disclose that fact to his solicitor before you go into interview with him.'

'After the last interview, we didn't anticipate him talking to us,' he replied.

'There's not a cat in hell's chance even with that revelation,' chortled Wilkie.

Charley was pragmatic. 'Well, there is no harm in trying, and we must give him the opportunity to explain why his DNA has been found. You never know. If we're lucky, he might tell you who he was transporting the weapon for to take the focus off himself,' Charley responded.

Charley turned next to Helen and Lisa. 'I don't anticipate Grace Westbrook speaking to us again either, but again, I want you to give her the opportunity to tell us, for one, why she said she was innocent and suggested her sister Sinead had set her up.'

Chapter Thirty-One

It was crystal clear to Charley, after sensing the team's restlessness at the debrief, that they needed to see some light at the end of the tunnel. They also needed to see their families, get some exercise, go to the pub, or just switch off for more than a few hours at a time, something that had not been possible since the start of Operation Danube.

Being a police officer meant that every day was varied and with it came many difficulties to overcome, but it was also rewarding after all their hard work to see the evidence come together and to put the perpetrators of crimes before the courts. Yet Charley knew only too well that being pushed to the limits was emotionally challenging, especially when dealing with man's inhumanity to fellow man. As she stood before the quiet group, free from joking around and banter this evening, she was reminded of the oath that they had taken. The words had meant so much to her at the time that she could still remember them verbatim:

'I do solemnly and sincerely declare and affirm that I will well and truly serve the Queen in the office of constable, with fairness, integrity, diligence and impartiality, upholding fundamental human rights and according equal respect to all people; and that I will, to the best of my power, cause the peace to be kept and preserved and prevent all offences against people and property; and that I will continue to hold the said office, I will to the best of my skill and knowledge discharge all the duties thereof faithfully according to law.'

Charley told her exhausted colleagues, 'The prisoners have had ample opportunity in interviews to explain why they have done what they have. I'm going to speak with Caroline at CPS. It's time to charge them and put them before the Magistrates' Court to be remanded in custody. However,' she said as she scanned the sea of faces in her audience, 'I do have one main concern, and that is that Chelsea Clough could be being held against her will, as suggested by Grace Westbrook.'

Mike disagreed. 'Of course, both she and Sinead should remain on our most wanted list, but after interviewing Grace Westbrook, I'm more than happy to believe that she's lying through her back teeth to try to save her own neck. She's concocted a story to try to make us believe that she's the victim, and thereby shifting our focus off her.'

Driving home, Charley felt that all she needed was her bed and a good night's sleep. However, she knew that her subconscious mind would fight for supremacy over her body and would eventually win. She sighed. What she would give to be soothed by one of her grandparents' fables. As an overexcited child, it was the only thing that could help when sleep wouldn't come easily to her.

As if thinking about them and their rigid belief in folk-lore had conjured it up, a white horse suddenly appeared, jumping a wall in front of her and bounding into the adjacent field. Charley's foot instantly touched her brakes, but the horse was long gone.

'The white horse...' she whispered as she sat up straight, remaining still, in the pitch-black for a moment. Her heart was hammering against her chest. 'A white horse... a sign of triumph of good over evil.' The job could be a blessing or a curse, surrounded as it was by shades of death and destruction. That night was one of the most restless she'd had in a while, and all she could think about was the victims, and how much she wanted justice for them.

The next morning, the mobile phone data was available. It showed Charley the frequency and length of calls made between Clough and the Westbrook sisters on the day of the murder and after. It also gave her the contact with Mick Dawson that she was seeking.

GPS mapping showed all three women as being in Slaithwaite on the day of the wedding.

By nine-thirty, Jerry Campbell was stepping into the interview room with Detective Ania Kierczynska and DC Sarah Blackburn. Campbell's defensive posture, sitting rigidly upright, indicated to them that his nervous system had kicked in.

Ania appealed to his better nature straightaway. 'We've known each other for years, Jerry, haven't we? I hope you're going to be honest with us in response to our questions.'

Nervous finger tapping, legs crossed, no eye contact. She could only assume that he was deciding whether to speak to them or not.

After a few anxious moments, Campbell lifted his head and looked Ania straight in the eyes.

'I will,' he said. He sounded genuine. 'I want to say from the outset that I didn't know that they were going to kill Bob.' He paused and the detectives remained silent. 'I liked Bob. He was good to me.'

'Can you tell us what happened?' asked Ania.

'Early on the morning of the wedding, the two sisters brought a package to what me and Bob called the tradesmen's entrance, the back door. Bob had just left. He'd been to collect the post and he was off to prepare himself for the wedding. The shop was almost empty by then, just rubbish and shelving remained, and since I wasn't going to the wedding – weddings aren't my thing – I had offered to finish clearing up. The estate agent was due on the Monday. Taped to the package, which was a drill box that the woman handed to me, was an envelope. I was told not to look inside under any circumstances. They said Benny Patterson would be along to collect it shortly. I didn't see no harm in passing on a parcel.'

Ania interrupted him. 'Now let's be clear, whatever was in the package was wrapped up?'

Jerry nodded emphatically. 'Oh yes, it was definitely wrapped up. Whoever had wrapped it must have used a whole roll of gaffer tape in the process.'

'What colour was the envelope?'

'It was a brown envelope that was fastened to the parcel with Sellotape.'

'If you were told not to look inside, how can you explain your fingerprints being on the bank notes found in Benny Patterson's possession?' Ania continued.

Jerry's face flushed slightly. 'I was being nosey. I opened the envelope and looked inside. I was worried it might be drugs, y'see, but I was glad to see it was money. I guess there was about five hundred quid. I put the notes back and resealed the envelope just before Patterson came hammering on the door, demanding it.'

'You know that after Bob Sullivan was murdered, Benny Patterson was arrested at the scene with a gun?'

Campbell bowed his head and nodded. 'Yes.'

'Why are you only telling us about this, now Jerry?' asked Ania.

When he looked up, his eyes were red-rimmed and teary. 'Bob had been murdered. Patterson had been arrested. I'm a coward. I didn't know the women, but I sensed they were all involved, and I thought I might be next if I didn't keep my trap shut.'

'Be honest – were you involved in Bob Sullivan's murder and that's why you declined the invitation to the wedding wasn't it?' asked Sarah.

A panic-stricken Campbell licked his dry lips. His eyes proceeded to dart from one detective to the other, finally settling on Ania's face. 'No, no, I had no idea! You've got to believe me.'

'You say you didn't know the women. Had you not seen them before?' Sarah asked.

Campbell fiddled with his fingers on his lap as he shook his head. 'No. Never.'

'How did you know your visitors were sisters?' Sarah probed.

'They looked alike and I think someone must have told me.'

Ania adjusted her sitting position. 'Okay, so you're telling us that two sisters came to the shop, the shop that's closed, and handed you a well-taped-up drill box with a brown envelope attached to it, with, you think, about five hundred pounds inside. The sisters told you that Benny Patterson would be collecting it from you, and you were curious enough to look inside the envelope, but you weren't curious enough to look in the box or to ask what it was all about?' asked Sarah.

Campbell nodded. 'Yes, that's it.'

'Do you know Benny Patterson?' asked Ania.

Campbell sniggered. 'Who doesn't? Local waste of space, druggie, weirdo, ex-con...'

'If you knew Benny Patterson, then why didn't you ask him what it was all about?'

Campbell hung his head. 'Because he's known to be a nasty and aggressive bugger, and I thought that he would have probably hit me as soon as look at me that day if I'd questioned him. Like I said before, I'm a coward.'

'Weren't you scared then that he would know that you'd looked inside the envelope?'

'Oh, no. I'm used to opening stuff up and resealing it. The envelope opened easily with a bit of steam from the kettle and the sharp end of a knife, and I sealed it back so no one would ever know I'd taken a peek inside.'

'Why did you count the money?' Sarah asked.

'I didn't actually count it as such. I'm used to handling bank notes. Five hundred pounds was just a guess. Like I said before, I was just relieved it wasn't drugs.'

'Did they pay you for handing the package over to Patterson?' Ania intervened.

Campbell put his fingers to his mouth. 'Yes, they gave me fifty quid to make sure that Patterson received it.'

'These people killed Bob Sullivan, and by doing what you did, you helped them to succeed. You told us you liked Bob; he had been good to you. Why would you do that to him?' Sarah said.

'I swear I DID NOT KNOW what was in the box! I used to hand parcels over to customers every day when I worked in the shop. I knew because I'd opened the envelope that it contained money, not drugs, and that was all I was bothered about.'

Ania leaned towards him. 'Jerry, look, all we want to know is the truth. Was there a gun in the box?'

Campbell raised his voice. 'I swear I don't know!'

Ania moved on. 'Did the women threaten you?'

Campbell shook his head. 'No, not as such, however they told me that they would know if Patterson didn't get it. They made it obvious that if he didn't receive it then I would be in bother.'

'When did he collect it?'

'Like I said before, shortly after they left. Minutes afterwards actually. They could have given it to him themselves and saved themselves the brass if they had waited.'

'Is there anything else you haven't told us?' asked Ania.

'No,' Campbell answered solemnly.

The interview was terminated.

–

Back in the incident room, they updated Charley.

'Do you believe him?' Charley asked them both.

'Well, he's never been the brightest button in the box,' said Ania. 'However, knowing him of old, I think he would be easily bullied into doing a deed for someone, especially if they were authoritative. I can see he might have been frightened of upsetting Benny Patterson too. Jerry has never been a fighter, and I guess that his disability makes him feel vulnerable…'

'Still, I would have thought if he was curious enough to look in the sealed envelope, he'd also have been curious to ask what was in the box.' Sarah paused for a moment thoughtfully. 'That said, he did say that the box was heavily sealed with tape.'

Charley collected the papers on her desk for her next meeting and thanked the officers. 'Let's leave him to think about what he's done for a while. He's connected both Grace and Sinead for us. I've been led to believe that Patterson is now on the mend and recovering well from his attack, and although he finds it difficult to talk, he is able to communicate. I'd like you both to go visit him in the prison hospital and see what he has to say about the shop and Jerry Campbell. That's if he co-operates at all.' Charley was thoughtful. 'A drill box covered in gaffer tape and the torn brown envelope were the only two things that we seized from Patterson's bedsit. I'm going to arrange for them to be taken to Forensics immediately. Who knows what we might find. Good work, you two.'

Charley reflected for a moment when they'd gone. She wondered whether Campbell would be better used as a witness. She scribbled down the thought to discuss with Caroline at CPS. She would be doing that within the hour, in respect of all presently in custody.

Break time, she said to herself as she reached for the kettle. Her mouth felt like the bottom of a parrot's cage.

Chapter Thirty-Two

When Annie arrived back from The Greasy Spoon, everyone converged around the large table in the incident room to eat their lunch while it was still warm. High in sugar, salt, saturated fat and calories, junk food might not be healthy, but it satisfied the hunger pangs.

Head swimming because of her upcoming telephone conversation with Caroline at CPS, she knew that she needed to get the salient points down, should she need to refer to them, to argue her view point on the charges for those in custody.

'The push to find Sinead Westbrook and Chelsea Clough remains priority. They can run but they can't hide forever. At some stage, someone will drop them in it, intentionally or not,' she said in a determined voice to the others, when she had finished.

She took a bite of her bacon sandwich. Then she set it down on her napkin and reached for her pen as she remembered something else. Caroline Marston was known to be decisive. Very rarely did she sit on the fence, and she hoped they could come to an agreement without a long, detailed discussion.

Glancing down at her notepad, she tapped it with the end of her pen. 'As you know, I'll be speaking to CPS this afternoon to decide what charges can be laid against each individual. Once the offenders have been charged, whatever the charges agreed, then we can update the victims' families.' Charley set down her pen, closed her notebook and reached out for the rest of her sandwich. Thoughts shared, Charley retreated to her office. She kicked the door shut behind her and set her mobile phone to silent mode in anticipation of Caroline's imminent call. The role of the SIO could be a lonely one on occasions. Charley had been warned before she accepted the position. As Detective Inspector, she was responsible for the control and the direction of the enquiry, and, as much as she had experts in the relevant fields whom she could call upon for their advice and opinions, the decisions were ultimately hers to make.

Two minutes later, Charley's phone rang, and she was instantly transported into professional mode. She placed her half-empty coffee mug on her desk and picked up the paperwork related to the investigation.

'With regards to Patsy Henderson and her involvement, I am in agreement with you that the evidence against her, at this time, supports the charges of assisting the offender, along with the illegal possession of the firearms and ammunition. The serious nature of these charges will ensure that she is remanded in custody until her trial,' said Caroline.

'Maybe further down the line we'll also secure enough evidence to further charge her with joint enterprise, or a further charge of assisting offenders, in respect of the murders not just the firearm, and knowing Sinead was wanted. That's, of course if we can prove she knew about them at the time,' said Charley. 'Moving on, what are your thoughts regarding Mick Dawson?'

'I think that the charges laid before Dawson should be the same as Henderson, with the additional charge of possession of Class A drugs with intent to supply,' Caroline replied.

Charley paused whilst she wrote the recommendations down. 'That brings us to Grace Westbrook,' she said, picking up her coffee.

'Let's get the drugs charge out of the way – which should be possession of Class A drugs with intent to supply, like Dawson. Then, onto the charge of murder. As I understand it, the telephone evidence puts her in Slaithwaite on the day in question. Her fingerprints were found in the flat that Chelsea Clough was renting, and then the confirmation that the DNA from the cigarette butt, recovered from the roof where the rifle was used to shoot Bob Sullivan, is also hers. Is there anything that I have missed?' she asked.

Charley pressed her lips together as she recalled. 'No, I don't think so. However, the rifle that killed Bob Sullivan was, we believe, only used once by Grace Westbrook. This would be one count of murder. Whereas Benny Patterson is presently charged with two counts of murder, one in respect of Bob Sullivan's death, which might therefore be amended, for clarity, to attempted murder. Although technically Patterson did shoot Sullivan four times, and at least one of the bullets would have killed him, just not as quickly in the end.'

Caroline's silence confirmed to Charley that she was considering her words. 'Mmm… I see what you mean. I am happy to support a charge of murder against Grace Westbrook. Anything else for me in relation to this enquiry?'

Charley took a sip of her coffee. She frowned, it tasted bitter and it was cold. Her eyes dropped to her notes. 'We've arrested Bob Sullivan's shop assistant, Jerry

Campbell. He tells us that the Westbrook sisters visited him at the shop on the morning of the wedding. They left money and a heavily taped box for collection by Benny Patterson, which he did shortly after they left. We know there was money in the envelope because Campbell admits to taking a peek, and his fingerprints were found on bank notes in Patterson's possession. However, Campbell assures us that he didn't look inside the box, he didn't know what was in it, nor was he aware that a murder was planned. I suggest that owing to the circumstances, he is better used as a witness for the Crown than be charged with assisting offenders, where it's unlikely to result in a conviction.'

'I agree if no further evidence to substantiate his involvement is forthcoming and he is able to identify the Westbrook sisters.' Caroline took a deep breath. 'All you need to do now is to locate the other two and get them locked up! Which, considering what you have already achieved, I'm sure is imminent.'

'They're circulated. We can't do any more until they stick their heads above the parapet, but believe me, we're ready for them,' replied Charley.

Caroline chuckled. 'I don't doubt it. By the way, I'll be in court to do the application for remand for the three in custody tomorrow.'

For some reason the SIO felt relieved that Caroline, whom she greatly admired, agreed with her on the charges, and was reassured by her professional approach and her confidence in her, but mostly she was grateful for her support.

'I'll make sure one of my officers is present tomorrow at court should you require anything further because I have no doubt that they'll be applying for bail.'

She paused to collect her thoughts before walking out of her office and into the incident room to update the others.

There was a twinkle in Mike's eye at the news. 'It'll be the first time that they've seen each other when they're in the dock together, won't it? I'll go and keep an eye out. It'll be interesting to see if anyone turns up at the remand hearing to see what happens to them,' said Mike.

Annie's head snapped around, her eyes meeting his. 'What, do you think Sinead or Chelsea might be there?'

Mike shrugged. 'Stranger things have happened.'

'I'm so glad we seized the drill box and the envelope from Patterson's place,' said Annie.

'What sort of detectives would we be if we hadn't seized the two things that stuck out like a sore thumb?' asked Wilkie.

'Ah, but others might have left them. Well done. Let's hope Forensics can obtain something from them,' said Charley.

Ricky-Lee picked up the ringing phone. His eyes found Charley's. He put the phone down. 'Boss, a British Transport Police Officer has contacted us to say that Chelsea Clough is on a train from Leeds to Manchester. We got cut off...'

Charley blinked. 'How does he know it's her?'

'Apparently she upgraded her train ticket and paid with a credit card that was in her name.'

'Did you get his mobile number? I presume he's observing her?'

Ricky-Lee nodded. 'They're in transit. No doubt he'll ring back when he gets a connection.'

All eyes were on the phone, willing it to ring. When it did, Ricky-Lee snatched it from its holder.

The train that Chelsea and the BTP officer were travelling in was said to be approaching Huddersfield train station. She had collected her belongings and was preparing to leave the train at the station. With no time for the team to get there, the BTP officer was told to arrest her on behalf of West Yorkshire Police for conspiracy to murder.

Words weren't necessary for Ricky-Lee and Annie as they grabbed the car keys. Within minutes, they were out the door and heading towards the train station.

–

As the train came to a halt, people began to get off, and when the BTP officer moved forward to arrest Chelsea Clough, a ferocious fight broke out between two male passengers. He had no alternative but to wade in to break it up, at which time he was assaulted, and he called for urgent backup.

By the time the detectives were on the scene, Chelsea Clough had left the train and disappeared into thin air.

In the office, Charley didn't have time to have any feelings on the matter as she moved into professional mode. She turned to Wilkie. 'We need copies of the CCTV that covers Huddersfield and Leeds train station where her journey began.'

'I wonder if anyone took her to Leeds station?' said Mike.

'Hopefully we will find out when we get the CCTV,' said Charley, 'but, one thing's for sure – she's not in Manchester and she's not being held hostage by Sinead Westbrook as her sister suggested.'

Mike agreed.

'Alert patrol to the fact that one of our suspects has just got off a train in town. We might have been close, but we weren't close enough. Get details of her credit card from BTP. Now that we know she's using it, get the Financial Investigation Unit to track her movements. It might be the one thing that eventually leads us to her.'

'Well, you know what they say boss – if we don't catch them on the swings, we'll catch them on the roundabout,' said Wilkie.

Within the hour, DC Ania Kierczynska and DC Sarah Blackburn had returned from the hospital wing of the prison, having visited Benny Patterson.

He had appeared happy to see anyone, Sarah told Charley. 'As if he was getting a social visit from us.'

'That may be owing to the fact that I told his solicitor to inform him of your visit, and to discuss with him the events that had unfolded since his arrest.'

Ania frowned. 'She wasn't present. She declined.'

Charley shrugged.

'What did he have to say?'

'He said he couldn't remember much before the attack on him, funnily enough. Nevertheless, as you asked, we told him that a second gun had been used to kill Bob Sullivan, and that a second person had been charged in connection with his murder.'

'Did he comment on the attack?'

Sarah shook her head. 'No, but surprisingly, he did confirm to us that he picked up the package left for him at Sullivan's shop, and when we asked why there, he told us that Jerry was known to be a soft touch, and he wouldn't refuse to pass on a parcel for a bob or two.'

Chapter Thirty-Three

Owing to the seriousness of the charges, coupled with the high risk that they might abscond, Mick Dawson, Grace Westbrook, and Patsy Henderson were remanded in custody at the Magistrates' Court. Mike reported back to Charley that the solicitors had tried exceptionally hard to get the offenders released on bail, offering stringent conditions such as the surrendering of passports, the promise to sign in at their local police station twice daily, and a surety of a substantial amount of money, to ensure that they would adhere to the conditions agreed by the summary court. However, much to the detective sergeant's great relief, the three magistrates were having none of it.

It was Wednesday morning and the information from Chelsea Clough's bank told Mike that she had once again used her credit card at the Asda supermarket.

A sea of blank faces and shrugged shoulders met Annie's gaze when she shared her thoughts. 'Why Wednesday?'

'Routine? Coincidence?' said Ricky-Lee.

'Routine or coincidence, it also tells us that she could be living locally. I want observations established at the supermarket,' said Charley.

By late morning, the news was in that Forensics had painstakingly unwrapped the gaffer tape from around the

Bosch drill box. 'In total, the three-metre length of tape used to wrap around it was extreme, to say the least, don't you think?' Eira said.

'That indicates to me that there was precious cargo inside that the sender only wanted the recipient to see.'

'Doesn't it just. Our findings show us four traces of DNA at various stages on the tape. Malcolm Dooley's was on the edge of the tape, as if it was he who wrapped the tape around the box. However, the best result appertaining to him is at both ends, where I guess he bit through it with his teeth. We also have Grace Westbrook's DNA and Benny Patterson's, the former at the beginning and the latter at the end of the tape.'

'Could be that our Mr Teflon eventually slipped up by providing the weapon for Patterson to use in the operation.'

'Remember, though, that unless you can tell me otherwise, his DNA on the tape only shows us that Dooley was present whilst taping the box up. We've found nothing to confirm that a firearm or ammunition was concealed inside.'

Eira's news was good, but as the SIO told the team, it was not a call for celebration. No one had said that a weapon and ammunition were concealed in the box. It was purely circumstantial and they had no evidence to prove it.

'Have you decided to speak to Malcolm Dooley about his DNA being found on the tape?' asked Mike.

Charley shook her head. 'No, not until the women have been arrested and we have had an opportunity to speak to them first.'

Mike looked surprised. 'You think that they might talk?'

'I'm counting on it,' she replied.

On the following Wednesday morning, Charley couldn't quite believe her luck when Chelsea Clough turned up at the Asda supermarket. Identified on the CCTV cameras in the security office by DC Wilkie Connor, he and DC Annie Glover approached her, then arrested her on suspicion of the murders of Bob Sullivan and Ralph Bateman, much to the amazement of the other shoppers.

Handcuffed on her arrest, she spoke only four words. 'I haven't murdered anyone.'

In the car en route to Peel Street Police Station, Clough remained silent. In compliance with the Police and Criminal Evidence Act, there were no questions put to her by the arresting officers.

Her public arrest had not been missed by the media, and almost immediately, Charley was being chased by Connie Seabourne from the Force press office, who asked her for a comment.

'I wish we got such a quick response from the public to an appeal,' Mike said when Charley told him. 'I'm going to put a statement out confirming the arrest on Operation Danube at the supermarket. The press won't be happy as that's all I can give them, but I can't make further comment because we've got the others in custody.'

Mike thought he saw a glint of feistiness in her eyes.

'Tell you what, I'm also going to release Sinead Westbrook's picture and tell them that we still want to speak to her. Perhaps this time we will get some reaction.'

'There's nothing lost. It might also put pressure on her to hand herself in,' said Mike.

'Huh, and pigs might fly,' Charley scoffed.

Charley was interested to hear what belongings Clough had when she was arrested, and whether she had given a current address to the custody sergeant when she was booked into the cells. Charley hoped that there would be a mobile phone and a key belonging to the address she had given.

Charley was in luck. The door key belonging to the property she was renting in Bradley Road, Huddersfield, was a stone's throw from the Asda supermarket.

On her monitor, Charley saw Chelsea Clough look disdainfully at her solicitor as they sat down next to each other in the interview room.

Two minutes later, Mike strolled into her office carrying two cold cans of Coca Cola. He handed one to Charley.

'Thought you might be in need of a caffeine boost because I know I am. Mind if I join you?'

Charley pulled the tab on the soft drink and drank thirstily. 'Just what I needed,' she said, smacking her lips. 'Be my guest.' She glanced up at the clock. 'Four hours since Clough's arrest. Have you any update on the search of her premises?'

'Not yet. Her mobile phone data is also being checked, along with GPS mapping, for her latest contacts and whereabouts until we can speak to the service provider for a more in-depth detailed statement that will take longer.'

Charley nodded towards the monitor. 'I'm glad to see she's being represented by a duty solicitor who hasn't represented any of the others.'

Mike scrutinised the interview room scene. 'She looks drawn and pale, her face was make-up free and her long dark hair was pulled back into a tight ponytail. Nothing like she was described by Wilkie when he and Annie had met with her at the studio.'

In the interview room, Clough and her solicitor sat with their heads together, talking quietly. DC Annie Glover shuffled her papers into a neat pile and put them down in front of her. DC Wilkie Connor coughed to get their attention.

'Mind me asking why you chose them to do the first interview with her?' Mike asked.

'It's because they've spoken to her before and I'm interested to hear what they think after speaking to her now that she's been arrested.'

The recording equipment was switched on, and as soon as the introductions had been made, solicitor Alice Brennan spoke.

'My client wishes to tell you her story, and I have advised her to do so.'

Charley turned to Mike, eyebrows raised, before turning back to the monitor.

'Is that right, Chelsea?' Annie said calmly. 'You want to tell us what happened leading up to the murders, as the photographer at the wedding, and afterwards?'

'Yes,' she said softly. 'As you already know, my step-brother was Reece Brown. I wasn't close to him. We never lived in the same household. However, when he died alongside Shane Dooley, I was his next of kin, so I had to be involved with the arrangements for his funeral. That's when I met Shane's dad, Malcolm Dooley, Shane's fiancée Sinead, and her sister Grace. It was a sad and emotional time. The killer was on the loose and everyone was angry and wanted revenge.'

Annie cut in. 'Sorry to interrupt. Does that include you?'

'Yes, I suppose I did, but I only wanted the person responsible for killing Reece caught and dealt with by the police. I guess that is sort of revenge in a way, but the others appeared to want more. They talked of burning down houses, and later it got bizarre when Tyrone Wells was actually arrested, charged with murder and remanded. They then talked about harming others close to him, so that he would suffer in the same way that we had. I thought it was the hurt and the anger talking. After the trial and conviction, when Tyrone Wells was sent down, I thought that was it. It was all over at last. I moved away and tried to distance myself from them, but they kept contacting me. Their world was nothing like the one that I lived in and I had no desire to swap.'

'So what happened to change that?' nudged Annie.

'I finished my photography degree, then about three years ago, I opened my own business in a semi-rural, post-industrial village described by others as one of the coolest places to live in the north – Slaithwaite. I had no idea that Tyrone Wells had relatives living in the area. Why should I? My contact with Grace and Sinead had all but died out. In all honesty, I was relieved to put that time in my life behind me. Reece and Shane's death was the only thing that we had in common. Then, one day, out of the blue, Sinead made contact shortly after Grace rang me and asked me if I'd be interested in doing the photography for a wedding here at short notice. Of course I was interested. It was work and the business had never really taken off because of the pandemic. I was barely keeping afloat with government handouts. I never thought that something sinister lay behind her request.'

Clough paused for a moment. The detectives waited in silence, anticipating that she hadn't finished telling the tale. 'It wasn't until they visited me that the sisters told me that the bride was related to Tyrone Wells. I refused to do it. I wanted nothing to do with anyone connected to Wells. That's when they became angry. They intimated that my best friend Fran and her baby were in danger, should I refuse to do as they asked. At first, I thought they were bluffing. Then they told me their address to prove they knew where they lived.'

Chelsea Clough began to cry, silently at first, but soon she was sobbing. 'Fran and I met at uni, and we shared a flat in the Midlands until she married Guy and I moved back north. Fran was more a sister to me than Reece ever was a brother... I wish I could turn the clock back,' she whispered.

'Do you want to have a break?' asked Annie.

Clough shook her head. 'No, I need to tell you this.'

'As you wish,' agreed Annie.

'At the time, I was still blissfully unaware of what the Westbrook sisters had planned. Stacey and Mark were a lovely couple and I enjoyed working with them on their wedding day plans.'

'Did you never wonder why they had asked you to be involved?' asked Annie.

Chelsea shook her head. 'No, I didn't. I did question Sinead's mood swings and that's when I learnt from Grace that Sinead was using drugs.'

'What about Grace?' asked Annie.

'Come to think of it, Grace appeared to be very interested in a wedding photographer's agenda on the big day. However, she was also very touchy-feely, and to be honest, made it quite obvious that she was interested in me. She wanted to know my plans… I had to confirm the venue, timings and locations where I intended to take photographs. She even suggested that I use the rose-covered latticework arch, already favoured by Stacey, so I was intending to use it anyway. Grace freaked me out. But, that was because I thought she was interested in being close to me, and that included being interested in my work, not the wedding.'

'What happened next?' said Annie.

'The day before the wedding, Grace telephoned to tell me that they needed to have access to my place, and they would come there before I left. I can remember thinking that I was pleased that they hadn't asked for a key. She said I was to go about my day as usual. She wasn't going to come on her own, so by this time, I just decided I would comply with their requests. The sooner that the wedding was over, the better.'

Wilkie cut in. 'Can I just confirm that you are telling us that at this time, you still had no idea what was going to happen?'

'Absolutely not. I had a feeling they were up to something but I had no idea what. I guess I just thought the less I knew, the better. Like I said, I couldn't wait for the wedding to be over, and for them to be gone from my life for good. When a man turned up and started firing a gun at the wedding, I couldn't believe my eyes.'

'Why didn't you tell the police after the shooting what you knew?' Annie asked.

'What could I tell them? I didn't know anything and I was afraid that if I spoke to the police, and they spoke to the Westbrook sisters about what I said, they might hurt Fran and the baby.'

'The sisters turned up at your place on the morning of the wedding?'

'Yes,' said Clough.

'Did they say anything to you?' continued Annie.

'I was all prepared to leave when they arrived. My gear was already in the car. The only thing that I remember from that morning is that Sinead was already spaced out of her head, whereas Grace was very alert, like she was on some kind of mission. She told me to have a good day as I left, and that they would be gone by the time I got back. I was very relieved. She also said that if anyone asked, I was to say that I hadn't seen them.'

'Were they there when you got back?' asked Wilkie.

Clough shook her head. 'No, they'd gone, and I knew that after what had happened, I just wanted to get away, as far away from them as I could, to somewhere they couldn't find me.'

'At any time did you see a firearm at your house?'

'No.'

'What about a pushchair?'

Clough looked puzzled. 'A pushchair? No, why?'

'Because apart from being shot by the gunman at the wedding, Bob Sullivan was also shot with a rifle from a nearby rooftop. We know that Grace Westbrook was on that rooftop, and we also know that she walked there and back with the rifle in a pushchair. The one that she used was found in your loft space. We also found an item near the storeroom in your home, which is part of a rifle.'

Chelsea Clough's face instantly drained of colour.

'I have never seen a rifle or a pushchair there. Never. If I had, I promise you I would tell you.'

'Your fingerprints are being checked against certain items, along with your DNA, so if you are lying, we'll soon find out,' Annie told her.

'I'm not. Honestly, I'm not. I just want this nightmare to come to an end,' she cried.

The interview was terminated.

Chapter Thirty-Four

Fifteen minutes later, sitting at their desks nursing mugs of coffee, Wilkie and Annie were joined by Charley and Mike to talk about the interview with Chelsea Clough and a way forward.

'Clough's story so far is completely feasible. I think she's telling the truth,' Annie said between sips of her drink. 'Her fingerprints are being checked against outstanding marks lifted. Apart from the rented property, they don't appear anywhere else. As far as her DNA, we will know the result in due course.'

Mike checked the list of DNA found and prints lifted just to be sure. 'No,' he said when he lifted his head. 'We've no evidence to dispute what she's saying, and the mobile data from the others' phones doesn't tell us a great deal about Clough, either. Her DNA will be checked but I honestly don't think that it will implicate her.'

'There's no doubt that her appearance suggests that she's still shaken,' added Wilkie.

'Maybe she was reluctantly involved through fear as she says?' said Charley. 'What's the opinion about her knowledge of the intention to kill?'

'I don't think for one minute she knew of the intention to commit murder,' replied Annie.

'I agree,' added Wilkie. 'There's no doubt that she was intimidated by Grace and frightened by the threats she made towards Clough's friend Fran and her baby, which ensured that she co-operated with them. I don't think that they confided their intention to kill either.'

'It could be that we misread her involvement, and like you say, Mike, we have no evidence to dispute her account of things.' Charley put her mug down on the table. 'Okay, Wilkie, Annie, next interview. I want you to ask Clough about her relationship with Grace. Tell her that you don't believe her, and let's see if she maintains her story. If she does, then she may end up being a good witness for the prosecution. Another thing – ask her who smokes.'

Mid-afternoon, the two DCs, Chelsea Clough, and her solicitor returned to the interview room and settled in. Clough was reminded by Annie that she was still under caution before the interview started.

'You know you have been arrested in connection with the murder of Bob Sullivan and Ralph Bateman, and earlier you explained to us about your involvement in the enquiry, so we now want to ask you some more questions surrounding the incident,' Annie continued. 'Do you know Benny Patterson, the man who was in the church grounds and who fired a weapon at the wedding guests?'

'No, I don't,' Clough said.

'Do you smoke, and do you know if any of the Westbrook sisters smoke?'

'Perish the thought. I detest the smell of cigarettes. However, I have seen both the Westbrook sisters smoke.'

'Do you know what brand of cigarettes they smoke?'

'They roll their own, but I wouldn't know what brand of tobacco they used.'

'Grace Westbrook tells us that she asked you to go to France with her. Were you ever in a relationship with her?'

'No. I told you that she seemed to be coming onto me, and yes, she asked me to go to France with her, but I never gave her any reason to think that I was interested in her or France. She's not my type. The only reason I played along, if she said I did, was because I was frightened of what she might do if I didn't.'

'I'm not judging you, Chelsea. I'm simply trying to understand what happened,' Annie told her.

'I'm not like Reece. He was the black sheep of the family. He started drinking and taking drugs at a young age, and from then on, was in and out of detention centres. I'm like my mum. She hated conflict and confrontation, and would do anything for a quiet life, which probably made him worse because she gave in to him. Sinead Westbrook's mood swings when she was on drugs frightened me, like I said. Grace just frightened me full stop. Their world isn't a place that I want to be part of. Not ever.'

Wilkie Connor stared at her in silence before speaking. 'Two people were executed at a wedding, and let's face it, you were the person that lined them up for the firing squad like lambs to the slaughter. We can prove that two of the murderers were at your place on that day. Do you really expect us to believe you knew nothing about it?'

Chelsea's eyes welled up and she was powerless to hold back the tears. 'I didn't line anyone up other than for the wedding photographs. I know what happened and I'll never be able to forget it, but you have got to believe me when I say that I didn't know what they were up to.'

'Or is that your story now that you've been caught? Are your tears for yourself or for the victims? Let's face it, you've had plenty of time to think about what you would say when we caught up with you, haven't you?' Wilkie said.

Her jaw tightened. 'No, it wasn't like that at all. I could never be involved in anything like that.'

'We're only interested in the truth,' he said bluntly.

Clough's hands went together as if in prayer. She was sweating. 'I'm begging you to believe me. I'm telling you the absolute truth.'

Wilkie twisted his face in a grimace. 'I don't believe you. This was a vendetta, a reprisal for the killing of Shane Dooley and your stepbrother Reece Brown, wasn't it?'

Tears rolled unchecked down Clough's cheeks as she realised what was happening. 'How many times do I have to tell you? I knew nothing of their intentions. I promise. I distanced myself from them at the earliest opportunity. I had no idea that the Sullivans were related to Reece's killer. These people scare the shit out of me. They have proved that they have eyes everywhere. Just look how long they waited to kill Mr Sullivan, and for what? Because he was a relative of Tyrone Wells? How... how macabre is that?' Chelsea would have continued had her words not been lost in gulps.

Her solicitor scowled at the detective, reached out and touched her arm. 'Do you need a break?' she asked softly.

Chelsea turned on her quickly and pushed the solicitor's hand away.

'No!' she cried. 'I just want them to believe that I wasn't involved because I wasn't.'

Stoney-faced, Wilkie's voice didn't falter. 'If that is the case, then why didn't you come to see us after the shootings to tell us what you did know?'

Clough took a couple of deep breaths. She appeared to gain some composure. 'You know what these people are capable of. They planned, and they schemed, and they waited for near on two years to kill a relative of a person who had wronged them just because they couldn't get to him for God's sake. If they thought for one minute that I'd been into a police station of my own volition to speak to you about them, I'd be dead. And so would my friend and her baby. Even if you got them, there would still be Malcolm Dooley's lot out there to come after us.'

Clough's solicitor cut in. 'I think my client does need that break now,' she said. 'Can we please get a glass of water or a tea?'

Wilkie Connor nodded. 'Okay, Chelsea, we are now going to terminate the interview.'

–

It was a relief to leave the interview room. It was hot and the atmosphere intense. The corridor was cooler and several windows were open.

'I notice you're not going on about how lovely she is anymore,' Annie teased Wilkie.

Wilkie only scoffed.

'Well, do you believe her?' Annie asked.

'Yeah, I think I do,' Wilkie replied.

'You can't sit on the fence. The boss will want to know. Yes or no?'

Wilkie held the door open for her to enter the incident room. 'I'd have thought that she would have had the nerve to come forward before now.'

'Really? She's right, she could have ended up dead. She still could if they get their hands on her. Like she says, being a grass is not acceptable in their world, where words are not enough to settle differences.'

In Charley's office, she and Mike were waiting with drinks and biscuits to speak with Annie and Wilkie.

'We watched and she's maintaining her story. Do we ask her to be a witness for the prosecution?' Charley asked when they entered.

Wilkie picked up the nearest mug of coffee from the table, reached for a couple of biscuits and eagerly shoved them in his mouth. 'We'll need to consider witness protection,' he mumbled.

'Looking at the evidence we have against the others, she might not be required,' suggested Mike.

'I think CPS would want to use her to show continuity. I'll speak to Caroline and see what her take on it is, then we'll make the decision,' said Charley.

'You saw that she's petrified of them, so I don't know how she'd cope in the witness box,' commented Mike.

'We can use a screen. They'll know who she is, but it might be less intimidating for her not to have to see them,' replied Annie.

Charley's eyes turned to Wilkie. 'You're quiet. What do you think?'

Annie turned to Wilkie, then looked at the plate empty of biscuits with a stunned look in her eyes and a drink in her hand.

Wilkie looked sheepish. 'I think she might surprise us and relish the opportunity to start a new life elsewhere under witness protection,' he said. 'What's left for her in Huddersfield?'

'Okay, let's get it all written up and onto the system. All we need for a full house now is Sinead Westbrook.'

Mike opened his mouth as if to speak.

'Don't worry, I haven't forgot about Malcolm Dooley's prints on the gaffer tape, he may be last but not least,' Charley said.

Chapter Thirty-Five

The outer office was buzzing with energy. People were walking about on the phone, waiting for printouts, photo-copying, and looking at computer screens. Nothing, however, was going to distract Charley from her discussion with Caroline at CPS. It ended in the mutual decision to bail Chelsea Clough and to further discuss whether she could be a potential witness for the Crown.

Minutes later, Annie turned from her computer screen when Charley emerged from her office.

'Speak with the custody sergeant, will you?' Charley asked. 'CPS have agreed that Clough ought to be released on bail with conditions.'

'Signing on daily, I guess?' asked Annie.

Charley nodded. 'Got it in one.'

Returning to her office, Charley logged onto her computer and began checking that the victims' families were up to date with recent developments. She was adding the latest news when the HOLMES team sergeant Steve Taylor popped his head around her door.

'Boss, Eira from Forensics has been trying to get hold of you. Says she's been trying for a while, but you've been engaged.' Charley's heart skipped a beat. Something told her that it was connected to new evidence she'd found – or not.

'I have news,' Eira blurted out when she picked up Charley's call. 'We have a further hit on the database for Malcolm Dooley.'

Charley felt colour flood her cheeks. 'From where?'

'You're going to love this. It's on the rifle. There was some damage to the edge of the stock. We discovered a minute trace of blood, which produced a different DNA profile from the one we identified on the weapon earlier.'

'You're certain it's Malcolm Dooley's?'

There was a tone of exultation in her voice. 'Absolutely. There's no doubt about it.'

As Charley said Dooley's name, Mike walked into her office. Thanking Eira, Charley replaced the receiver. Mike sat down, his eyes eager and questioning.

'Eira's connected Malcolm Dooley through DNA to the rifle that killed Sullivan. We need to liaise with our counterparts at GMP. I'm sure they'd like to assist in the search of his home when we go to arrest him.'

—

Charley was standing in the kitchen toasting a slice of bread for a belated lunch and discussing Dooley's arrest before her meeting with Connie when Ricky-Lee hurried in.

'Sinead Westbrook's turned up at the front desk, and Marty wanted you to know that her legal advisor is Barrister Charles Pompous.'

The toast popped up and Charley turned to Mike, butter knife in hand. She glanced up at the clock.

'Would you do the honours? I've that meeting in five minutes,' she said.

Mike Blake made his way down the steps and let himself into the reception area. Marty looked up from behind the counter and nodded in the direction of a brown-haired young woman wearing skinny jeans with a rainbow-coloured T-shirt and flip-flops.

She was sitting on a bench fixed to the floor and the furthest from the door. Her hair hung in a tangled mess about her face, and she seemed oblivious to her surroundings, immersed in her own thoughts.

Towering above her protectively was a rotund bald bespectacled older man dressed in an expensive-looking dark striped suit. Although the weather didn't look like rain, he had a long green raincoat draped over his arm and an old worn briefcase in his other hand.

Mr Pompous introduced himself, and his client. When he spoke, his jowls shook, and he adjusted his wire-framed glasses. If Sinead thought arriving with a barrister was supposed to faze Detective Sergeant Mike Blake, then she was wrong. Sinead Westbrook was arrested for the double murder within seconds of her standing.

Walking down the corridor towards the bridewell, Mr Pompous asked Mike when his client would be interviewed.

'It may be a while, but the custody sergeant will inform you once she has been booked in,' Mike said.

'Don't you know that I'm an extremely busy man,' Mr Pompous said.

'Obviously, you can wait or return when we're ready.'

In the meantime, Sinead Westbrook had consented to her fingerprints and DNA being taken. The team had a lot to speak to her about, and they had the advantage that she didn't know what the others had said. She also didn't know what evidence the investigation team had managed to secure. That was something only she and her legal team would find out when disclosure was given.

Two hours after her arrest, they were ready to disclose the evidence they had against his client to Mr Pompous, prior to starting interviews. Mr Pompous made it clear that he was not happy.

DS Mike Blake would interview Sinead, accompanied by DC Annie Glover.

As Charley watched the interview from her office, she saw Mr Pompous. It was always nice to put a face to a name.

'You came to the police station with your barrister today knowing you were sought by the police in connection with a double murder at a wedding. On your arrival, you were arrested for your part in these offences, as well as for the possession of a firearm, along with ammunition. Have you any comment to make at this time?' asked Mike.

Sinead looked grey. She was trembling and clasping her hands together in an attempt to steady them. Her voice quivered as she spoke. 'No comment.' She kept looking at Mr Pompous for reassurance.

'Three years ago, your fiancé Shane Dooley was murdered, and the murderer for that crime is now serving a life sentence in prison. You, with your sister Grace, decided that you would seek revenge by shooting and killing a distant relative of his as the man celebrated his daughter's wedding. Whilst you and your sister used the rifle, you also paid a local man to use a handgun. The rifle used was recovered hidden in your car.'

'No comment,' she said, squirming slightly in her seat. Pompous nodded his approval at her answer.

'We can prove that you left the gun, which Benny Patterson used, at Mr Sullivan's shop for him to collect. He did this, and then shot Bob Sullivan and Ralph Bateman with it in the church grounds. We also know that you and your sister paid Jerry Campbell, the shop assistant at Sullivan's, for his help in handing over the package on the morning of the wedding. We have evidence that puts you in Chelsea Clough's photographic studio in Slaithwaite. We can also prove that the weapon found hidden in your car was the rifle used to kill Bob Sullivan. As you can see, there is a substantial amount of evidence to connect you to these crimes. Do you wish to make any comments or a statement about what we have told you?'

Sinead Westbrook made no comment. The interview was terminated.

Two further interviews took place with Sinead Westbrook to give her further opportunities to answer any of the questions, but her reply of 'no comment' remained constant.

At the custody desk, in the presence of her barrister, DC Annie Glover read out the prepared statement to charge Sinead Westbrook in connection with the murder of Bob Sullivan and Ralph Bateman and related firearms offences. Although there was no evidence to suggest she pulled the trigger on a firearm, there was evidence to show her being complicit in the murders.

Her only response was, 'No comment.'

She was going to be taken back to her cell until her appearance at the Magistrates' Court, where she would be taken for a remand in custody, just as her co-accused had been.

Mr Pompous spoke reassuringly to her. 'It's alright, don't worry. I'll see you tomorrow morning when, as I said, we will be applying for bail.'

'Good luck to him with that,' said Ricky-Lee when Annie relayed the conversation to the team.

In the incident room Mike was sitting back in his chair next to Wilkie and opposite Ricky-Lee. He cocked his head to one side. 'Don't be too sure. Mr Pompous isn't one of the leading and most expensive barristers for nothing. That said, he will need to convince the magistrates that she won't abscond or attempt to interfere with any witnesses. The detective sergeant counted on his fingers the number of points on which the magistrates could remand a person. 'The fact is, Sinead handed herself in, so he'll argue she is unlikely to abscond.'

'That's only because her picture went out to the media,' interjected Wilkie.

'He might offer up someone who is willing to put up a substantial monetary surety. She hasn't been convicted of a serious crime before and hasn't interfered with any of the witnesses that we know of, so why would she do so now?' added Mike.

'But, she's charged with murder and possession of a firearm and ammunition used in the crime. What magistrates are going to grant her bail?' Wilkie argued.

'Bail isn't about examining the evidence against her, or whether she is pleading her innocence. Let's face it, we are not looking for anyone else now are we?'

Wilkie was silent for a moment, his face flushed, his brow wrinkled, mouth turned down.

'We still haven't caught up with Malcolm Dooley and he's connected to both firearms, isn't he? So, there are people still to be arrested, when we prove their involvement,' he said with a smile. 'And, that might just seal the remand for us.'

'We just need to be sure,' said Mike.

'You know what they say, m'old mucker, they're all innocent until proven guilty. You do remember that bit of the law?'

'Alright Mother Teresa,' he replied.

Mike remained stoic. 'Let's just all keep positive shall we?'

It was necessary to keep Caroline Maston updated as to what was happening with Sinead Westbrook, and in her office Charley was making that call.

'Thank you,' said the crown prosecutor. 'Forearmed is forearmed. All I can do is put the evidence before the court, and let the magistrates decide where she resides until her trial.'

Whilst the others had been talking, Annie had been checking out the details that Sinead Westbrook had given to the custody sergeant. The address she had given was in the name of a Karen Foster. Turning her screen for the others to see, she pointed to the known woman's details.

'Maybe we need to visit her and find out who she is? We also need to search Sinead's last known address to see if there is any more evidence to connect her to the crime, don't we?' she asked, looking up at the clock. It was ten past six.

Chapter Thirty-Six

Multi-ethnic Moss Side, Manchester, was an inner-city area that was reportedly likened to London's Brixton. Therefore, Charley did not take the night visit lightly. She worked through a hundred scenarios and what-ifs in her head en route with Annie to speak to Karen Foster. However, in the end it all turned unexpectedly simple when one of Mike's contacts, the Mancunian detective Eddie Wilbur, who knew the area and its people well, agreed with Mike to go with them. Darkness had all but fallen on Manchester when Annie and Charley pulled up at the agreed meeting place behind the GMP CID car under one of the few unbroken streetlamps at their meeting place. The sun was, however, still bright enough to peek beneath the clouds and give a fiery orange hue to the rundown estate. It looked remarkably serene and beautiful.

Leaving the cars behind, with Wilbur's partner on guard, Wilbur led the way towards the high-rise apartment block, halting young children that were playing among the cars. Annie, originally from a village in the countryside, looked mortified. She saw, as many others had before her, a disaster waiting to happen.

As they walked, bikes met cars moving at great speed on what Wilbur called the 'rat run'. Once or twice,

Charley caught Annie putting her hand to her eyes in expectation of an imminent accident.

Wilbur saw the women taking an interest in the car park full of abandoned cars, tents, and cardboard boxes. 'Shelters by homeless people and drug users,' he told them.

A gang of youths were congregated at the bottom of the litter-strewn stairwell and on the landing leading to Karen Foster's flat. Although they were rowdy, they appeared to be harmless, laughing and shoulder-barging each other.

'If you can't behave, be careful,' Wilbur told them. A few respectfully acknowledged him with a Nazi salute. It was without doubt that Wilbur was giving the West Yorkshire detectives a free pass into the known no-go area, and for that Charley was extremely grateful.

As soon as the detectives were out of sight, the youths could be heard shouting and swearing and Wilbur raised his eyebrows. 'If we can make this quick, partaking in drugs, crime, and alcohol has begun and it's not a pretty sight.'

Wilbur rapped at Sinead Westbrook's friend's door and stood back. He retrieved a handkerchief from his pocket and covered his nose. Annie eyed him, puzzled.

'Why—' she began when a petite, round-shouldered old lady with salt and pepper hair and dark glasses answered.

Charley screwed up her nose and Annie gagged when she got the first strong waft of the smell coming from within. They were both thankful that they hadn't had time to eat.

As she closely peered at the detective's credentials, she was assured by Wilbur in his strong Mancunian accent that the two women were police officers.

'It's the drains, again,' Karen said by way of an explanation for the smell. She took one slow step after another down the hallway, turning her head slightly to glance over her shoulder as much as her stiff neck would allow when she spoke. 'I don't notice it now,' she continued.

Suddenly she stopped outside the door to what looked like a bedroom, although one room could not be distinguished from another owing to the clutter. 'I don't suppose you lot have any clout with the council?'

'I'm sorry, we're from West Yorkshire,' said Charley.

'Ah yes, the bizzy said. I believe Sinead was from West Yorkshire,' she said, a smile in her voice.

Charley turned to Annie, who was close behind her. The SIO's hopes were raised. Charley could see that there was no bulb in the ceiling light, but the light at the end of the corridor appeared brighter. Or was it that her eyes were becoming accustomed to the dark?

In the lounge, she could make out a portion of greasy chips and lumpy gravy in a broken tray on the arm of a heavily stained, threadbare chair. The carpet looked as if it hadn't been vacuumed for months. Finding her seat by the touch of her hand, Karen flopped down with a big sigh of what sounded like relief and contentment.

'Do you mind if I carry on eating my supper?' she asked after regaining her composure and her breath. 'My grandson brought it for me from the Pakistani chippy. They're cold because he forgot to deliver them straight away. Said he'd had an errand to run. If I'd have said that to my grandmother, I'd have got a clip round the ear,' she chortled. 'He's not a bad 'un, though. At least he comes to see I'm alright. I don't know what I'd do without him when my lodger's not here. She looks after me good and proper…'

Annie took a tissue from her pocket and covered her nose, breathing through her mouth. Charley frowned. Annie shrugged her shoulders, nodding her head towards the old lady. 'She can't see. She's blind,' she mouthed.

'There must still be some stuff of Sinead's here. If you want to look for it, be my guest,' Karen said, when Charley asked for confirmation that Sinead had lived in the flat.

'So, where did she sleep?'

'Mostly on the sofa,' Karen said, her mouth full.

It was true, there were a few bits of younger women's clothing, but nothing to confirm they were Sinead's or that she lived in the flat. Was it possible that she had used the flat as a bail address?

'Can you remember how long she's been here and when you last saw her?'

Karen shook her head. 'I wish I could help you,' she replied, when Charley asked her if she'd sign a statement to the fact. 'Although it might not look like much to you, I value what I have.' She leaned over the arm of her chair and indicated for Charley to move closer. 'I'm not ready to meet my maker just yet, which is no doubt what I would be doing, and pronto, if I did what you asked,' she whispered.

–

It was midnight before Charley and Annie arrived back at Peel Street Police Station.

Annie made a drink of tea, struggling to rid herself of the smell in Foster's flat. 'I can't imagine Sinead living there. Nobody could get used to that smell. It's impossible. It can't be healthy.'

Charley was busy writing up the notes from the visit. 'That's the least of my concerns,' she replied.

Annie shook her head sadly. 'I know, but we can report it to the council, right?'

'We can, but I don't hold out much hope of anything being done, do you? Considering the state of the rest of the estate?'

Chapter Thirty-Seven

Despite the late night, the next morning Charley was up before the alarm woke her. The briefing set for eight o'clock was to update the team on the previous night's developments and to discuss the court hearing for the remand of Sinead Westbrook. They had everything covered.

As much as Charley was feeling jubilant to see the offenders eventually charged thanks to the diligence and determination of her team, she knew that the investigation was far from over. They had yet to arrest, interview, and charge Malcolm Dooley for his part in the enquiry, and still had to prove beyond doubt to a jury at Crown Court that they were all guilty of the crimes for which they had been charged. So she had to keep a lid on it. Any slip-up, no matter how minor, from the preparation of the file to the witnesses taking the stand, was potential for the defence to find a chink in the prosecution's armour and which might cause the case to fail.

Annie yawned. 'I'll never get my head around the judicial system,' she said to Ricky-Lee who was sat next to her as they waited for the briefing to begin.

'In what way?' he replied.

'Well, it's not fair that we have to disclose our evidence whether we have used, intend to use, or don't use it to the defence for them to decide whether it's relevant or not. Yet the defence doesn't have the same responsibility.'

The appearance of the Divisional Commander in the incident room caused everyone to sit up straight. As unusual as it was to see an officer of rank and file in an incident room, Bobbie Stokes was there to thank them for their dogged determination to bring those responsible for the horrific crime in their community to justice.

Once the briefing was over, Mike and Annie walked round to the next block of buildings that incorporated the Magistrates' Court to support Caroline Maston from CPS with the remand application for Sinead Westbrook.

There was building work to the court building and as they turned the corner Annie grabbed Mike's arm, dragging him into the road to avoid a ladder. A driver pressed his car horn. Annie grimaced at Mike's scolding. 'It's bad luck,' she said.

'Don't you think, that it's equally true that you may get run over by a vehicle as you step out into the road to avoid walking under that ladder?'

Low hanging clouds had turned the sky a pale grey, which matched the sombre mood, as silently, along with several others they walked up the court steps, towards the automatic door. Some entered the building, others remained outside taking one last breath to fortify themselves, put out their cigarette, or end a phone call.

In the foyer each eyed the next with suspicion until it was possible to ascertain who was friend or foe and on the right side of the law – criminals didn't come with a dress code.

Annie looked around for the police presence as they looked for a seat near the courtroom.

'Where's the designated police officer these days?' she asked Mike.

'Not enough resources I guess.'

Whilst Mike took a call, she rested her head against the wall avoiding eye contact with those around them and stared up at the rows of bright light in the ceiling, because there was nothing else to do while they waited, other than read the noticeboard, which consisted of nothing more than health-and-safety posters or court listings. However, despite appearances her focus remained keenly trained on the door that led to the courtroom.

Suddenly, the mood in the foyer changed as the clock struck ten and the court usher opened the door to announce that the case for R. V. Westbrook was about to commence. A couple of reporters that she knew to be from the local newspapers, followed the detectives into the courtroom – exchanging one seat for another at the back of the room.

Mike and Annie walked to the front of the courtroom, where Caroline Maston was in conversation with the magistrates. She smiled when she saw them. Mike indicated to the seats behind her. 'We'll sit here should you require anything.'

'Thank you,' she replied.

Seated, Annie took a good look at Mr Pompous, Sinead's defence barrister, whose job it was to ultimately drive a wedge in their cases, but this morning it was about getting his client, Sinead, bail. Dressed in a white shirt, black tie and a pinstriped three-piece suit he stood, as did everyone, as the three magistrates entered, and took up their positions, at the front of the courtroom.

Caroline remained standing when everyone else sat back down, and commenced to lay before the magistrates the case to remand Sinead Westbrook into custody, until her trial. The crown prosecutor then went on to outline the circumstances of the offences, and latterly reinforced the reason for the need for the remand to be in custody.

When Caroline had finished, she sat, and Mr Pompous stood, introducing himself to the magistrates. His face was serious and his voice brittle, like he was itching to say something to make himself look good. Then he announced, curtly, that his client would ultimately be pleading not guilty to the charges against her.

Mike turned to Annie. 'Nothing more than we expected. There's money to be made with a trial.'

Annie's eyes were on the dock where Westbrook's reaction was to fold her shaking hands on her lap and bite down on her bottom lip. Caroline Maston didn't flinch either, on hearing the somewhat surprising suggestion of a plea at this stage, considering the evidence stacked against his client.

Annie leaned towards Mike and whispered in his ear. 'I wondered why she got a barrister instead of a solicitor to act on her behalf. Must be costing her a mint.'

'Her prerogative, if she's paying, although she'll no doubt get legal aid and so some of it will end up coming out of the public purse,' he answered. Mike took a deep breath as Pompous turned his attention to some papers in his hand and began to lay the grounds for the bail plea to the magistrates.

'Your Worships, my client came into the police station of her own volition after hearing that the police wished to speak with her, and I hope that you will give her credit for doing so, not many would. Also, she is willing to comply with any instructions that the magistrates may feel necessary to enable her to be released on bail today:

surrender her passport or sign on once or twice a day at the police station. It would be no problem to her and I have every confidence that she would do so. She will not interfere with the police investigation or be in touch with witnesses. In fact, she has agreed to reside in the next county.' He paused, waiting to see if he could see a reaction from the magistrates, but there was none, so he continued with a dramatic sweep of his arm towards the door which led out into the foyer. 'I also have someone waiting to give evidence, on oath, as to the good character of my client, and who is willing to deposit fifty-thousand pounds as surety of Sinead Westbrook's attendance at any future hearing or trial, if Your Worships feel that it is right that they should hear from this witness who is here to assist the court this morning.'

Mike rose as if to leave. 'Follow me. Let's see if we can see who has that sort of money to lose.'

Following Mike, Annie could see the DS rummaging in his suit pocket, and he exited the courtroom with his mobile phone in his hand.

The foyer was hushed but busy with people stood and sat waiting to be called into court. One man lay near the door, his head on his coat, with his eyes closed. Annie was always amazed at the various arrays of clothing, from the new suit bought for the occasion to the football shirt which seemed to be popular this day. All seats were taken. The bin by the coffee machine was already overflowing with plastic cups.

Mike stood in a corner, as far away as he could get from the rest, dialling Charley's number. Annie had his back. It was blatantly obvious to him who would offer up such a substantial amount of money for the likes of Sinead

Westbrook. Anxiously, he waited for Charley to pick up and turned to scour the room for Malcolm Dooley.

At the sight of a muscle-bound black-leather-clad minder, standing head and shoulders above the rest just inside the entrance, Malcolm Dooley, stood next to him, was hardly trying to make himself inconspicuous. He was wearing a high-necked black jersey under a long camel wool coat. He was clean shaven, his hair gelled back against his head and sporting sunglasses – ever the look of the hardened criminal, even in the height of summer.

The detective sergeant turned to the wall to speak to the DI and explained to her what had been said in court, and that he could now see Malcolm Dooley and his minder in the court foyer. 'I'm going to ask Caroline to ask the magistrates for a ten-minute adjournment,' he said hurriedly. 'We will need backup to arrest him.'

Having heard the applications by both parties, back inside the courtroom the magistrates had taken a brief adjournment. Mike tapped Caroline's shoulder to gain her attention, and quietly, but hastily informed her about what was occurring. Immediately the CPS prosecutor leaned over to speak with the court clerk and asked her if the magistrates would extend their break for a little longer.

Mr Pompous was blissfully unaware of what was about to happen.

Back out in the foyer Mike was pleased to see that backup were arriving in the shape of five uniformed officers who approached an unsuspecting Malcolm Dooley.

DI Charley Mann had chosen the tradesman's entrance. When she entered the foyer through the door marked private, she headed straight for Dooley, flashing her warrant card. 'Malcolm Dooley, you are under arrest in connection with the murders of Robert Sullivan and Ralph Bateman and the illegal possession of firearms.'

Dooley looked sideways at his minder, then back at Charley to laugh in her face. 'Is this some kind of joke, lady?'

'Look behind you and you will see that it isn't.'

There was panic in his eyes when he turned to his minder on seeing officers within cuffing distance of them. Without warning, the minder lunged at Charley, attempting, to head-butt the DI.

Charley had been on the end of a Liverpool kiss before. She swiftly stepped to one side. Then, in one fluid movement, she found the back of his head with one hand, and his arm with the other. She toppled the giant of a man to the floor.

With cheers from the onlookers and arms flaying, along with threats aplenty, the minder managed to get to his feet. He showed his gold teeth in a snarl, but struggled to make contact with his fists. It was lucky for the police officers who had come to Charley's aid because he was wearing mean-looking knuckledusters.

A uniformed officer drew his taser and warned the minder to put his weapon down. He was not for giving in, though.

Taser fired, it felt to Charley like the building shook as once again the giant of a man hit the deck. This time, he was restrained.

Meanwhile, Malcolm Dooley was in cuffs, but he kept lashing out with his feet in a feeble attempt to scupper the inevitable. Annie had come off the worse for wear with a kick of a size twelve shoe to her shin.

'You have no idea who you're dealing with,' he shouted at the top of his voice.

Caroline Maston had stepped out of the courtroom on hearing the commotion, to see two men being ceremoniously marched out of the court foyer and to the waiting police cars by a group of uniformed officers.

'Would someone like to explain what's going on?' she asked, only then realising that it was Detective Inspector Charley Mann who was on her haunches looking at DC Annie Glover's bruised leg. The DI raised her voice so the Crown Prosecutor could hear above the ongoing chatter. The fight had caused quite a stir.

'We've arrested Malcolm Dooley, the person who was going to be Sinead's surety in connection with the murders, and also his minder for public order and assaulting the police. So he will be in custody for some time, he won't be standing surety for anyone. In fact he will be charged in relation to the murders too.'

Caroline looked shocked, but her frown soon turned to a smile. 'Really? I'm going to enjoy seeing the look on Pompous's face when I relay that news to the magistrates,' she said. She turned on her heels to hurry back through the door into court, ready to resume the remand hearing. Caroline asked the clerk, to ask the magistrates if they would re-convene as there was new evidence, that may affect their decision. She took great pleasure in explaining what had just occurred, which meant that the surety offered by Mr Pompous on behalf of his client was no longer an option.

Mr Pompous's eyes immediately found the dock where his client stood in shock. Flustered, and body twitching he addressed the magistrates, through gritted teeth. 'I understand this to be the case. However, I can assure you that I was totally unaware of any of it.'

The magistrates exhibited an affected manner, the Chair speaking for the others when she told the audience that they would return when a decision had been made.

'How is it?' Charley asked Annie as she helped her to her feet in the foyer.

'Sore, but worth it,' she said, smiling through the pain. 'But next time, will you pick on someone your own size?'

Charley stifled a giggle. Mike headed back into court to wait until the remand hearing was over.

When Wilkie arrived to pick Annie up and take her to the hospital for a check-up, Annie placed an arm around his shoulders and he walked her slowly to the door.

'You ruined Dooley's day, apparently, Percy Shaw tells me,' he said.

'He'll be even more annoyed when he knows his black Hummer MD 13 is heading for the pound,' she replied.

'Hurry back,' Charley called after them. 'There's an interview to conduct!'

Chapter Thirty-Eight

With Malcolm Dooley arrested and in custody, Charley was able to get a warrantless search of his house. She was keen to get that underway before they spoke to him. And with his custody clock ticking, as always there was some urgency.

Charley still had her phone in her hand when Mike returned from court to give her the news that Sinead Westbrook had been remanded in custody. He also brought paperwork that required her signature.

Head down, pen in hand, signing one document after another, she spoke fast to update the DS. 'I've spoken to GMP and they're happy to do the search on our behalf. I've given them specific instructions as to what I'm particularly looking for including a copy of Dooley's handwriting. Percy Shaw is the custody sergeant on duty and he's informed me that Dooley and his minder are in the cells, and the barrister has been in touch. He says, surprisingly, neither of them are happy bunnies.'

Mike shrugged as he sat. 'Nothing unusual there then. Who was the minder? Do we know him?'

'I don't. His name is Thomas Delaney. Loads of previous, mainly assaults, but there's a warrant for his arrest for non-appearance at Crown Court on a wounding charge, no bail.'

'Mmm. Must have thought he was safe over the border.'

'Or he was following orders. The drug barons don't just control the small, weak and fragile. Anyone can be an addict.'

Mike caught Charley smiling as she was concentrating on her signature. He asked her why she was smiling.

'Apparently, Percy says that he had trouble getting Delaney through the cell door. They are quite small when you think of it.'

Mike laughed. 'I bet he didn't go in quietly either.'

Charley shuffled the signed papers into a pile. Picking them up from her desk, she handed them back to Mike. 'No, but I'm told he's quietened down now, like they all do eventually.'

'Being alone and locked up in a cell is a very sobering place, so I'm told,' Mike mused.

Charley stretched her back and breathed in deeply. 'We'll get them interviewed in a while. I'm of a mind to let uniform deal with Delaney and let you and Wilkie interview Dooley. I don't know if Annie will be fit to return to work…' she said, looking out only to see Annie hobble through the door on crutches.

Mike followed her gaze. Raising his eyes to the ceiling, he smiled knowingly. 'You can't keep a good man down. Does Dooley know that his house is being searched?'

Charley scoffed. 'He will do by now. I told Percy to give him the news, through the door hatch if necessary. He'll not be pleased, but he'll have to get used to not being in control, won't he, where he's going?'

Mike turned to leave. 'As the old adage goes, "If you can't do the time, don't do the crime," comes to mind.'

The incident room, previously bustling with a blend of high anxiety and copious amounts of stress, was now abuzz with productivity. An abundance of hot sweaty bodies were working as one to get a result, but now with a positive end in sight. People walked purposefully to and fro across the room. There was a hum of pertinent conversations. No one was eating, no one was doodling while they talked on the phone, no one had a glazed look on their face whilst staring at their computer screens. The room exuded energy that had been brought about by the unexpected news that Mr Teflon, Malcolm Dooley, was in custody and behind the eight ball.

They had a lot to talk to Dooley about, now that forensic evidence had linked him to the murders of Bob Sullivan and Ralph Bateman. His appearance at Sinead Westbrook's bail hearing, with the intent of standing surety for his late son's fiancée, also showed them their allegiance to her.

Ricky-Lee had involved himself in the search of Dooley's Hummer.

'It's clean,' he told Charley when he returned with more paperwork. 'What a monster that car is. I wonder how much it does to the litre?'

'I wouldn't worry, you're hardly likely to own one,' she replied, a slight smile taking shape at the corner of her lips.

Winnie announced lunchtime by clearing space on the large table in the incident room. She brought drinks and sandwiches, without asking or fuss, which ultimately allowed Charley to brief the others of her decisions over a bite to eat.

Refreshed and bellies full, when the old lady returned to clear up, Charley grabbed her arthritic hand.

'Thank you,' she mouthed, but as always, Winnie brushed her thanks off as not needed.

'I keep telling you, someone's got to look after you lot,' she said, but Charley knew that the old lady had started her working day long before most of the others much younger than her had, and her shift ended at noon. However, Charley also knew that her repetitive act of kindness wasn't for the others, and it didn't tell the whole story of how Winnie had loved Charley's dad and had carried on looking after his daughter after his death. Although Winnie had every reason to hate her father for building a life with another woman in her absence, Charley's mother Ada, she had loved him enough to let him go and give him her blessing.

The incident room staff was so busy that the short break for Charley meant that her desk was already covered in an assortment of disorganised papers when she returned.

Meanwhile, Annie was sat at her desk working. The younger detective was just as eager as the others, despite the pain, to be part of the proceedings. Mike and Wilkie were huddled over Mike's desk finalising their preparations for the interview with Malcolm Dooley.

'With regard to his DNA on the gaffer tape,' said Charley. 'We won't be telling his brief where it was exactly found in disclosure,' she said. 'I'm hoping he will tie himself up in knots.'

The men smiled. 'Of course not.'

'Have you got any update regarding the house search?'

Charley smiled. 'We are in possession of his handwriting. There is no doubt that he was the one who wrote the threatening unsigned letter received by Tyrone Wells in prison. Of course, we'll need an expert's statement to confirm this to the Court. But, let's say from a visual point of view, it is strikingly similar.'

'Yes!' the detectives said in unison.

When the interview was about to start, Charley settled down to watch on her monitor and asked Annie to join her. If the interview didn't go as expected, she could be the next to go into the interview with Dooley. The more she knew, the better and Charley knew that she would also want to see what was taking place.

'When we've charged Dooley, I'm going to personally update the families and explain to them what the future holds in terms of the trial, and how far away that is likely to be,' Charley told her as the door of the small sparse interview room slowly opened and they watched the four men enter.

'Twelve months. It's a long time for a case to be heard in Crown Court, isn't it? I can't imagine how that must feel for the witnesses, and how many times they must think about seeing their nemesis again. Never mind giving their evidence against them whilst they are there. And of course the potential repercussions.'

Eyes on the monitor, Charley nodded. 'Keeping them onboard is going to be a struggle, but doable. I have every faith.'

'Nobody wants to go to court to give evidence a year after the event, do they?'

'I agree, it's a big ask.'

'I've found that the general public think that once the offender has been caught, it's job done. They're surprised when I tell them that it's just the beginning for us to prepare the file, to then share with the offender's legal team, for them to work on a defence. I still struggle to get my head around it myself.'

'The law is an ass. However, as you are well aware the onus is on the prosecution to prove the guilt beyond doubt.'

Whilst the men were getting seated and comfortable for the upcoming interview, and the recording device was readied, Annie picked up the list of witnesses involved in the case from Charley's desk. 'It never ceases to surprise me how many people get caught up in a murder trial.'

'It surprises me how many get involved in aiding and abetting a murderer, too.' Charley looked thoughtful. 'Do you think that they would if they knew from the start that they could be tried and dealt with the same as a principal offender?'

Annie shrugged. 'Who knows?' she said and paused, still looking at the list. 'So many lives ruined, but the degree of planning and patience that's been put into this crime especially... to pull off an act of revenge beats a lot. Let's face it, Tyrone Wells was convicted and serving his time for his crime when this was planned and executed. Senseless.'

'There are no winners in this game, we know that. Look at Benny Patterson, he was willing to throw himself on the sword for a few quid, for his next fix.'

'I wonder if Grace Westbrook was raped by Shane Dooley, or did she just have sex with him to rile Sinead?'

'Who knows, she could have loved him as much as Sinead for all we know.'

Mike Blake's voice introducing himself for the purpose of the recording device alerted the two women to the screen.

'Looks like they're about to start,' said Charley, eagerly.

–

Malcolm Dooley had been in custody for four and a half hours by the time Mike cautioned him. Dooley was leaning forward, his elbows on the table and his chin on his fists.

'You have been arrested for your involvement in two murders that took place at a wedding in Slaithwaite. The father of the bride, Robert Sullivan, and Ralph Bateman both died on that fateful day from gunshot wounds. Do you want to make any comment about these deaths?' Mike asked.

Dooley shook his head. 'I don't know who you're talking about. However, my legal advisor has informed me that my DNA was found on the gaffer tape that was wrapped around a box that had a gun inside that was used to kill someone. All I can say about that is that I've probably handled several thousand rolls of gaffer tape in my time. In fact, it's a joke amongst those who know me – how much I use it. But that doesn't say that it was me who wrapped up the box in question.'

'Someone, yes, but not just anyone, because we know that Sinead and Grace Westbrook delivered that box to be handed to one of the gunmen, Benny Patterson.'

Dooley pulled a face. 'Never 'erd of 'im.'

'But you do know Sinead and Grace Westbrook? Do you want to tell us how you know them?'

'Sinead was my late son's fiancée, and so yes, I know her and her sister too.'

'You also know that Bob Sullivan was a distant relative of Tyrone Wells, don't you? He murdered your son Shane Dooley, as well as Reece Brown.' Mike paused for a brief moment. 'I think you got the Westbrook sisters to do your dirty work in your vendetta against Tyrone Wells,' Mike continued.

Dooley leaned back in his chair, a smirk upon his face. 'That's rubbish!'

'I think that the reason you chose the wedding of Bob Sullivan's daughter Stacey for that vendetta was because

Shane and Sinead were due to be married when Shane was killed.'

Dooley's jaw tightened. 'What a load of bullshit.'

Wilkie cut in. 'Can you tell us why you sent an unsigned letter taunting Tyrone Wells in prison, and in the process also let him know that his family were targets?'

'You're just trying to stitch me up.' Dooley sat up straight and turned to Mr Pompous, who was sat at his side. 'What am I paying you for? Are you going to let them accuse me like this?'

Mr Pompous opened his mouth as if to speak, but Mike cut in.

'You know that we are searching your address, Mr Dooley? We have samples of your handwriting to compare against the letter. This will be going to an expert who we are confident will confirm that this is indeed your writing.'

When there was no reaction, Mike continued.

'You and I know that what we are telling you is the truth. However, I can understand that you have a reputation to live up to. You can't let anyone get one over on you and still hold your head up, can you? Getting women to do the dirty work for you is bit low, though, even by your standards.'

Dooley's palms clenched into fists. 'For God's sake, this is utterly ridiculous. Either fucking charge me or let me go.'

'We know you wrapped up the box with the gun inside. Like I said, your DNA is on the gaffer tape.'

Dooley's eyes half closed. 'Look, I'm bored now. I've explained that away.'

'Ah, but how do you explain the fact that your DNA was not only found on the edges of the gaffer tape, where granted, you could have just picked it up, but it was also found at the beginning, the middle and also at the end of the length of tape, where only the person doing the wrapping would have touched?'

Dooley shuffled back in his chair, silent. Was that sweat on his furrowed brow?

'We also know that at this wedding, the other weapon used to kill a person was a rifle. This weapon has been recovered. Can you explain how your DNA is on that too?'

Charley could see from her monitor that Malcolm Dooley was getting angry. His nostrils were flared and his breathing more noticeable.

Dooley shook his head. 'Then, you lot must have put it there.'

Wilkie took the baton. 'Let me assure you, Mr Dooley, this is no fit-up. This is retribution for your vengeance against Tyrone Wells, the killer of your son Shane, who also worked for you. No matter what it took, you were going to get even. You did that by killing a totally innocent man, which you didn't even have the balls to do yourself. The women were both emotionally invested and drug dependent – not that it condones their part in the heinous act, but you did supply them with the weapons and ammunition to carry out your plans. Didn't you?'

Dooley jumped up from his chair, much to the surprise of Mr Pompous. 'So fucking what?'

'Sit down,' Mike told him. 'We haven't finished.'

Mr Pompous looked up at his client like an adult looking at a petulant child, and after a few moments Dooley sat down.

Charley looked across at Annie. 'Well, what did we expect? For him to admit to anything we put to him?'

'Book 'em, Danno. There's a drink with my name on it,' Annie said to the monitor in her best American accent.

Back in the interview room, Mike wasn't done with Dooley.

'Not only did you involve yourself in the executions, you waited patiently to ensure it was done at the wedding that was cancelled not once, but twice over two years. I'd call that premeditated, wouldn't you?'

'Call it what you fucking want,' Dooley replied.

Mike had been in enough interviews to tell when the accused had finished talking, and with the crossing of Dooley's arms tightly across his chest, and the silence, he terminated the interview.

Meanwhile, in the DI's office, Charley was still laughing at Annie. 'I bet you don't even know who Danno is,' she said as she switched off the monitor and helped her to her feet.

The pain in Annie's leg was less obvious now that the painkillers had kicked in. Or was it the adrenaline that was pumping through her veins?

'I do so! *Hawaii Five-O* happened to be the favourite cop show of one of the nuns at my school. We all had to suffer Steve McGarrett quotes on a regular basis.'

At the debrief, they talked of Dooley's motivation and associates and celebrated his carelessness and mistakes. They critiqued their own performance, assessed their strengths and weaknesses, and tried to figure out how to function better as a team.

–

Afterwards Charley spoke to Mike alone in her office.

'Well Mike, we got there in the end. Who would have thought on the morning of the wedding how it would end?'

'Maybe if Benny Patterson's gun hadn't jammed he might have got away? However, now he will be staying where he belongs behind bars, recovering from the attack on him that he sustained in prison.'

'Until he upsets someone else. I don't see his incarceration being uneventful, do you?'

Mike grinned. 'No, I don't.' For a moment he was thoughtful. 'I've been thinking of Sinead's involvement. She was Shane Dooley's fiancée, but apart from delivering a box for Patterson to Sullivan's, with Grace, which she may or may not have known contained a gun, possibly a very tenuous link of her being present on the roof with her sister when the rifle was fired, if we are to believe Grace that she shared Sinead's cigarettes, she didn't have further involvement did she, or none that we know of anyway?'

'No, if she was on the rooftop when Grace shot Bob Sullivan then she must have got there under her own steam because we know from the CCTV that she didn't walk with Grace, who pushed the pram containing the rifle, through the village.'

'According to Chelsea Clough she was out of it on drugs when she arrived at her studio that day, so maybe that was more by chance than management though.'

'She must have forgiven her sister whatever relationship she had with Shane Dooley.'

'I feel sorry in some respects for Chelsea Clough, entering the murky world of her half-brother after his death, and then being used and threatened by his errant friend's family, through no fault of her own. I'm hoping that they don't need to call her at the trial. That way she can get on with her new life.'

Charley was not optimistic, 'You and I know that they aren't going to plead guilty. It'll be a six-week trial no mistake. But, at least they are locked up for now.'

'We both also know that sadly someone will already be in the wings to step into Malcolm Dooley's shoes though, that's how it works. Even big drugs barons are indispensable.'

'And, he'll still be running operations from the nick, no doubt.'

'No doubt we will uncover more intelligence in the coming months as we continue to work on the file, but for now I think we deserve a large drink, don't you?'

Mike stood to leave as Des Ryder tapped on the SIO's door.

'Come in,' Charley called out.

Des Ryder's face was emotionless. 'Bob Sullivan was laundering money through his business. Not on a massive scale, but quite a few thousand,' he told them.

Charley raised her eyebrows. 'So, he was actually washing money through it?'

'Looks like it started around about the time that the pandemic hit. His business spiralled downwards, and it is at this time that he started putting dirty money in.'

'Could it have been from Tyrone Wells?' she asked.

'We are still in the process of trying to unravel who the accounts belong to.'

Mike turned to Charley. 'Well, we can't pursue him because he's dead.'

'No we can't, but we like to tie up loose ends,' she replied. 'Des, share the intelligence with whoever needs it, and I'll speak to his daughter Stacey, and DC Helen Weir the family liaison officer in the case. Stacey may wish to speak to you before she decides whether to tell her mum or not.'

—

Celebrating their comradeship and a drink in the pub was the order of the day and a chance for Charley to say thank you for the team's support and hard work. A gesture, not a celebration, that would happen once those responsible were convicted at a future date in Crown Court. Whilst there was elation for their success, for Charley, it didn't take away the sadness for the lives destroyed on that fateful day. But, at least, now, the families of the deceased knew who the culprits were, what happened, and why. Hard as this was to comprehend.

'I've got a family wedding in a fortnight,' Mike said to Charley after a glass or two. 'I don't think I want to go alone. Fancy being my plus one?'

Charley chuckled. 'Relax and enjoy it. Celebrate the day as it should be celebrated. Murders like these are rare. You should know that by now. Just remember to wear your bulletproof vest.'

'You haven't answered my question,' he said coyly.

'Yes, yes, I'd like that very much,' she replied.

Wilkie raised his glass to Charley. 'And another one bites the dust, boss.'

'The sad thing is that someone else will be ready, and more than willing to step into Dooley's shoes, and continue to destroy lives, violently abuse others and even kill – all driven by the need for power, and greed.'

Acknowledgements

Our special thanks to Michael Bhaskar, Kit Nevile, and everyone at Canelo for their hard work and commitment to making this Detective Charley Mann novel the best it can be.

To our literary agent David H. Headley at DHH Literary Agency, who 'found us' and continues to support us, believes in us as writers, and is as passionate about our storytelling as we are about writing him stories.

To David's PA Emily Glenister – always at the end of the phone with a cheery voice, and the boss's ear!

To Mark Swan, for a brilliant cover design.

To Laura Burge, for her detailed work on the copyedit.

Thanks also to Judith Kay and Pamela McNulty whose contribution to *Vengeance* we are very grateful for.

We couldn't have done it without you!